DON'T SAY A WORD

Also by David Mark

The Sal Delaney mysteries

WHEN THE BOUGH BREAKS *

The DS Aector McAvoy series

DARK WINTER
ORIGINAL SKIN
SORROW BOUND
TAKING PITY
DEAD PRETTY
CRUEL MERCY
SCORCHED EARTH
COLD BONES
PAST LIFE *
BLIND JUSTICE *
FLESH AND BLOOD *
THE BURNING TIME *
PAST REDEMPTION *

Novels

THE ZEALOT'S BONES (*as D.M. Mark*)
THE MAUSOLEUM (aka THE BURYING GROUND) *
A RUSH OF BLOOD *
BORROWED TIME *
BLOOD MONEY
INTO THE WOODS
SUSPICIOUS MINDS *
CAGES *
PIECE OF MIND: A MEMOIR
ANATOMY OF A HERETIC
THE WHISPERING DEAD *

* *available from Severn House*

DON'T SAY A WORD

David Mark

SEVERN
HOUSE

First world edition published in Great Britain and the USA in 2025
by Severn House, an imprint of Canongate Books Ltd,
14 High Street, Edinburgh EH1 1TE.

severnhouse.com

Copyright © David Mark, 2025

Cover and jacket design by Nick May at bluegecko22.com

All rights reserved including the right of reproduction in whole or in part in any form. The right of David Mark to be identified as the author of this work has been asserted in accordance with the Copyright, Designs & Patents Act 1988.

British Library Cataloguing-in-Publication Data
A CIP catalogue record for this title is available from the British Library.

ISBN-13: 978-1-4483-1532-1 (cased)
ISBN-13: 978-1-4483-1533-8 (e-book)

This is a work of fiction. Names, characters, places and incidents are either the product of the author's imagination or are used fictitiously. Except where actual historical events and characters are being described for the storyline of this novel, all situations in this publication are fictitious and any resemblance to actual persons, living or dead, business establishments, events or locales is purely coincidental.

No part of this book may be used or reproduced in any manner for the purpose of training artificial intelligence technologies or systems. This work is reserved from text and data mining (Article 4(3) Directive (EU) 2019/790).

All Severn House titles are printed on acid-free paper.

Typeset by Palimpsest Book Production Ltd.,
Falkirk, Stirlingshire, Scotland.
Printed and bound in Great Britain by
TJ Books, Padstow, Cornwall.

The manufacturer's authorised representative in the EU for product safety is
Authorised Rep Compliance Ltd, 71 Lower Baggot Street,
Dublin D02 P593 Ireland (arccompliance.com)

Praise for David Mark

"Mark is a superbly gifted writer who creates a bleak, unforgiving setting, deeply damaged characters, and a plot that ramps up the violence, tension, and suspense to an almost unbearable level before an explosive ending that will leave readers utterly shattered"
Booklist Starred Review of *When the Bough Breaks*

"Masterfully plotted"
Kirkus Reviews on *When the Bough Breaks*

"An outstanding read for those who like their crime thrillers gritty, graphic, and gripping"
Booklist Starred Review of *Past Redemption*

"A dark, creepy, twisted mystery that will keep readers awake far into the night"
Booklist Starred Review of *The Burning Time*

"An involving, nail-biting police procedural from a masterful storyteller"
Kirkus Reviews on *Flesh and Blood*

"[Delivers] the kind of grisly torture and murder scenes that have rightly linked his work with that of Val McDermid"
Booklist on *Blind Justice*

"Polished prose, lovable recurring characters, and a stunning revelation make this a mystery to savor"
Kirkus Reviews Starred Review of *Past Life*

"A fine police procedural . . . Ian Rankin fans will be pleased"
Publishers Weekly on *Past Life*

"[Mark is] on the level of Scottish and English contemporaries such as Denise Mina, Val McDermid, and Peter Robinson"
Library Journal Starred Review of *Cruel Mercy*

"To call Mark's novels police procedurals is like calling the Mona Lisa a pretty painting"
Kirkus Reviews Starred Review of *Cruel Mercy*

About the author

David Mark spent seven years as crime reporter for the *Yorkshire Post* and now writes full-time. A former Richard & Judy pick, and a *Sunday Times* bestseller, he is the author of the DS Aector McAvoy series, the Sal Delaney police procedurals and a number of stand-alone thrillers. He lives in Northumberland with his family.

www.davidmarkwriter.co.uk

For my three witches. You are my protection spell.

'So they took Jeremiah and cast him into the cistern of Malchiah, the king's son, which was in the court of the guard, letting Jeremiah down by ropes. And there was no water in the cistern, but only mud, and Jeremiah sank in the mud.'

Jeremiah 38:6

'Our citadels are placed conspicuous to outward view . . . but within are secrets.'

From *The Changeling*, by Thomas Middleton and William Rowley, 1622

PROLOGUE

Three weeks ago

He squeaks a finger across his teeth. Jimmies a nail between incisor and canine. Probes a molar with a slug of tongue. Unearths something meaty. Swallows it down.

He peers into the darkness. Slows down as he snatches a glimpse of spiky hedgerows, of potholes deep enough to hide a body. Makes out the mass of forest to his left, his right: branches reaching out across the pitted road to hold gnarled, winter-black hands. Glances up at a swollen, pearlescent moon. Thinks of D-cups clad in white satin. Thinks of giants. Of bare feet and wrinkled, grimy soles.

The wipers screech across the grimy, bug-smeared glass – a leaf caught by the stem between the rubber and the blade. He thinks of sharks. Thinks of swimmers waving, drowning . . .

The buzz at his thigh: **I want you. I can't wait much longer** . . .

He raises his fingers to his nose. Breathes in the wet-metal hum of tartare, plaque; some lingering carbohydrate; a sugary drink.

Are you nearly here? Don't keep me waiting. I won't wait 4 eva.

He sees his watery reflection give a little leer. Smirks through his likeness, eyes on the road. Grins, child-like, absurdly excited.

A flash again, the phone still on his thigh. The sat-nav flashing, rotating. Makes himself snort with laughter as he imagines the automated voice telling him that he's in the middle of pissing nowhere.

He picks up the phone. Thumbs in a response.

Moments away, I swear. Just past Hdn Brdg.

He glances up and down as he types. Gives a little jerk of the steering wheel as a branch whips against the windscreen, smearing raindrops, shedding green needles. He swallows the sudden burst of panic. Tries to stop himself from jiggling up and down. God how he wants this. Needs this. Deserves it.

Should I take my knickers off now or do you want to see how pretty I look . . .?

He bites his cheek. Squeezes the steering wheel. Decisions, decisions.

A burst of static from the radio: the hiss and parp of talk radio. He prods at the console, unsure what to press. This isn't his car. These aren't his clothes. This isn't his life.

Disco music, now. Electronica. Sudden visions of synthesizers played on guitar-straps: high fringes and rolled-up jeans. He sees himself at university, stripy vest and petrol-blue jeans, greasy arms above his head, spaghetti legs, bright eyes.

He shakes it away. Bites down. Pokes a finger and thumb into the pocket of his dark jogging trousers, looking for the piece of gum that he used up and spat out three hours back. He wonders if they'll want to kiss him. They haven't said. Told him all the other things they want him to do and which they are going to do to him, but nothing about lips and tongues and mouths. He shouldn't have let himself eat. Should have turned up primped and fresh, cologned and minty – the way he was when he plucked the keys from his uncle's desk and walked into the low evening sun.

Getting cold, luvva-boy. Thinking you're a time-waster. Thinking u've pussied out.

He presses his toe down on the accelerator. Glances again at the sat-nav. Lifts the hem of his T-shirt and squeaks it across his teeth. Imagines himself polishing a mosaic.

He feels the two sides of himself arguing, queasily, in his belly. He shouldn't be here. Not really. People here wish him ill. Wish him harm. Wish him dead. He tells himself again, more urgently this time, that he's making a silly mistake. He's letting his desires override his caution. Pushing down his sanity, even as it screams that this is a set-up – that, at best, he can expect to drive home again unsatisfied but unhurt. Shakes his head, angry with himself. No, Mahee, no, there are thousands of people that live near here. Anybody trying to set him up would at least try to be sneaky about it. Anybody luring him to a secluded spot in the wilderness would have the sense to make it somewhere further away from this place, these people, with its memories and debts and obligations and rage, and . . .

Is that you?

He looks down at the sat-nav. He's a little blue dot, blinking on a white line, inches of green either side; a sickle of river a little way beyond the red circle. He's parallel with the Roman wall though he can't make it out in this thick, deep dark.

He makes out a body of water to his right; a sheet of hammered tin that holds the moon's reflecting with an eerie stillness. Hears the mournful bleating of an animal in distress. Breathes in the sheep shit and rotting-crop fug of a landscape that appears entirely uninhabited. Feels a brief surge of good feeling. God, he's actually made it. Actually got here. He's really going to do it this time. Really going to press his flesh against that of another. He's going to lose himself in someone; going to muffle the din in his head by muffling his ears with cool, welcoming thighs.

He pulls in at the little gap in the fence. Glances up at a sky the colour of prune juice and tobacco spit. Thinks of wet earth.

'No,' he says, out loud. 'No, don't spoil it, Mahee. You deserve this. All you've been through, all that you've lost . . .'

Hot acid rises in his throat. He twitches. Presses his flabby cheek into his shoulder, pushing his jaw out until it hurts at the hinge. He turns the music up a notch, hoping he can distract himself before the bird calls. Curses himself as the sound begins to drill into the place where skull meets spine. It's an unearthly shrieking: a raucous cawing that seems to be in front and behind and inside him all at once. The first time he heard it his eardrum perforated – he'd bled into the receiver of the work phone. A cruel trick, according to his colleagues. A warning, according to the grandmother in whom he had confided. *The Ulama*, she'd said, one knobbly hand clutching at the folds of her blouse. The Devil Bird. A feathered banshee: its shriek presaging death.

'Stop it! Forget about it for one night. Forget all of it. Forget what you did and what you were. Lose yourself in pleasure, you silly fat man.'

The car bumps over a cattle grid. He enjoys the vibration. Turns the radio off just before the DJ can ruin the moment. Pulls forward, a spiky hedge to his right; endless damp nothingness to his left

I c U.

He switches off the ignition. Makes fists. Glances at himself in the rear-view mirror and tells himself not to spoil this. Don't let the nerves get in the way of the pleasure. He feels a sudden, desperate urge to urinate. Feels something moving in his guts.

He picks up his phone. Smirks at himself. Thumbs out: **Take them off.**

He steps out of the car. Puts his phone in his pocket. Feels wet grass on the bare space between his trainer and his cuff.

Breathes in the wet air and burnt petrol; the sheep shit and stirred earth. He puts a hand in his pants and readjusts himself. He doesn't want to disappoint. He's talked a good game these past weeks. Made himself taller, leaner, better endowed. He hopes they've done the same. Hopes they're a little lumper than their picture; that the images are a few years out of date. He's not sure he'll be able to do himself justice if they're as attractive as they are in the snaps. Hopes they treat truth as a spectrum, just like him.

The phone pings in his pocket.

Oh you pretty thing! Come on now. Give me what I want.

He locks the car. Walks as steadily as he can across the rutted field. On his left, a sudden burst of movement; a white tail bobbing between chocolate-brown trees.

Looks forward. Big bright halogen bulbs flare and flash. Slugs and tadpoles dance upon his dazzled lenses. His foot finds a divot and he almost trips, gathering himself. He smiles madly, half-embarrassed, half-giddy. God, it's really going to happen. He's really going to be allowed to have this; to lose himself; find himself. God, he doesn't care what they look like, taste like, smell like; he just wants contact, tough, wants to bite and be bitten; hungers for the red meat of mingled flesh.

His pocket pings again. He grabs for his phone. A picture message – the vibration enough to send a Pavlovian thrill through his extremities. Wonders what they've got for him. What treat they're going to show off for his pleasure.

He opens the picture. Stops walking. Stares at the image through a little gathering cloud of icy breath.

The image shows his own outline. Shows his silhouette, walking forward, moving across the field towards the parked car to where his every pleasure is about to be brought to life.

There's a moment when he despairs at the sight that he presents; when he looks at his puddled middle, his hunched shoulders; the liminal gleam of light bouncing off his bald skull; a moment when he sees himself for who and what he is.

He turns, squinting into the darkness.

In his hand, the phone pings. He looks down.

I'm sorry.

A rush of movement. A column of meat and bone, hair and skin. A hand chopping down, falling like an axe.

And then he's on his back, and there's blood in his ears, and shit in his hair and the hot reek of animal piss in his nostrils.

Only when he stops wriggling, does the creature truly begin its work.

Article from *The Guardian*

'He's Innocent,' Says Desperate Mum

14.02.2019

Tara Myers sits at a living-room table overflowing with campaign literature. They represent an adult life recorded in headlines: setbacks, tragedies, brief flarings of hope. There are photographs of the time that family and friends took a bus to prison to celebrate her son Theo's twenty-first birthday; clippings of newspaper interviews; a BAFTA-winning documentary.

Theo Myers was sentenced to life for the murder of a homeless man in a gang attack in Middlesbrough in 2013. He was one of two men convicted of the killing after a 'joint enterprise' prosecution in which there had initially been multiple defendants. He has always claimed he was nowhere near the scene and had never met the victim. It is, he claims, a catastrophic case of mistaken identity.

Tara says Theo is a victim of police incompetence, legal malpractice, and the intransigence of the Court of Appeal.

Theo was 19 when Matthew Thurrock, 29, was killed. Theo, then studying drama at Northumbria University, had been in Middlesbrough for a drink with his father the night of the sickening attack. He did not know the victim, but was placed at the scene by two witnesses who thought one of the men might have been the 'friendly, long-haired lad' with whom they had shared a conversation at the bus station earlier that day. He gave his name as Theo and spoke of the performing arts course on which he was a second-year student. Questioned by police, having witnessed the attack, they mistakenly gave Theo's name.

Theo was arrested on a Wednesday – picked up by police as he walked from his halls of residence to a morning lecture. Terrified, bewildered, Theo followed the advice of the duty solicitor, replying 'no comment' to every question put by detectives. He and his family believed that police would quickly see that a mistake had been made.

In October 2014, Theo, by then 20, was given a life sentence and jailed for a minimum of twelve years.

Tara and husband Paul were devastated by their only son's conviction. Tara said: 'I couldn't eat, couldn't sleep. I couldn't leave the house. I just closed in on myself. He's done nothing wrong. He's a shy, sensitive lad who loves acting and reading and has never been in a fight in his life. They all but picked his name out of a hat. Even when he was arrested we thought it would all get sorted out, but they just wouldn't listen. We know he wasn't there but they're refusing to listen to us. That's why I've had to fight – why I've had to get over myself, pull my big girl pants on, and start making a nuisance of myself. They won't get away with it.'

Tara's campaign was emboldened by the involvement of veteran legal campaigner Alec Devlin, who has been involved in overturning a number of high-profile convictions and is involved with the influential Juris Project, which believes there may be dozens of wrongly convicted individuals in the British penal system.

Devlin said: 'From the moment he was arrested he has been mistreated and badly served. The solicitor he was assigned during his interviews told him to just say nothing – to go "no comment" to every question put to him. Obviously if he'd put his side of the story then, they'd have seen at once that he wasn't at the scene and that would have been the end of the matter. By the time he started talking, nobody believed him and half of the evidence that would have exonerated him had gone missing.'

Tara says: 'His dad's not really coping. He knows to his very bones his son didn't do this and yet he's stuck in a cell. Paul is very protective of him and can't stand the thought of him being caged like that. Theo's never wished harm on anybody. He'd met up with his dad because Paul was missing him and going through one of his low spells and needed to spend time with him. Theo loves his dad to bits but for them I don't think anything's been the same since the moment they said goodbye that night. Somehow, the police think Theo got across town, joined up with a gang of known drug-dealers, and then went and kicked a stranger to death for the fun of it. It makes me sick. Paul can't even visit him; he just comes apart.'

Theo was placed at the scene by two witnesses. Didier

Mabuse, at the time 19, and Constance Andrysiak, at the time 17, told police they saw Theo kicking Thurrock as he lay bleeding from numerous blows. Both have since written to the Juris Project offering their assistance with the appeal. Both claim that the police pressured them to name names and that all they ever told them was that one of the attackers had the same trainers as the young drama student they had spoken to earlier in the evening.

The jury at Teesside Crown Court heard that the attack was an act of revenge by a group of youths, for an alleged assault carried out on one of their members by Thurrock. Of the youths initially charged, prosecutions were only secured against two individuals. The other man, Lawrence Boden, initially told the jury that it was Theo who carried out the attack. He has since admitted to perjuring himself and claims he had never met Theo before they saw one another in the dock. He claims to have been pressured into implicating his co-accused by his defence counsel.

PART ONE

ONE

Sunday 18 May

Redburn, Langley, South Northumberland

The water tastes of blood. Of earth and metal. Of ash.
    He gasps, trying to move his face away from the rushing, sucking tide.
Swallows. Retches – nostrils full of brimstone; bone.
    He squirms. Slithers. Reaches out with his mangled hand, fingers stretching – a spider in a rictus of agony.
    Brick, now. Stone. Slime and moss and unyielding earth. Bones. Iron against his hip. Earth in his mouth, his eyes, ears, nose.
    He burrows into the wet clay. Anchors his bare, bleeding feet against the brick. Pushes himself deeper into the opening. He gulps down the water that cascades down the gently curving passage. Glugs down gutfuls of the briny, iron-laced flood. He stops, sensing movement. He is beyond fear, beyond rational thought, but some primal part of him acknowledges the nearness of threat. He angles his head away from the rushing water, pushing his face hard against the slimy stone. His half-blind eyes widen, mouth jerking open, trapped hand clawing against his own skin. Wave upon wave of worm-tailed horrors skitter and screech, pat the raw flesh of his face: needle-sharp claws in his hair, on his back, his legs, wriggling past him in a chittering brown deluge. He screams into the earth. Wriggles. Jerks.
    Above him, a stone shifts. Another. He starts to rock back and forth, his whole body an implement; a tool crafted for the sole purpose of widening this too-small space.
    He claws again at the clay in front of him. Pushes his head further forward. Tries to close his ears to the screams that emanate from the little chamber behind him.
    Onward. Deeper. His nails crack, joints rupture. He feels the meat being rashered from his body with each inch of ground gained. He feels nothing now. He has discovered that pain is finite. He has

endured all that a body can endure. He exists in a perpetual state of exquisite numbness; his entire being somehow anaesthetized and aflame.

Something gives. Ahead, a rock is displaced by his questing palm. A gust of cold air caresses his skinless fingertips. Raises the flesh upon his bare arm.

For a blessed moment, his brain clears. For an instant, he knows himself. Knows where he is. Who he is. What has been done to him. There is a moment when he feels anger flare in the cold coils of his gut. It galvanizes him, floods him with the strength to wrench and writhe and push, worming his way through the narrow tunnel like a grub burrowing into rancid flesh.

Her voice, muffled, helpless: 'Please . . . it's rising . . . don't leave me . . .'

His scrabbling foot snags a piece of masonry that feels more solid than the others. He pushes himself forward. Feels his trapped hand find a pocket of space. Turns himself over, pulling his hand through the mud and the rain and the mass of wriggling bodies to pop into the cool air above his head. He grabs blindly at the brick. Pushes himself up. He feels metal. Old iron. A circle and spokes. He thinks of ribs. Skulls. The chatter in his skull.

Thinks: *Blindworm*.

Thinks: *forgive me.*

Fear propels him. Fear sells strips of flesh from his bones.

Hauls.

Drags.

Scrapes.

Bleeds . . .

There is no witness to the resurrection. No apostles or weeping penitents gather in the ceaseless, tumbling rain, to watch the fallen rise. The severed thumb of one grey-green wall stands as grave marker. Drowned dandelions and the whitewashed flecks of madly bobbing daisies are the funeral blooms that adorn this unquiet grave. The only psalm sung is the bacon-sizzle hiss of rain upon rock, upon stone, upon the metal bones of the rusting tractor parked lopsidedly between the hawthorns: a dragon assaulting the highest tower of a fairy-tale castle.

Nobody sees the hand punch through the sodden earth, splayed fingers in spasm, nails clutching soil.

Nobody sees the hand become an arm; become a blood-black

head, shoulders. Nobody sees the earth spit out its captive: this emaciated, mud-slimed thing – slithering free of the earth like a baby animal; a helpless fawn that staggers and kicks and lies in the teeming rain; eyes staring up at clouds that scud and roll above this vast, scarred landscape. Only the charcoal-black trees huddle as bent-backed mourners at the graveside, staring down into the darkness of the pit: hunch-shouldered, trembling in their grief.

When he rises, he is more clay than flesh. He is misshapen. Malformed. The chamber has remade him. Baked him. Made him anew.

He turns sightless eyes upon the old castle wall. Whips his head to the right. A car? *Sweet Jesus, could it be rescue . . .?*

He turns and lurches through grass that clutches and grabs at him: each tug at his feet and ankles a fleshless hand, rising from the grave to ensnare him, drag him home.

He feels a sharp, gritty firmness beneath his soles. Feels puddles splash his legs.

There is the sensation of light. A sudden onrushing gust of wind and rain.

Metal.

A sicking moment of impact, collision.

Then there is just the wet earth and the hot blood and the sensation of slipping, sinking, oozing back into the wretched blackness.

He knows what awaits him.

Bites down upon his tongue until his teeth touch.

Lets the blood clog his throat; his excised tongue a peach-stone in his throat.

Die, he begs.

Please die.

He will get his wish.

But not yet.

TWO

Tynedale Terrace West, Haltwhistle

8.44 p.m.

S al Delaney sits with her back against the bathroom door, knees pulled up as if braced for impact. She can't make out the letters on the screen of her phone, but she can't stop typing. Her thumbs make her think of the claws of fighting crabs, waving, jabbing, lunging at the keypad. She writes as if she is bleeding ink.

'You all right, Sal?'

She pushes her back harder against the door. Squeezes her knees together. Bites down hard.

. . . **wouldn't matter what I said or did so why am I saying or doing anything and why am I putting myself thru it when my best is so much worse than they deserve** . . .

'Sal? Was it the sausage rolls? I told you the dog had been licking them?'

Sal feels as though her head is underwater. Feels like there's static in her ears. She snatches one hand away from her phone and presses her knuckle into the groove between her eyebrows. The headache runs all the way to the nape of her neck. She wipes a hand under her black curls. Feels sweat and grime on her skin.

'Just shout if you need anything, OK love? We've got Robert doing Boney M., if you fancy an aneurysm . . .'

She puts her head back against the door. Wishes herself into the wood. Recoils as a sudden memory blurs her vision. Dagmara, all red hair and moon boots, kneading at her scalp with her short, muddy fingers. Hears her as clearly as if she were whispering in her ear.

'Bastard things, migraines. No bugger can really tell you where they come from. Chocolate, according to some people, but that's the medical profession for you. Always trying to kill the things that make it all a bit better. You lay yourself down on the wood and stay still as you can. Gravity'll do the rest . . .'

Sal closes the file on her phone. Slips it into the pocket of her big baggy cardigan. Taps her fingers against her breastbone, removing another dusty patch of faded ink from the washed-out band T-shirt. Closes her eyes and waits for the room to stop spinning, her heart to slow down. Waits for the woman who killed her mam to slither back beneath the locked door in her memory.

Slowly, she pulls herself up. There are creaks from her joints, a crack as she puts her weight on her bad hand. She glares at it like an enemy. She's not far past forty. Doesn't think she should have a bad hand. Doesn't think the bad weather should play havoc with her joints. Doesn't feel like the barometer in the hallways should be able to predict her migraines with such uncanny accuracy. Shouldn't be affected by things like atmospheric pressure and lunar cycles.

Sal fumbles her way to the sink. Places her palms on the porcelain. Forces herself to look into her own eyes in the little toothpaste-flecked vanity mirror behind the grimy taps. Sees round glasses, curly hair; flushed cheeks; a mucky kind of tan that makes people question whether she might have any 'exotic' blood. She doesn't know the answer. Knows only that she's half monster. That her skin fastens up around a warring multitude.

'Sort yourself out,' she mutters, shivering suddenly. 'Wipe your eyes. Go play Mum. You can do this . . .'

She studies her face again, slowly moving her reflection this way and that, trying to catch it out. Sees the sweat on her top lip and across her brow; the crumbs on the front of her T-shirt, junk food in her teeth. She stares hard at her reflection. Waits for him to appear. Waits for the moment when her twin looks back.

'Sal!'

She closes her eyes. Listens to the muffled whump of the karaoke machine. There's a raucous yelp of laughter somewhere beneath her: better people, having a better time.

She risks another glance at her reflection. Sees the spots in her hairline; the dried skin around her nose; the cracks in her lips. The darkness beneath her eyes are smudges of charcoal, the grey at her roots a carpet of snow in a burnt forest. God she's tired.

'That's it, I'm coming in.'

Sal opens the door before Elsie can put her shoulder to it. Greets her with a bright-eyed smile.

'You look like you've got electrodes wired to your cheeks,' says

Elsie, appraisingly. She's a stout, no-nonsense woman whom an artful toddler could realistically recreate out of two balls of clay. She's wearing a glitzy, silver-sequinned dress. She's got her hair in what she refers to as an *up-do*. To Sal, she looks like a cross between a glitter ball and a pineapple.

'Sorry I was so long,' mutters Sal, trying to push past and into the corridor. 'The girls OK?'

She flinches, cross with herself. She'd read a book recently that suggested using terms like 'the girls' stripped them of their individualism and might cause self-worth issues in later life. 'Nola. Lottie.'

Elsie frowns. Puts her head on one side: a mechanic looking under the bonnet of a banger. 'Joining in. Having fun. Lottie's doing "Oom-Pah-Pah" from *Oliver* next. Won't start until you're there.'

Sal flinches again. Feels her heart twitch as if poked. 'And Nola?'

'You know teenagers,' says Elsie, with a shrug. 'Glued to her phone. Looks like the Grim Reaper in that bloody hoodie but she's doing her best. She smiled when Denise hit the high note in "New York, New York" and Kevin started barking like she'd stepped on his tail.'

Sal lets herself smile. Shrinks a little. Fiddles with her fringe. Tries to untangle her necklaces – an open book on a silver chain twisted around the string of multi-coloured beads that Lottie made at Art Club. Gives up, fingernails too short, the skin picked raw and ugly at her thumbs. Feels Elsie soften her gaze. Elsie's been a copper longer than she was a person. Knows when somebody is struggling. Knows when they need a friend, when they need a drink, and when they need more than anybody else can provide.

'You're doing good, Sal,' she says, and means it. 'You've given those girls something to live for. Given them hope. Given them a place to feel safe again.'

Sal looks past her. Looks at the family photos arranged haphazardly on the woodchip-covered walls. Looks at so many photos of so many smiles: Elsie's whole family tree; gummy babies and whiskered ancestors, monochrome farmwives and splendid, prom-dressed teens. Sees only what Lottie and Nola will never have.

'I shouldn't have brought Lottie,' says Sal, and a sudden wave of dizziness seems to rise up from her gut. She's empty. Wretched. Gorged herself at the paper-plate buffet so that everybody would see she was taking care of herself, then made her way upstairs to throw it all up again. It's the only thing she can control.

'Lottie's a diamond girl,' says Elsie, putting a hand on Sal's arm. 'They both are. A credit to you.'

'To Lewis,' she says, automatically. 'To their mum.'

Elsie makes a face. 'You've raised them, Sal. You're the one who's taught them right from wrong. You know I wouldn't wish what happened to the poor bastard on anyone, but Lewis was always more of a McDonald's and swimming kind of a dad. It was always you they turned to when things were going wrong.'

Sal shakes her head. Bites down until it hurts. She doesn't want kind words. Can't stand to be comforted. Detective Inspector Lewis Beecher is in a specialist head injury unit forty miles south. He's learning to walk again. Talk again. Trying to remember who he is and what was done to him by a killer who Sal didn't reach in time. His ex-wife, Jasmine, sits in a cardboard box on Lottie's bedside table. She survived the attack that had almost cost Nola her life, but the infection she picked up in hospital succeeded where her vicious boyfriend failed. Their children, these not-quite orphans, became hers almost by default. Social services made it plain – they had nowhere to go other than Lewis's ex-partner, their not-quite stepmum. She hadn't wanted to step into the gap. But she wasn't letting them go into care. She's raising them alone, in the house that Lewis threw her out of just weeks before the attack that left him in a state of suspended animation.

'Come on, eh? Give us a song. You do that Kate Bush one beautifully. And you love that book, don't you? Withering Slights, or whatever.'

Sal twitches a smile. 'I've gone off it,' she confides. 'I think it gave me an unrealistic idea of what love's supposed to feel like.'

Elsie flares her nostrils. Slaps her on the forearm. 'You do talk some shit, my lass. Come on, eh? Just enjoy yourself for a bit. Forget all the outside noise. Have a Cadbury's Finger and a bowl of cheese balls. Open the ouzo if it helps. Go and play with the dog. Parenthood isn't all guilt and denial, y'know. You're allowed to relax.'

Sal lets herself be led down the little hallway and follows Elsie down the stairs, stepping over the jumbled piles of letters and laundry that have been optimistically placed on the stairs for the next person going up. She looks up as a sudden blast of cold, damp air caresses her face. Breathes in tobacco, dead leaves and rain.

A broad-shouldered young man is standing on the front step,

leaning against the door, smoking a roll-up and watching the rain fall through the big yellow cone of light. For a moment, he's Jarod. He's Sal's twin. He's the boy who protected her; the man who felt her every joy and sorrow; the brother who fled the one place he felt safe when Sal discovered what had been done to him, and by whom.

'Fag?' asks Will, looking past his auntie to Sal.

'I don't think you can say that any more,' smiles Elsie, opening the living-room door and letting the sound of Van Morrison blare into the corridor. It's quickly drowned out by a roar from the assembled party guests, all demanding to know why Elsie has taken off her party hat. She's fifty-six years old today.

Sal joins the teenager on the step. Listens to the slap of rain upon brick, upon tarmac, upon the fat leaves of the rosebushes in the little yard. Looks out at the row of houses opposite: warm lights and soft air, light reflecting off the gleaming metal of a line of nose-to-tail cars.

'Not moved on to the vape, then?' asks Sal, doing her best, as Will sets about rolling her a cigarette. She doesn't think Nola and Lottie are aware she smokes. Isn't sure that they would give her explanation much credence. She's not addicted to nicotine, but her twin brother is. She feels this need the same way she feels so many of his other compulsions and hungers. Shares his nightmares whenever she loses the fight with sleep.

'There's nothing cool about vaping,' says Will, stretching his neck so that the rain can better soak his face. 'Looks like you're playing a kazoo.'

'You're too young to even know what a kazoo is,' says Sal, taking a draw of nicotine into her lungs. 'What are you now? Nineteen?'

'Twenty,' says Will. 'Packed a whole load of living into the past year. Been reading a lot. Politics. History. Philosophy. The kazoo.'

Sal leans back against the door. Blows out a cloud. Feels the sparks in her lungs. Feels Will looking at her; the same appraising eye as his auntie Elsie.

'I'm all right,' she says, unable to maintain eye contact. 'We're all all right.'

Will shrugs. He's a student in York and has travelled back north to celebrate his auntie Elsie's birthday and to have his laundry done. Sal's known him since he was a nipper. Isn't sure whether to treat him like a friend or somebody for whom she has a sense of responsibility.

'Lottie's doing better than I thought,' says Will. 'What they went through . . .' he shakes his head. 'It's true, isn't it? About Dagmara?'

Sal stiffens. Squeezes the roll-up between finger and thumb. Nobody mentions the name around her. Nobody speaks of the well-intentioned killer whose murders did so much good. She shakes her head, mouth a tight line.

'It's not . . . not like you heard . . . she didn't . . . I mean . . .' she trails off. Feels Will put an arm around her. Smells sweat and Lynx Africa, damp cotton and smoke. Lets herself be held. Takes comfort in the arms of a lad half her age, whose surname she doesn't recall.

The door behind her swings open. Lottie pokes her head out. She's wearing a party dress, her eyes bright, cheeks pink. There's chocolate around her mouth. She grins at Sal. Sees a hug and joins it, pressing her little plump body against Sal's legs, face upon her hip. She says something that Sal can't make out, a muffled demand for attention, an audience, and a duet.

'Having fun, sweet-pea?' asks Sal, stroking her hair. 'I heard you from upstairs. Soooo good.'

Lottie looks up, grinning. 'I got to sing one with a rude word in it! You know the Thrift shop one? I got to do the four-letter word bit. I did the accent and everything!'

Sal squats down. Puts her palm on the girl's warm, glittering cheek. 'You're having fun, then? You're glad you came?'

'Elsie's the best! And Kevin is, like, the cutest dog ever. I fed him a sausage roll and Nola said it was cannibalism because he's a Dachshund and I said in that case it was cannibalism whenever she ate a cheesy Wotsits, cause that's what she is. Was that OK? That's funny, yeah? Not mean?'

Sal puts her head against Lottie's. Breathes in Ribena and corn snacks, processed meat and home-made trifle. She suddenly realizes that she hasn't recorded either of the girls singing yet. She's due to see Lewis again soon – to show him the latest photographs and videos of his daughters in the hope that some kind of light returns to his dull eyes. Realizes she hasn't even taken a picture of them all in their party clothes, even if her own outfit is jeans and a cardigan and Nola had flatly refused to be extricated from her black hoodie. Only Lottie has made the effort: fondant-coloured fingernails and sparkly lip-gloss, glitzy hair-slides and a necklace bearing her name. She deserves to be celebrated. Deserves to have her moment slapped on social media so that other mums and dads can give a thumbs-up and a heart and say that she is 'absolutely gorgeous'. The copper in her knows that putting pictures of children on social media is like throwing a black pudding into a piranha tank, but sometimes the prevailing winds are just too strong to stand against.

'You haven't got a mean bone in your body,' says Sal, rummaging in her pockets for her phone. 'You're the kindest, sweetest, loveliest . . .' she breathes her in and mimes a big frown . . . 'the stinkiest!'

Lottie giggles as Sal tickles her. They share a big grin. Share a moment. Sal unearths her phone, telling herself she's doing OK; that she can make herself sing a Kate Bush medley and down a couple of Proseccos. That she can focus on here, on now, and not on the maelstrom of what-ifs and wheres that have feasted upon her these past months.

Her smile fades as she looks at the phone. Six missed calls from work. One from Uncle Wulf. She isn't sure which one she wants to listen to least. They'll all want something from her. All be asking for more than she can give. In the centre of her head, a voice.

Dagmara.

I can make it all go away, Sal. Listen to me. Let me soothe you. Let me help you forget . . .

She turns away from Lottie. Listens to the voicemail. Listens to the pleas from her boss, Claire. A favour. Nobody else. Know you're not due back from leave until midweek but there's really, honestly, nobody else, and it's not far, not really, and if she doesn't moan she'll buy her a book token and make her a banana bread with chocolate pieces, the ones she likes, and . . .

She looks back at Lottie, who is waiting expectantly for her stepmum to finally join the party.

Sal calls back. Tells her she'll do it. There's just something she has to do first.

'Come on, little one,' she says, hanging up. 'Let's start "Running Up That Hill" . . .'

THREE

B6305, near Langley, Hexham

9.32 p.m.

She holds the steering wheel like a garrotte: her fingers white, palms chafing, sweat smearing her wrists. She glares through the rain, the steam, the darkness. Sees branches grab for the wing mirrors. Hears the pneumatic hiss of rubber scything through dark, stagnant puddles.

She shouldn't be driving. She's sober, but the medication makes her in turns drowsy and hyper. She keeps grinding her back teeth together. Jiggles her feet on the pedals. Feels the tension shoot from her locked wrists to her braced shoulders.

Shouldn't have left them, she thinks. Shouldn't be here. Shouldn't be this close to the place where the people she loved came to harm.

'I think I can see you now . . .'

She's got the cold, miserable police constable on hands-free. He bleeds out of the console of the almost roadworthy Subaru Outback, his voice gruff, manner morose. She isn't sure she knows him. She's pretty sure he knows her.

'Aye, if you just ease off as you come down the bend. That'll do it.'

Sal mutters under her breath. She doesn't need advice on how to drive. Everything else, perhaps. But not driving. She's been a dab hand behind the wheel since she was nine.

She slows and turns as instructed. The quality of the darkness seems to shift. It's been pitch dark most of the way here but suddenly the gloom is absolute; the air thick, close. She thinks of molasses. Of crow feathers. Thinks of the place she grew up, twenty minutes further into the valley. Thinks of Uncle Wulf, cold and alone in the farmhouse where she found brief respite, and which she had to vacate when she took responsibility for the girls – social services being understandably cautious about letting Nola and Lottie set up home with a convicted killer, even if he does happen to be the best person she knows.

She flashes the lights into full beam. Feels a perverse trill of pleasure as the squat, round-shouldered uniform raises his hand to his face and squints into the glare. What was his name? Pressley? Priestley? Pressman?

She opens the door and enjoys the swirl of rain against her face, glasses misting over with tiny particles. She gives a jerk of her head. 'Alan, yeah?'

'Aye,' he says, giving her a once-over. 'Priestfield. Took long enough, didn't you? Been sitting here since I came on shift.'

Sal kills the engine. Climbs down from the driving seat and pulls her collar close. Pulls her lanyard from her pocket and drapes it around her neck. Tucks it inside her luminous coat.

'Sal, isn't it?' asks Priestfield, moving to the side of the van so it provides a temporary windbreak from the biting gale. 'Delaney?' He sucks spit through his teeth. Sal sees the pastry in his canines. Smells pork. Lynx Africa. A pain-relieving muscle gel. Wet clothes.

'Do you want to talk me through it?' asks Sal, ignoring him. 'And maybe move the cordon back another fifty feet, eh? There's a residential school not far off. Staff will be coming in early. Let's preserve what we've got while we've got it.'

'Haven't got much of much,' grunts Priestfield, rolling his bowling-ball head on his thick neck. 'Whole thing's nowt. Rich prick wasn't paying attention. Could have been worse, could have been a fuck-load better.'

Sal finds a woollen hat in the pocket of her overcoat. Pulls it on and tucks her curly hair out of the way. She catches a glimpse of herself in the darkened windows. Sees her brother. Sees her mam.

The PC has a face that seems to exist in a state of stop-motion scowls – an endless repertoire of scornful twisted lips and wrinkled brows. He grumbles the way other people might whistle.

'I told them, it's not more than a doddery sod going into a wall. Bad spot, isn't it? That wall's been down more than it's been up. Not a job for us, is it?'

Sal continues to ignore him. She doesn't begrudge him his grumbles. He's cold and miserable and has spent the past hour sitting in his patrol car waiting for the control room to locate a collision investigator able to take a look at a patch of dark, twinkling road, halfway between Hexham and Haydon Bridge. She'd grumble too.

'He's gone to hospital, has he?' asks Sal, waving an arm. She can make out the tail end of a 4x4, wedged into the space between a farm gate and a thick, black-trunked oak. She hasn't quite got her bearings. Can't quite picture how this spot will look in daylight. She knows there's a farm in the next fold of valley. Pictures a big, medieval slab of a place; thick walls and crumbling battlements sitting incongruously beside grain silos and sheep pens. They're near the fancy hotel, best she can tell. Pictures suits of armour and flaming torches, polished breastplates, pikes and swords. She and Lewis went there for tea one snatched afternoon. She'd watched him pick at the fancy little finger sandwiches; watched him ordering more tea with a little dollop of cream on the end of his nose; a chunk of jammy scone stuck to his second-best shirt. She'd loved him so fiercely it unnerved her. She wonders what she feels about him now. What she'll decide when she actually has time to stop and work out what she thinks.

'Old boy didn't want to go to hospital. Didn't want to toddle on home neither. He's bloody chatty.' Priestfield makes the word sound like an unspeakable character flaw.

'What's the story, then?' asks Sal, getting her bearings. She turns on her torch and shines it on the wet road, looking for broken glass, tyre tracks – anything that can help demonstrate whether a criminal act has taken place. She squats down, changing the angle of the torch. She can just make out where the driver hit the brakes. She takes a step back, watching the dark road twinkle like iron ore. She starts taking pictures. Opens up one of the images and expands it. There's a smear of red upon the dark road.

'He swerved?'

'One swerved like a bastard, my dear,' comes a voice from a few paces away. Sal looks up and makes out the shape of a round-shouldered, barrel-chested man: big beard, thick hair, *Daily Telegraph* forehead. He's wearing a battered tweed jacket over a checked shirt that strains around his swollen stomach. He's holding a spotted handkerchief in his left hand, dabbing it to the slight cut below his hairline.

'Sycamore Le Gros,' says the man, in a voice that is all old money and Shakespearean syntax. Waves at the land around and behind him. 'Landowner, for my sins.'

Sal recognizes him at once. He used to donate to Weardy, the Youth Initiative run by Dagmara which helped hundreds of troubled youngsters work out who they wanted to be. He was kind to Jarod when he moved back to the valley. Even shook Wulf's hand when he ran into him at the feedstore in Hexham shortly after his release. Told him that everybody deserves a fresh start and that he wouldn't be joining in with the multitudes of pitchfork-wielding locals who wanted to run him out of the valley for good.

'Salome, isn't it? Good lord! Good lord but it's a small world. And gosh, look at you! Frail little thing, weren't you? Good to see a bit of meat on you, what? Never had an appetite for this super-waif nonsense. Give me a woman with shot-putter arms and pit-pony legs, eh?'

Sal slips into her professional mode. Doesn't let herself look at Priestfield, who's snuffling into his hi-vis coat.

'I'll need you to stay behind the cordon please, Mr Le Gros,' she says. 'We have your details, if you want to get that injury looked at.'

'Barely broke the surface, Salome. I've got skin like leather. Don't be worrying about me.' He stands a little too close to Sal and she finds herself sniffing the air.

'No blood alcohol,' mutters Priestfield, as a harsh gust of wind slices down from the hillside.

'Haven't touched the stuff in six and a half years,' says Le Gros, huffing on his fingernails and buffing them on his jacket. 'Haven't enjoyed a day since, but apparently by quitting drink, I get to live longer. Can't help thinking it's because every day without a drink feels like an eternity, but there you go.'

Sal isn't sure how to reply. She starts to gently manoeuvre him back to the side of the road but he doesn't move. His eyes glitter darkly in the moonlight. There's an intensity to his stare.

'Dagmara, eh? Now there's a dark horse.'

Sal gives the same polite smile with which she greets all questions about the youth worker who earned an MBE for her decades spent caring for the region's waifs and strays. Despite the best efforts of the senior figures at Cumbria Police, rumours have spread about the full extent of Dagmara's level of intercession. On paper, Dagmara has suffered a stroke and is being cared for at a private hospital offering facilities not dissimilar to those being used to piece Lewis Beecher back together. Weardy is temporarily closed – her number two, Jarod Delaney, having vanished around the time Lewis and Dagmara were both the victims of near catastrophic head traumas. Sal can feel her twin. Knows that he lives. Knows that she misses him. Misses Lewis. Misses Dagmara . . .

'As I said, Mr Le Gros – if you could just let us get on and do our jobs, yes? Are you far from home? Could my colleague drop you somewhere?'

Le Gros gives a theatrical bow. Points towards the slowly rising hillside. 'I'm yonder. Could be home and under the covers in a moment or two, never fear.' He gives Priestfield a look that suggests they haven't warmed to one another. 'You might be more receptive than your colleague, young lady. He told you, yes? About the zombie?'

Sal takes a moment. Runs the sentence back through her head. 'Zombie?'

'He reckons he saw a zombie and swerved to avoid him,' mutters Priestfield. 'I mean . . .'

'A zombie, Mr Le Gros?'

Le Gros gives a big, Brian Blessed laugh. 'I'm using a utility word, Salome. I don't know how else to describe it, other than to say it looked like something you see in zombie films.'

Sal frowns. 'And by "zombie" . . .?'

'Half naked, rotten, dragging themselves along on stumps. I'm trying not to say zombie again.'

'You're saying you swerved to avoid a figure in the road?' She turns to Priestfield. 'That sounds like useful information.'

'I'm willing to accept that it wasn't a zombie,' concedes Le Gros. 'I'm not going to start that rumour. But there was definitely some bugger in the road who didn't look at all well.'

Beside her, Priestfield sighs. 'Do you see anybody?' He points at the hawthorn which overspills on to the road from the dark, damp field. 'Hear anybody?'

'I'm growing rather tired of this man,' confides Le Gros, leaning in conspiratorially but making no effort to lower his voice. 'I only hung around in the hope of speaking to a grown-up. Duty done, as it were. I'll leave it with you.'

Sal feels a strange throbbing sensation in the hinge of her jaw. Feels the migraine starting to wrap its steel bands around her brow. She realizes how ill she feels. How empty. How fizzy and exhausted all at once. She wants to go home to the girls. Wants to ring the hospital to be told that Lewis is doing better – that he wants to come home. Wants to call Dagmara's facility to be told that she's passed away, peacefully. That it's over. That the past is finally going to leave her be.

'OK, is he?' asks Le Gros, angling his body to exclude Priestfield and asking the question of Sal with what seems like genuine concern. 'Wulf? People are leaving him be, are they? I had a word, but you know what people can be. And you're OK too, yes? That brother of yours . . . what was his name?'

Sal doesn't want to have this conversation. Doesn't want to ask which of her many siblings he remembers.

'Wulf's trying to move on with his life,' says Sal, tightly. 'Helping people. Making up for lost time, I suppose.'

'Heard he'd buddied up with that other poor bugger. Paul's lad. Theo, isn't it?'

Sal can't bring herself to tell Le Gros that she's at work, a professional; good at her job and eager to get cracking. Can't bring herself to be rude, even when the alternative makes her feel like she's coming apart.

'They've been through similar things,' she says. 'Wulf's helping him put himself back together.'

'Talented lad, that one,' says Le Gros, shaking his head. 'Performed at Whitley Chapel Parish Hall when he was no more than seven and he brought the house down. Songs, dancing, characters. His dad was so bloody proud of him. What he lost, what was taken from them – I read in the *Telegraph* he's not even getting compensation!'

Sal hears Priestfield mutter something under his breath. Realizes that she's damp and cold and caught up in a conversation she doesn't want to have.

'He's got his name back, at least. More than Wulf's got. At least Theo's been proven innocent.'

'Mud sticks,' says Le Gros, shaking his head. 'That family. Almost ruddy Shakespearean. Anyway, good on Tara for carving out a little happiness for herself, that's what I say. He's a braver man than I. Bloody tragedy what Paul did to himself but I'm not one of these nosy sods who goes prying in other people's business. She's got a second chance at happiness and she's taken it. Bugger the rest of them, that's what I say.'

Sal thinks about Theo's mother, the housewife who led a high-profile campaign to secure her son's release and whose husband killed himself when he lost faith. She married her co-campaigner, Alec Devlin, within a year. Sal remembers reading that Theo attended his father's funeral in handcuffs – that prison guards had to keep wiping his tears away as he sobbed for the father he adored, wrists shackled together behind his back.

'Nobody ever really knows anybody else's story,' says Sal, hoping to take cover in banalities. 'I'll tell Wulf you were asking after him. And I know Theo's looking for work if you might have anything that he could . . .'

Sal stops, suddenly, as the wind drops and she makes out the faintest whisper of an unexpected sound. It's a keening, a distant, muted whine. She thinks of injured animals. Thinks of dying rabbits, twitching and snuffling into themselves.

'Did you hear that?' she asks, turning to Priestfield.

'Hear what?'

'No, listen . . .'

She strains her ears. Tries to pick up the sound again. She's about to dismiss it when it comes again: plaintive, lost.

'That's the sheep,' says Priestfield, automatically. 'That's just sheep . . .'

Sal ignores him. Steps over the tyre tracks and finds a gap in the line of tangled hawthorns. Covers her face with her hand. Pushes in through the spikes and bars.

Only as the thorns close behind her, as the darkness sweeps up, does she acknowledge the whiff of blood.

She pushes deeper. Hears Priestfield grunting far behind her, complaining, carping. She winces as a thorn snags her hair.

She smells him first. Smells the rotting, rancid flesh: a sweet, shitty fug that climbs into her mouth and throat and fills her head with thoughts of dead meat.

A flash of skin. A block of flesh. Ugly, ravaged skin.

She gasps, takes in a deeper lungful of the foul stench.

For a moment she can't make sense of what she's seeing. Can't turn the mass of lesions and wounds and open sores into something human.

Sal reaches out to steady herself. Tries to cover her nose and mouth, the light spinning in haphazard helixes and whorls.

She leans over the rotting, twisted body, bound in brambles and hawthorn, laid out in the wet grass. Her whole heart fills with compassion, with pity. Nobody should endure this. Nobody should die like this.

There comes a desperate, ear-splitting screech: a sound that makes her think of barn owls, of final breaths; of agony and fear unimaginable.

And then the thing in the grass grabs her wrist.

FOUR

Hagman's Farm, Alston Moor

10.12 p.m.

The voice emerges half strangled, a throat held fast by a boot. The sound emerges from the place where the mouth should be, lips touching the ragged patchwork of leathery scraps. Blind eyes blink, milkily, in the mismatched slits scored into the wrinkled, stinking material.

'. . . their screams were the sweetest of songs. With each breaking bone I served my lord. With each burnt heart I served him. Each time the hammer struck the nail and I felt the tender flesh separate beneath the metal, I was performing a duty no other man could perform. I made both art and science of death. I learned what a human being could endure. Were I to have used similar artfulness in song, my ditties would still be hummed to this day . . .'

The figure twists. Writhes. Drags its crippled leg in a pained semi-circle, lurching suddenly forward. The light of the flickering fire finds its mirror in the rotting swatches of skin.

'Come with me, dear traveller. Step into the past with the creature they called Blindworm. Take my burned, bloodied hand and follow me to the bowels of Redburn.'

The creature straightens. Places a hand on its hip. Readjusts the hessian sacking which clings to its twisted shoulders. The voice that emerges is gentle. Soft.

'I'm thinking it might be too ghoulish,' he says. 'Hot, too. I've overdone it, haven't I? They're going to hate it.'

He takes a fistful of the crude, ill-fitting mask. Yanks it off. A fine-featured man emerges: tousled black hair and strikingly blue eyes. He drags off the rest of the outfit. Slumps, dejectedly, in the spindly chair by the fireplace, knocking over a pile of discarded papers as he does so.

'Sorry. I'm just . . . nervous.'

'I can't say whether they'll like it, Theo. But I can tell you it's very good. You're very good. If they don't go for it, that's their loss.'

'It is ghoulish though, isn't it? I mean, when you think about what they'll have heard.'

'They heard the wrong story and now they're learning the right one. You're an innocent man. Behave like one.'

'Says you,' smiles Theo.

'Aye, well.'

Wulfric Hagman rubs his big pink palm over wet black fur. Feels the nervousness bleed out of the Border Collie whose head lolls drunkenly on his lap. Tips isn't much of a sheepdog. Jarod, her true owner, always thought of her as a well-intentioned moron. Were there a sheepdog exam, Jarod reckoned old Tips would be on to her final resit and the careers adviser would be suggesting she consider a qualification in health and social care. But she's kind and gentle and doesn't care that the man who looks after her in her master's absence is a convicted killer and gullible accomplice to a dozen unsolved murders.

Give it a rest, Wulf. None of it's your fault. You've got a good heart, that's all. Too big for this world. Caused you no end of pain. Did some good with it, though. Did some good along the way . . .

Hagman winces, grinding his teeth. He tastes Calendula. Soup. Tobacco. Tastes the low, peaty fug of the golden fire, smouldering in the hearth.

Shut up, he hisses, inside his head. *Stop it. Nobody's listening to you any more, Dagmara . . .*

Hagman tries not to let himself convey his thoughts through his touch. He has a horrible feeling that, one day soon, Tips will look up at him and give a disappointed shake of the head. She'll turn her back and walk out the door. He knows such thoughts are maudlin and self-pitying. He also feels as though he is well within his rights.

Not listening, are you Wulf? Drifted into yourself again. Poor sod's come to you for help and you're not even looking at the silly bugger . . .

'. . . honestly think she's going to do something stupid . . . I know it's not like your situation but maybe, I don't know, if you just talked to her . . .'

Hagman gives his attention back to the young man who sits in the other rocking chair in front of the smouldering open fire. They are in the flagstoned, low-ceilinged kitchen of the dark little farmhouse where Hagman grew up. The windows are small, the glass thick, and every spare surface is taken up with jars and demijohns, multi-coloured bottles and opaque containers. Dried herbs hang from the metal hooks in the ceiling. Rag rugs cover the grey, uneven floor. If placed in a frame, nothing in the scene would suggest the twenty-first century. Hagman, with his soft cords, his open-necked shirt and cardigan, his bald head and thick beard, could be mistaken for a gentleman farmer. Theo Myers, with his thick, slicked-black curls, his wide blue eyes, his waistcoat and blue suit jacket, has the air of hopeful suitor; a wistful romantic making a pitch for some absent maiden. Hagman cannot help but see the world through such a lens. For two decades he was a prisoner, locked up for a crime he believed he had committed. He taught himself to make up stories, to turn snapshots into scenes from whimsical tales. He thinks it might have saved his sanity. Either that, or driven him mad.

'. . . know you've got problems of your own, but look, I'm out, aren't I? I mean, that's what it's all been for and she just won't . . . she just won't leave it . . .'

Hagman watches as the younger man takes a final swig from the big glass tankard in his hand. It contains cleaver-water. It's good for the lymph nodes. Good to flush out the system. Theo has twice asked him for the recipe. Twice giggled, madly, when Hagman has told him that 'cleavers' is another name for the weed commonly known as sticky jack, or sticky willy. Theo was only 20 when he was sent to prison. Thirty when he came out. His maturity levels tended to oscillate.

Hagman rubs at Tips's head once more. The daft dog's been out in the downpour, barking up trees and sniffing around in the outbuildings. There's still a trace of Jarod in some of the murkier corners. She hoovers it up with her nostrils – comes home looking confused, bewildered, bereft. Hagman endures a memory: Tips arriving home three days after Jarod left the farm on the quad bike to go and confront the woman who twisted his mind into vermicelli. Remembers the blood on Tips's muzzle; the whimpering as Hagman ran his hands over her sore ribs, tender pads. He wishes she could tell him what she knew. Whether her master, his friend, is still alive.

'Sorry Wulf,' says Theo, coming to a stop. 'I'm just going on, aren't I? Like you haven't got enough problems without me adding to them. It's just, like . . . you calm me down, y'know? I can't put it any other way. You're like . . . you know when you hug a tree, or plant a shrub or something, and you feel all kind of *at one* with everything for a moment. You're like that. Is that too much, mate? I mean, if it is, I'll shut up, but I thought maybe you could do with hearing it, or something, and . . .'

Hagman lets himself smile. Closes his eyes while he does so in case Theo pulls a face he can't endure. 'It's a lovely thing to hear, Theo,' he says, quietly. 'Means a lot.'

He opens his eyes. Theo has cocked his head. He's staring at him, earnest and intent.

'You can make her feel better, yeah? Or just explain it all. Just tell her to leave it be. I'm home. There's nowt more to be done. I just want to live. She's got a chance at a bit of happiness and all she's doing is looking back and I can't move forward while she's . . . while she's telling me every day what she's lost, what was taken from her, from me . . .'

Hagman nods, despite himself. He's made countless promises not to get involved. He just can't help himself. He's never been good at saying no.

'I'm not just turning up uninvited, Theo,' he says, taking a sip from the dainty cup that rests on a mismatched saucer on the pile of books at his side. It's tepid. Bitter. He can taste the red clover and honey. Can almost get a sense of Jarod, grinding and decocting, steeping and dead-heading, making his wellness elixirs while fighting the demons in his head. Feels Tips stiffen at his knee. Raises his hand from the dog's head lest the sense of disquiet pass from one to the other.

'I'll bring her to you,' says Theo, sitting forward, his manner excitable. 'She knows who you are. How you've helped. I'll tell her it's part of the process or something. That you've asked to meet her. That it'll do me good. I mean, you should have met before now, really, given all you've done for me.'

Hagman directs his gaze to the mound of books at the far end of the table. He can't look the lad in the eyes while he's keeping secrets. Hates himself for not being able to tell the younger man why he's so reluctant to meet his mum. He let them down. Let down every bugger on his patch when he decided he'd rather die than live without Trina Delaney. If he'd still been a copper, maybe Theo's life would have gone very differently. He knows Tara's would. Reckons a lot of bad things wouldn't have happened if he'd just stuck to doing a job he wasn't even particularly good at.

'We've nothing to talk about other than the case,' says Theo. 'It's like being a teenager again sometimes. We don't like any of the same stuff, haven't even got the same memories of the same events. I thought maybe after Dad, after all this, maybe she'd start to see me – who I really am, but she still looks through me sometimes, and then I think about Dad and what he wanted to tell me and I get this feeling like I'm among strangers – like a cuckoo in a nest, you know?'

Hagman jumps as a log snaps in the fireplace, a shower of red and gold falling like the last days of autumn. Wonders when he would go back to, were he so permitted. How far he would project himself into the past if he were given the chance to change just one thing. He shouldn't have agreed to talk to Theo, he realizes that now, but Jane from the Juris Project had been so damn insistent and he'd been feeling so bloody lonely since Salome left, since Jarod took off, since Dagmara, well . . . since Dagmara revealed what she had done. He'd been tempted by the notion of a friend. He can't even go to the local shops without somebody calling him a killer. Can't park the old 4x4 in Allendale without coming back to flat tyres and abuse drawn in the mud on the windshield. The idea of a companion had been appealing. Jane had been clear enough in her instructions. Keep him from going mad. Keep him positive. Keep him on the straight and narrow. Hagman is long past the stage of questioning life's absurdities, but the fact that he, a convicted killer, is being tasked with the emotional well-being of a murderer found innocent on appeal, is not lost on him.

He gives Theo another glance. He likes having him here. Hagman doesn't see his own children. Doesn't see any of the numerous stepchildren who once called him Uncle Wulf. But Theo fills a space of some kind in his life. He looks forward to his visits, to his nearness. Likes sitting by the fire and chatting about life and death and all the things in between and after. Sometimes they play chess. Occasionally they'll sit in silence, each reading a book, the only sound the cracking of the logs in the fire and the turning of dry pages. Theo has tried to help him with the running of the struggling little sheep farm, but he's not got much of a gift for outdoors work. He'd harboured dreams of becoming an actor before he got himself arrested. He likes to draw now. Sometimes he'll sit with a stick of charcoal and scribble towers and turrets on empty packets and scraps of paper. He's covered the transcripts of Hagman's court appearance with so many smudgy black daubings that they are all but illegible.

Hagman doesn't mind. He's given up on the idea of his conviction being overturned. Thanks to Sal, he knows the truth. Knows he didn't kill Trina Delaney. Knows who did, and why. And that's enough. That was all that ever mattered to him. He can take the insults, the vandalism, the abuse and loneliness. Can take it all and more. All that matters is the certainty that he didn't end her life.

'You reckon this week will be all right, Wulf?' asks Theo, eagerly. He's sitting forward in his chair, animated and giddy, the reflected light of the fire flickering on one cheek so that for a moment it seems as though he is being slowly devoured by flames. 'Alec will thank you for it if I get the gig, I promise you. I think he regrets getting me out, truth be told.'

Hagman gives the required smile. He hasn't yet encountered Alec Devlin, though he's read about him here and there. First saw his name when still inside – author of an opinion piece in *The Guardian*. He's done a lot for the unjustly convicted. Taken on the authorities and won more often than he's lost. Fights the good fight. It was his tenacity that saw Theo's conviction overturned. His refusal to quit which ensured the young man was set free. Theo hasn't yet opened up about how he feels that Alec is now also his stepfather – the comfort he offered Tara Myers in the wake of her husband's suicide becoming a love story along the way. Theo doesn't quite live with them. He keeps his things at the converted barn they share near Langley Dam, but he sleeps most nights in the little glade to the east of Hagman's farm. He's pinning his hopes on a position up at Lumley Castle, cos-playing the role of fabled thirteenth-century madman and torturer, Blindworm. Hagman has performed countless incantations and invocations to try and swaddle the lad in hope and possibility, but he doesn't really believe that the castle's owners are going to employ somebody who's best known in the valley for killing a homeless man on a drunken night out. The fact that he's been exonerated counts for little in the court of local opinion.

'It's like I'm a disappointment, or something,' says Theo. 'All she wanted while I was inside was to have me home. Well, I'm home, aren't I? I mean, we won. I'm out. It was bad enough when she kept grabbing me, hugging me like I was going to disappear. But this . . . the way she is . . . so angry, distant. I mean, she's got a chance at happiness, hasn't she? It's like she doesn't want to let me become her son again. It's like she just wants me to be this, what was the word . . . ?'

'Avatar,' says Hagman, quietly.

Theo nods. 'Yeah, an avatar for injustice. It's like, now she's won, she doesn't know what to do with the prize.'

'She put a lot of herself into fighting for you, Theo. It's going to take time.'

'We don't have time, Wulf. She's sixty-four. Alec is nigh-on seventy-five. I'm not saying that's geriatric, but we can still make good memories. I just want her to let herself be happy.'

Hagman fights the urge to reach across and put his hand on Theo's. Wonders whether, in such moments, the young man feels the presence of his own father. Wonders when the lad will talk about the weight of guilt that dwells within him; about the sure and certain knowledge that if it were not for his conviction, his father would still be alive.

Hagman sits back in the rocking chair. Strokes Tips's ears. Feels the weight of responsibility settle inside him. It was the same when he was a police officer; the same when he was a convicted killer looking out for those more vulnerable than himself. Couldn't leave well alone. Had to do the decent thing.

He watches as Theo glances at the clock. It's getting late. Sees Theo throw a glance at the window, at the hard rain hammering the dark glass. He starts picking a hair off the front of his jacket. He always dresses smartly when coming to see Hagman. Likes any excuse to put on something a little more formal; an outfit with flair. He works part-time in a warehouse on an industrial estate just outside of Prudhoe. It's got little in common with the dream he sustained himself with during incarceration: West End dazzle and the chance to lose himself in performance. Instead he drives a forklift. Wears trainers and jogging suits. Eats his lunch in the disabled toilet so he doesn't have to answer the questions from his workmates about the worst things he saw, about the killers and rapists with whom he shared a wing; about his feelings towards the bastards who lied on the stand and put him away. They've all read the articles. All listened to the podcasts. One or two even went across to the Sage in Gateshead to watch the play inspired by his conviction and subsequent fight for justice. He's told Wulf how it feels; told him how much of a let-down he knows himself to be. The hot, constant burn of knowing he's not nearly as interesting as the things that have happened to him.

'You can stay, if you like,' says Hagman, affecting nonchalance. He doesn't know whether he hopes he'll stay or leave. Isn't sure whether he wants company, or blessed isolation. 'Proper roof. Proper bed.'

Theo gives a big warm smile. 'You're a good egg, Wulfric Hagman. Weird phrase that, isn't it? Don't know where it came from. But no, you're all right. I'll get off. It's dry inside the tent, I've told you. If Alec asks, I was in bed an hour ago, yeah?'

Hagman notices the way Theo breaks eye contact when he mentions the campaigner who set him free.

'I saw that,' says Theo, with a little grin. 'Looking into my head, weren't you? Looking for truths.'

Hagman reaches forward. Picks up the metal poker and moves the logs around in the fire. Glances up and sees the flames dance in the young man's eyes.

'Looking in your head?'

'All that guided meditation; lucid dreaming, unlocking memories, keeping others closed . . . it was her that showed you, wasn't it? *Her*.'

Hagman gazes into the fire. Thinks of Dagmara. Of his closest ally, only friend. God he misses her. He feels half-made without her. Feels like uncooked dough.

'I can't talk about her,' says Hagman. 'I made a promise.'

'She did it though, yeah? Killed all those people? All those bad people who did bad things? She did that, didn't she? Even let you take the blame for one of them, yeah? You can tell me, Wulf. All of it. I mean, I've told you. You'll feel better. Just let it out, yeah?'

Hagman sits back in his chair. Feels the young man's gaze. Feels Tips return her head to his lap. Rubs at her ears. Doesn't realize how hard he's doing it until she yelps.

'I can't,' says Wulf, his throat suddenly dry. 'I made a promise.'

Theo gives a laugh, as if the older man has just admitted to believing in the Tooth Fairy. 'A promise? Twenty years they took, mate. Twenty years! And they still say it was you. I mean, you're the one who should be getting the pay-out, not me. What I went through – it's nowt compared to what was done to you. And you're one of their own. A copper! I mean, how do you stop from wanting vengeance? I know we all say the right things in interviews and stuff but, Christ, there are times when I think about what I would do if I ever saw them again; what I would do to them if I had the chance . . .'

Hagman can't be sure, but for a moment it sounds as if two voices are talking at once. Something hard, something malevolent, seems to bleed into Theo's voice. The gentle, animated young man becomes something else; something other. His eyes seem to darken, two black coals smouldering in the crucible of his skull.

'You did what I asked, yes? Wrote the words? Said the words?'

Theo nods, his whole manner sincere. 'Write the things I want to let go of on the leaves you gave me. Put them in the jar. Think about it hard. Place it in running water, or like, a stream, ideally – not the bath . . .'

'Has it helped?'

Theo smiles, tiredly. 'I don't know. Maybe I'd have been worse if not. Maybe I should stop trying to be positive and just let the anger out. That's what Mam says I need to do. Be angry. She says that's what sustained her; that Dad gave up when he let his anger drain away. I don't know. I don't like thinking about it. Thinking about how lonely he must have been in those last days.' He flinches. Wrinkles his nose. Grips the leather mask in his hand.

'There's no peace to be found in vengeance,' says Hagman, quietly. He feels suddenly uncomfortable. Feels a sudden urge to be rid of his visitor. To go back to the quiet and the loneliness.

Theo shakes his head. His face clears. He smiles, eyes wide. 'You're right,' he says, breezily. 'Best keep the dark thoughts away, eh? Who knows where they might lead? And I'll bring my mam, yeah? You'll help her, won't you? Help her let go of some of it? I mean, it's killing her. Killing all of us.'

Hagman strokes Tips. He'd give anything to swap places with the dog right now. Would love to be fed and cosseted, stroked and protected. Would do a damn better job at herding the sheep, too. Has no doubts that Tips, if somehow permitted the opportunity to walk around in Hagman's flesh, would do a far better job at being a person.

'Yes,' says Hagman. 'Yes, of course.'

Hexham Courant

'No compensation for man locked up for over seven years for a crime he didn't commit'

13.08.2024

After spending over seven years locked up for a murder he did not commit, Theodore Myers's conviction was finally quashed – and yet not a penny of compensation has been paid still. This week there was another blow for a man who deserves more than a grudging apology.

A miscarriage of justice victim who was jailed for almost eight years for a murder he did not commit has called for the abolition of the government's 'brutal test' for compensation.

Theo Myers, 31, was speaking after a devastating judgment was handed down in the European Court of Human Rights in Strasbourg. He and his legal team attempted to overturn a system that has in the last eight years blocked ninety-three per cent of people whose convictions are quashed on appeal from being compensated.

It was the latest chapter in a long-running scandal for the Stocksfield man, who was a promising drama student hoping for a career in the West End when he became the victim of mistaken identity that devastated him and his family. Theo's father, Hexham farmer Paul Myers, took his own life while his son was still inside.

Mr Myers, who now lives in rural Hexhamshire with his mother and her new husband, legal campaigner Alec Devlin, said in a statement: 'I have been fighting a murder case of which I am entirely innocent. Still today I have not received a single penny for the seven and half years I spent in prison. The brutal test for compensation introduced in 2016 needs to be abolished; it goes completely against what this country should stand for.'

Mr Myers's mother, Tara, said: 'He's innocent. Everybody knows he's innocent. He's been unequivocally cleared. So to withhold compensation for all that he lost – it's so cruel that I don't think I can endure it. I truly thought that when he walked through those gates we could pick up where we left off but what's been done to him – what we've all lost – there's no compensation in the world for that. Even so, he deserves to have some recompense for it all. What's he supposed to do with the rest of his life? What are any of us?'

Mr Myers's legal team were able to demonstrate that he was nowhere near the scene of the fatal attack, and that he had been the victim of poor legal counsel and levels of police incompetence. He is presently working part-time in a warehouse and has been unable to resume his earlier dream of a life in theatre.

FIVE

Sal stumbles backwards, hand rising to her face. The scent of rotting flesh pushes into her nose and mouth like a fist. She blinks over and over, each tiny moment of darkness an attempt to wipe away the horror.

Alive, she thinks. *It's alive . . .*

Every instinct is screaming at her to run. For a moment she is nothing but primal energy; a hunter-gatherer facing something unclean; something unknown and rancid.

She hears herself speak. Hears the better part of herself take control.

'I'm Sal. I'm a police officer. Can you hear me? Sir, can you hear me?'

Course he can't fucking hear you, Sal. Course he can't. Look at the state of him! Best thing you can do is end things for him, you know that. Cruel to do owt else. Nowt heroic about saving this life, girl. Nowt noble about giving this poor bastard a future. Do the decent thing, love. Pinch his nostrils and his gob and tell your mates he were dead when you found him . . .

Sal screws up her eyes. Makes fists. Ignores the voice as it fills her skull with poison.

'That you, Sal? What you got?'

She turns, startled. Gasps, gratefully, as Priestfield waddles forward out of the darkness, the light from his phone glaring into his broad, rain-soaked face. 'Jesus, could you not have said? Standing there like a bloody lemon, I was. What you . . .'

He raises the light. Illuminates the half-made thing. 'Fucking Jesus . . .'

Sal feels herself snap back into control, the voices snatched away like steam.

'He looks like . . . a zombie. Jesus, Sal, is he alive? He can't be alive . . .'

'Call it in,' demands Sal. 'Urgent. He's got a pulse. It's weak but it's there.'

Priestfield is staring, hunched, mouth open. 'Look at him. Sal, just look at him!'

Sal ignores him. She fights down her revulsion and moves closer to the man. He stares, eyes like slices of lemon, pupils barely there. His stump of tongue moves grotesquely in the black, filthy maw: teeth sitting in a mulch of purpled, bloody gum. She turns her face away as the stench of corruption pushes deeper inside. She pulls a pair of gloves from her pocket. Fumbles at the wet material, pushing her fingers and thumbs into the wrong holes. Runs her hands over the man's fragile, twisted form. He's bone and sinew, gristle and gore. He lurches, as her hands touch his wrist. Twists and jerks forward, squawking blindly.

'It's OK,' she hears herself. 'We're going to get help. Can you tell me your name? Sir? Can you tell me your name?'

At her side, she hears Priestfield retching. Sees the cone of light shiver, the illuminated raindrops vibrating like a paused VCR. She finds herself tapping her chest. Rubs her finger and thumb together, the nitrile material squeaking against her skin. She centres herself, the way Dagmara taught her. Breathes. Drama breaths, that's what she'd called them. In for three, hold for three, out for three. Centre yourself, girl. Take control . . .

Hears Jarod, the faintest whisper in the centre of her skull: *Don't be afraid. I've got you.*

She cocks her head. Moves closer. Tries to make out the details in the ruination of the man's face. Thinks: tattered trousers, bare feet, bare chest; grazes to the bone; blood on the toes, the stumps of finger; flesh missing from the forearm; the bicep; filth grimed into stewed-tea skin . . .

'He look foreign to you?' asks Priestfield, wiping his mouth. 'Under it all, like? He look . . .?'

She turns towards Priestfield's voice. Opens her mouth to speak.

The hand shoots out again. Catches her around the wrist: a wet mouth, toothless gums. Jerks like a noose.

She feels her feet slip and slither in the wet grass. Slithers on to her side, one hand thrown out for support. She jars her elbow. Feels her phone skitter away into the damp grass. She tries to yank her hand away. Every cell in her body is recoiling from the bad-meat touch of rotting flesh. But the grip is too strong. Bony fingers encircle her wrist. She feels manacled. Feels as though the contact will eat to the bone. He lurches again. Twists. His other hand slithers up her body. Finds her hand like a blind predator seeking prey.

'Get off her! Get off!'

Priestfield tries to pull her free. She uses her elbow to push him back. In her head, legion voices, screeching in harmony.

And then one bloodied, fetid finger is moving over her palm; her skin a stylus. She shudders at the touch. Feels concentric circles tickling her skin; shudders at the wet-spider caress.

'Urgent assistance required! Urgent assistance required!'

The man lurches again. Sits up like an electrified cadaver. The mouth twists. Oozes. Drools. A stream of vomit sprays from the slack, black mouth.

Sal squirms away, hauling herself free. Fights down her own rising bile. Looks, with horror, at the pool of vomit illuminated by Priestfield's quivering light.

Sees meat.

Scraps of flesh.

Sees something that might be an ear . . .

Hears Jarod. Dagmara. Mam.

Someone wanted this.

SIX

It moves like a spider. Moves as both predator and prey.
  Here, in the soggy blackness at the edge of the little stand of trees, it stalks, scuttles: a hand puppet on a bedroom wall.
It knows this terrain. Knows where to stand. Plants its feet in the well-trodden tufts, the unslimed stepping stones across the stream; stamping down the barbed wire and brambles that snag. As it moves, it seems to knit black threads between the dark trunks of ancient trees . . .
It ducks under the branches of the old beech tree and into the sloping field. It turns its black, lipless face towards the ghostly white lambs that bound, chubbily, at the far end of the field, huddled in with their bleating mothers, hunched by the wall that offers little protection from the ceaseless, swirling rain.
It moves with greater purpose now. Feels its breath become more ragged, heart begin to pound. Its gait appears to change, one leg suddenly dragging, an arm rising, as if the creature were suddenly feeling its way in pitch blackness rather the leering yellow moon which spills a tallowy light across the dark, slick fields.
It pauses. Looks down towards the far-off strip of road. Lights flicker, on and off, yellow and blue. It cocks its head.
A movement, to its left, a sudden blur and a splash as something dark and sleek and worm-tailed plunges from the long grass and into the flooded furrow, surface shimmering as if made of crow feathers.
For a moment, it stands transfixed. Watches, stomach roiling, as it sights a tail, slimy and grey-pink, snout breaking the undulating surface; bead-black eyes and mud-slicked fur; an urgency to the way its claws scrabble at the rising water.
Thinks: *the ruin.*
Thinks: *they couldn't . . . not after this long . . .*
It moves forward. Moves faster now. Makes for the great jagged splinter of burnt timber and toppled stone. Makes for the ruin.
Breath hot now. Hot and foul. Its nostrils, its mouth, flooding with the mingled tastes of acid; chemical; bile. It breathes in a

trapped mouthful of its own foulness. Regurgitates its own stench as a pain grips its gut. It begins to move faster towards the bulk of the grey-black tower wall: bare windows and weed-fined arrow slits glaring out like an eyeless face. Trees grow in its shelter; great gnarled hawthorns and twists of bramble; great purple-headed thistles bursting from the long grass like spears.

It stops short. Stares ahead, rain coming harder now, striking its face. Begins to lurch forward, past the wall, stumbling over the toppled masonry, the splashing down through the flooded beck, muddy ground sucking at its limbs as it squelches madly, over the little rise, and slithers down the grassy blanket to the thicket, all briars and deadwood, spiky twists of teasel, bindweed, artfully arranged around a mound of earth. Here and there are piles of masonry; sheets of corrugated metal; lengths of rotten timber studded with crucifixion nails; scribbled symbols scarred deep into the crumbled wood.

It stops still. Turns away from the stretch of rock and earth and grass and thorns and lets its gaze follow the glugging, inky ribbon of floodwater as it surges down the flooded slope. Sees brown fur: black as it moves out of the moonlight.

It stumbles at the water's edge. For a moment, it sees itself. Sees through the leather eye-slits and the crinkled patchwork of fetid leather. Sees what it is beneath.

Thinks: *stop pretending . . . stop listening . . . stop this madness!*

It rubs its gloved hands over its featureless face. Feels the sodden earth soak and pull at its feet, legs, knees – as if the ground was trying to pull it inside. It has a dizzying, high sensation; a burst of delirium. Sees high walls and gleaming torches, richly adorned tapestries and maids in billowing gowns. Sees low ceilings, flickering candles. Smells the meat fat and sweat; the smoke; hears again, an echo of the rain; the sizzle of meat on the spit. Sees this dark place, this tomb beneath the earth. Remembers the splinter of bones; the thud of flesh on rock. Hears again, the yearning pleas; the softening, fading calls for mercy.

Thinks: *you're pretending. Making it easy for yourself. Trying to ensure you get a moment's rest from the black thoughts that are going to hound you every day of what life you've got left, you worthless, snivelling . . .*

It cocks its head. Hears the sirens grow louder. Pushes on, leaping awkwardly across the fast-flowing floodwater. Stops, perfectly still. Looks down at the crumbled mound of broken black fur.

Sees the toppled bricks. The patch of freshly turned earth.

It considers the corpse. Feels its sodden, twisted form. Feels the broken bones. Looks again at the exposed patch of ground.

Quickly, it crosses to the entrance to the hole. Peers inside. Sees blackness. Smells rotten meat and sheep shit. Smells something dead.

It begins to rearrange the stones. Heaves boulders and blocks of mossy, brittle masonry into an uneven ridge around the patch of disturbed mud and stone.

There is a moment, as it wedges an old, age-weathered piece of rock into the space in the earth; a moment when, for a second, it thinks it might just be able to make out a sound.

Hears a distant, buried voice breathe 'Mahee'.

Then, in pitiful amen: a solitary 'please'.

It stamps the rock down. Pulls a length of timber from the pile and tries to sink it into the sodden ground. It breaks under the weight.

Sirens again. Louder now. Voices, inside, outside. The sound of static and rain and the mournful shivering of the gathering trees.

Thinks: *there's still time.*

Thinks: *must be dead. Must be.*

Looks at the rat, back broken. Considers, for a moment, the man must have had to wriggle and claw and scratch; the horrors and misery and the scrabbling claws of the evil-eyed vermin that had shown him the way . . .

It turns and walks quickly back up the slope. Its actions become less lurching, less pained. It begins to walk like a man.

As it enters the trees, it pulls off its face. Puts it in its pocket.

Later, when it lies in its bed and stares, unseeing, into the darkness, it will return to this place. It will think its way back here, this little patch of rocky land, and it will wonder if perhaps, there mightn't have been another way. Whether what it is doing, is wrong.

Blindworm will provide the only answer he cares to hear.

Blindworm will ask: *who next?*

SEVEN

Hagman doesn't really sleep. There are moments when he drifts into a vague, liminal state of consciousness, but he never truly gives himself over to the dark. Things wait for him in that deep, silent space.

Here, now, he sits in the high-backed chair, eyes closed, letting the light of the dying fire flicker upon his broad face and gleaming, razored skull. He twitches whenever a log cracks in the hearth; one of the old damp timbers stretches and settles. He still sleeps like a prisoner. Still keeps one eye on the door. It took him six months of freedom to let go his grip on the sock full of batteries that he used to protect himself on the inside. Ex cops aren't popular in prison. Nonces neither. He carries the cartography of his transgressions – re-set bones and stitched skin, knees that ache on cold mornings; one cauliflower ear sitting lopsided on his skull in a grisly mess of cartilage.

He strokes Tips with his foot. Rubs his belly. Lets himself wonder. God how he'd love to peer inside the dog's head and drain her of her memories. She knows what happened to her master. Saw what occurred when Jarod confronted the woman who made him believe he was a killer and who twisted his brain into a tangle of loops and garrottes. There was blood on her muzzle when she arrived home – shivering, whining – eight miles across a snow-blanketed landscape from the remote village hall where Jarod was last seen alive. The police found blood on the ground. Too much blood to bode anything but ill.

He feels Tips stiffen. Opens his eyes. Watches the light change beyond the small, black windows, peering out through the glass and the drying leaves and the rain-jewelled cobwebs. Sees the yellow cones of light through spotlights across the yard: flashes of corrugated roof, black brick, great skeletal hulks of tractor, digger, rotavator – mechanical dinosaurs long since dead in the foot-thick mulch of mud and sheep shit.

'Sal,' he says, softly. 'Don't worry.'

He closes his eyes, and lets himself breathe. Calms himself.

Glances up at the clock. It's a little after 2 a.m. He wonders if this is it. Whether she's here to break the news that one of them is dead. Dagmara. Jarod. Perhaps Lewis. Wonders if today's the day she slaps the cuffs on him and tells him it's all been a mistake. He's due back inside.

It takes several minutes for the door to open. He imagines her sitting there in the driving seat, head against the steering wheel, fighting the urge to come home. He pictures her glancing up at the mangled caravan where she briefly made her home when Lewis kicked her out, too horrified by what he had learned about her past to commit to the future he had once promised. *Lewis*, he thinks. *If it's one of them, I hope it's Lewis . . .*

The door opens. Sal creeps in like smoke. Stands for a moment in the frame of the doorway, curly hair soaked to melted plastic against her pale face, her glasses calligraphed with rain and grime. He angles his head. Manages a half-smile.

Wordlessly, Sal pulls off her boots. Crosses to the counter by the sink. Fills the kettle, lights the range. She lets out a long, slow breath. Settles into the seat opposite Hagman's. Rests her stockinged feet on Tips's warm, monochrome fur.

'Out late,' says Hagman, eventually.

Sal doesn't speak. Just sits in soft, sad silence. Occasionally she pinches her nostrils with her finger and thumb. Hagman watches the firelight dance on the lenses of her glasses. Looks at the pink-rimmed yellowness of her irises. Smells something bad rising from her damp clothes; a mustiness; something peptic and carnal.

'Bad one,' says Sal, at last. 'Worst one in a while.'

Hagman feels himself relax. Sinks into the chair. He knows why she's here. Knows what she needs him to be. She's been a proper copper tonight. She's witnessed something terrible. Can't go home and play Mum until it's out of her system. He's a safe space for her – a place to decompress lest she carry the toxins of her reality into the family home.

He listens as she speaks. Holds her as she cries.

Thinks: *a strange kind of happiness, this.*

You're a fucking psycho, Wulf. Not fit to be let out.

'Met a friend of yours,' she says, absently. 'Sycamore Le Gros. Bet he got teased at school, eh?'

'Not likely,' says Hagman, getting comfy. He thinks upon the rich landowner with the personality big enough for two. 'You'll probably have heard the stories already, and I can't tell you them without blushing, but let's just say, they've not had dull lives. None of them. You can trace them back to Edward I, apparently. They love telling the story. I heard they'd commissioned a proper book about their fascinating past and all the great men of their line. Sycamore's running out of time, I reckon.' He looks away, unable to keep his tone light. 'Like visitors from another time, some of these old families. His dad, well . . . I'll let you ask somebody else so I don't have to squirm.'

You're a waste of space, Wulf. Already hiding things. Already lying . . .

He watches as Sal tries to rouse herself. Sniffs back another potential deluge of tears. 'He's fine. Got a fright.'

'Nothing he can't take,' smiles Hagman, remembering the stories told to him while he was still a probationer. Thinks of his old mentor – the man who showed him what not to do. 'Callum Whitehead and him were pals, once upon a time. Maybe still are – though I doubt it if Sycamore felt able to give me a kindly glance. Whitehead's cronies are still under orders to make life as miserable for me as they can.' He looks at the ceiling. 'Not that I'm moaning . . .'

'He's gone quiet,' says Sal. 'Whitehead, I mean. Shushed everything up. All the old handshakes and nods and winks – quietened it all down. Even managed to keep Quinn in a job.'

Hagman looks into the fire. Thinks of the dark-haired woman who had tried to arrest him for multiple murders: very much the gun for retired Chief Superintendent Whitehead's bullets. Instead, he had saved Quinn's life, resulting in a truce that neither trusts. He knows Whitehead will carry a grudge to the grave. Hagman sometimes wishes he had spent less time healing his emotional traumas. Sometimes he would still like to feel hatred for the brutal street thug who beat him half to death when he thought him guilty of the murder of Trina Delaney, and who went on to become one of the most formidable voices in the upper echelons of Northumbria Police. Even in retirement, he wields power. Hagman just hopes he wields it against him, and not Sal.

'Everything that happened to Lewis . . . all the cut corners – she didn't lose more than a couple of ranks. Callum wangled Quinn a job with Cumbria's Criminal Investigation Department. You should see her in the corridors, clip-clopping along like a prize bloody unicorn, like the cat who got the cream.'

'Those mixed metaphors are beneath you,' says Hagman, trying to make a joke of it. His forced smile slips into his beard. He lets out a sigh. 'But she didn't get the cream, did she? Lewis didn't even recognize her when she poured her heart out to him. Recognized you though, didn't he? Lit up like a proper old-fashioned bulb when you sat by his bed.'

'Everybody's talking,' says Sal, into her knees. 'Saying things about me and Lewis and . . . her. And I've got to be so careful. One wrong step and the girls . . .' she runs out of words and air. Shakes her head.

Hagman tries to think of something to say. Thinks of Le Gros and a story surfaces. 'Did I ever tell you about Sycamore's grandfather? Mean old sod but had to admire his stamina. Lumley Castle in the Seventies, right – it wasn't quite such a fine and upstanding establishment as it is today. Some of the medieval banquets they held there during that time, they were more like Gomorrah on a Bank Holiday weekend than a night out. They had the lot, you know? Jesters, serving wenches; knights in armour bouncing maces off one another's heads. Like a Roman orgy, if you believed the stories. Le Gros popped his clogs there – in his eighties, he was. Proper regular, all told. His wife thought he went out to see the beagle society over at Haydon Bridge, but every other bugger knew how he spent his leisure time. They reckon he died with a smile on his face but the three serving wenches he was with at the time were a bit less impressed.'

Sal raises her head and smiles, dutifully. 'Is your friend doing OK? Theo?'

Hagman finds himself chuckling. Settles himself in his chair.

'He's auditioning for a role as a tour guide up at Lumley Castle. Decided to audition as Blindworm. Torturer in chief for Edward I. Almost certainly fictional, but that doesn't really matter eight hundred years down the line, does it? He did his audition for me earlier – in full Blindworm get-up. Scary voice, leathery mask, talk of blood and tears and the like.' He pauses. Swallows. 'Asked if it was a bit ghoulish.'

Sal makes a face. 'Might be good publicity, if it got out. But I can't see them going for that. Poor lad.'

Hagman puts his head back. Closes his eyes. Listens to the ticking of the clock, and the creak of the casters on the uneven floor.

'Thanks,' mutters Sal, as she starts to drift. 'For this. For . . .'

'Don't mention it,' says Hagman.

He sleeps soundly.

Wakes with a smile.

EIGHT

Dalston Road, Carlisle

Magdalena Quinn tenses as the arm snakes around her waist. A damp nose nuzzles through her dark hair and into her neck. Kisses find her neck. Teeth clamp down upon her earlobe.

'Found you.'

She reminds herself that she's meant to like this. Reminds herself that Tino expects a little appreciation. She presses herself against him. Puts her hand over his and squeezes.

'Just getting some air.'

She's standing in the little yard at the back of the tall, narrow property. The yard belongs to the downstairs apartment but there's a metal fire escape leading down from the back of Tino's flat on the first floor and Magda knows that the downstairs neighbour is always asleep by this time of night. She should have the place to herself. Should be able to stand here, in the dark, in the rain. Should be able to climb up on to the terracotta pots and look out across Dalston Road to the big, bay-windowed property where Lewis Beecher's kids are being raised by the fucking devil.

'You're soaked,' says Tino, at her ear. He's got a nose like a happy spaniel. Something like a day-old ciabatta pokes at her hip. God, she thought she'd seen him off for the night. Thought she had time to take in the view.

'It's one of the best feelings,' breathes Quinn, slipping into character, reaching back and giving Tino a squeeze. 'You never let the rain find your skin and just revel in it?'

She hears him thinking. Hears him trying to come up with an answer that will get the aloof, untameable bit-on-the-side back to bed.

'Only thing better would be a hot drink,' says Quinn, before he can come up with something disappointing. 'I clicked the kettle on before I came down. You couldn't, could you?'

She gives her attention back to the rain. Watches the black sky ripple and shimmy as a billion drops of hammering rain pummel every surface. She enjoys the noise; the tiny little hoofbeat sounds of water on metal, on prick, on earth; rippling the grimy, light-reflecting puddles in an endless onslaught. She stirs a puddle with her bare foot. Arches her leg, showing the gymnast's curve of toned calf. At her old nick, they used to call her 'the Succubus'. She'd have made a complaint if she hadn't liked it so much.

'You'll come back to bed after?'

'Of course, sweetie. Wild horses couldn't stop me.'

She feels him withdraw, giving her backside a slap like she's a good little pony. Swallows, painfully. Realizes she's got through the exchange without having to look at him. Hopes she can achieve the same when she goes upstairs and slips beneath the gaudy covers of his cheap divan bed. She's got a horrible feeling he's starting to fall in love with her — that he wants more from their union than brief couplings and the occasional dirty text. She'd despair, if she could summon the interest. Would wonder what the fuck the world was coming to, if she gave a shit about anything other than the monster across the road.

She reaches into the pocket of the coat she snatched from the peg on her way down the sodden metal stairs. It's Tino's. Smells like him: detergent and cigarettes, spicy food; that particular male miasma of deodorant and football socks. She finds his vape. Takes a suck of cherry menthol and breathes out a great curling plume of white air. Hears the door above click closed. Lets herself cross the little yard, dark hair plastered against her fine features, tangling in her earrings, clinging to her tanned skin like pitch. Climbs, barefoot, on to the terracotta pot and snatches a glance over the brick wall. The lights from the main road reflect in the jagged glass bottle shards that stud the brickwork. She wonders whether she'd take the homeowner's side if some burglar ripped his scrotum trying to take off with the microwave. Decides she probably wouldn't offer an opinion; would no doubt let somebody of a lower rank deal with it. She's got no time for the petty stuff. Wouldn't waste her considerable gifts on something that any PC with a warrant card could clear up.

She grips the lip of the pot with her feet. Glances down to check that she's not about to topple backwards. Admires the prettiness of her own toes. Lewis had liked her toes. Said so. Asked her the name of the shade. Whore-red, she'd told him. He'd blushed and got all giddy with himself, not sure what to say or how to say it. She'd just kept her eyes on him, little half-smile twisting her lips. God he'd been easy to reel in. He'd have given himself over to her – body, soul, chapter, verse – if the sob story across the road hadn't dosed him up on guilt and pity.

She glares at Beecher's house. There's no car in the driveway, no lights on upstairs, just a soft yellow glow from the front room. She chews her lip. Readjusts her position for a better grip on the brick. *They're not back yet*, she thinks. Not back from the party.

She reaches into the other coat pocket and closes her hand around her mobile phone. Checks Elsie's Facebook feed. Navigates her way to Nola's social media accounts. Magda's got half a dozen different identities online. Knows how to make new friends without arousing suspicion. Gives a little smile as she finds the photograph uploaded by Elsie's biker husband forty minutes before: half a dozen happy adults holding cans of lager and wearing party hats; two kids with matching curly hair gripping microphones and singing with their eyes closed. Nola's wearing her dad's hoodie.

'Where are you, Sal?' she asks, quietly. 'Where . . .?'

She ducks down as a blue van glides wetly down the silent road, sending up waves of dirty spray. Watches, heart thudding, gooseflesh rising on her bare skin. Watches the vehicle slow outside Beecher's. Sees a big lad, mohawk and leathers, bovine shoulders, carrying a sleeping Lottie from the passenger side. Watches as Nola steps down, hood up. There's a mumble of conversation. She watches the big man fumble for keys, little Lottie draping her arms around his neck.

She knows the man from Elsie's personnel file. They've been married a dozen years. He's got a record for violence, some motoring offences. Good egg now, by all accounts. Rides with a motorcycle outfit that raises a small fortune for good causes every year. Loves his Elsie. Would do anything for her – even driving Beecher's girls home after a can or two too many.

Christ, could it be this easy? Could she really fuck Sal over with so little effort? One quick call and she could have a dozen uniforms here. Could do for Salome and Elsie and put a big fat smile on Beecher's bulldog face. He can't tell her what he wants, not properly, but she knows men. Knows what he's telling her, deep down. He doesn't want that rotten bitch raising his children. He knows what she is. Her brother too. She hadn't realized how important he was to her until he told her he wasn't interested. She's trying to make sense of it. Trying to work out what he really means.

She realizes she's clutching at the glass. Feels a sudden warm wetness upon her palm. Ignores it. Opens the camera on her phone and reels off a dozen shots of the pitiful tableau across the street. She'll show him, next time she visits. Will tell him that she's going to make sure that Sal gets what's coming to her.

She turns back to the yard. Sees Tino standing there, mug of tea in his hand, looking at her like she's a wild animal. She stiches on her smile. Gives him a playful grin, the same seductive wiggle she'd used to get his attention the first time.

'What were you . . .?'

'Thought I heard someone,' says Magda, stepping down and moving towards him. She puts a palm on his cheek, the one she didn't cut on the glass. She looks into his eyes and reads him like a pop-up book. He's never had a woman like Magda before. Isn't sure whether to object to these little peculiarities. Wonders if they come as standard on intense, beautiful white women. He's Venezuelan. A quiet chap. Hard-working and nothing special to look at. He doesn't want to rock the boat.

'You're ringing.'

She looks at her phone. Spies the drop of blood on her palm. Licks it, absently, as she takes the call, her voice taking on a more feline aspect as she purrs her hellos in the way Callum Whitehead likes.

'Callum,' she breathes. 'I was just thinking about you.'

She listens, holding Tino's gaze, as the old man catches his breath. 'That moment,' he says, after a bronchial pause. 'The one I told you was coming. It's here, love. It's here.'

She listens, smile spreading, a warmth in her belly. An old pal of Whitehead's has witnessed an incident out towards Lumley Castle. It's got potential to be something high profile. Something big. Going to need some careful handling. Going to need somebody with experience.

She hears the smile in his voice as he saves the best until last.

'Sal Delaney found with the victim. He refused to let go of her hand.'

For a moment, the smile on Magda's face is one of pure pleasure.

'Of course, sir.'

NINE

Monday 19 May, 8.18 a.m.

Sal didn't sleep much. Twisted herself into knots. Made herself sick. Clutched the bedsheet like it was the edge of a cliff.

'It's bubbling over. What do I do? It's spilling!'

'We have to go, Lottie!'

'I haven't got my book bag. Was there homework? We're doing vertices.'

'You're still doing vertices? How can you still be doing vertices?'

Sal busies herself with packed lunches: slicing carrots and peppers into batons so they look pretty when she puts them in the bin after school. Tries to focus on the static hiss of conversation between the two gently bickering sisters. Takes stock. She's in the kitchen. Lewis's house. Her house, after a fashion. She's making herself a second cup of coffee with the fancy machine she doesn't quite know how to work. Her phone's still charging. She's got to get them to the bus stop. Got to top up their online accounts so they can have school lunches. Needs to take off Lottie's nail polish so there isn't another barbed comment in the Friday newsletter.

'Press the button,' snaps Lottie, at her little sister. 'It's going everywhere. Sal. Sal!'

Sal grasps a cloth from the draining board. Knocks a plate with a flailing elbow and winces as the air-dried crockery teeters and tumbles into a mini avalanche. Only one mug hits the terracotta tiles. It shatters like glass: the handle ricocheting off to clatter against the door to the biscuit cupboard.

Silence descends. Rises. Fills the space.

'That's Dad's,' says Nola, at last.

Sal wipes up the coffee. Picks up the pieces. It's a mug that came free with an Easter egg. Kit-Kat. It's split down the middle.

'We'll get him another.'

'Won't be the same.'

Sal looks at her reflection in the rain-speckled glass above the sink. She barely recognized herself. She sees Jarod. Sees Mum.

Pitted hollows, dark eyes; a sternness to the hinge of the jaw. Her glasses sit askew on her nose. She must have worn them while she slept. Wulf had brought her a tea around 6 a.m. Told her there was enough hot water for a shower if she needed it. She'd mumbled her thanks and left in the clothes she'd slept in. Made it back in time to be able to tell herself that the girls hadn't been left unattended all night. She reminds herself to listen to the voicemail from Elsie: a litany of apologies and explanations – a promise that nobody knew, nobody saw, it'll all be grand, don't worry . . .

'We can take him to the pottery place in Hexham,' says Sal, scalding her lip on a slurp of frothy coffee. She wipes the wetness from her nose. Takes another gulp. 'You know, the one where you paint the plates or the mugs or the dog bowls. We could make him a new one.'

'He'd hate that,' laughs Lottie. 'Can you imagine Dad trying to paint a teapot? He'd have his tongue out, the way he does when he's concentrating . . .'

The air in the kitchen seems to coalesce into an approximation of the absent Lewis Beecher. For a moment, it's like he's really in the room, drinking his tea, taking a bite of a fried egg and hash brown sandwich with sweet chilli sauce, dripping yolk down his shirt, swearing and laughing and telling his girls that he isn't fit to be let out.

Sal searches for the right words. Feels the familiar tide of gilt. Hears Jarod's voice, telling her to stop blaming herself. She's these children's saviour, not their abuser. She saved their dad's life.

Didn't do a very good job of it, did you, young lady? Didn't get there in time, did you? Not their mum, neither. Didn't even get Dagmara put away for what she did. Didn't stop Nola and Lottie from losing a part of themselves. You know what they did, and why, and you know what it will do to them when they remember . . .

She bites down. Takes another slurp. Feels the liquid sloshing in her empty stomach. Sees storms and tides and porthole windows and wonders if she should just throw up in the sink and call in sick.

There's a sudden vibration from the charger by the empty fruit bowl. She's been ignoring it for the past half-hour. She's not in until 2 p.m. today. Her boss, Claire Graves, has done a good job of keeping her from frontline duties since she came back to work and has already sent two voicemails apologizing for not being there to keep her from being called out to the horrors on the country road. She's promised to find out why the on-call Road Traffic Accident investigator had been bypassed and what confluence of fate and misfortune had led to her becoming involved. Sal fancies it can wait. She doesn't want to think about it any more. She's still got the stink of the man's rotting skin inside her nostrils. Can still feel the bloodied stump of finger moving in scratchy, urgent circles over the damp skin of her palm.

'Can you sign my homework diary?' asks Nola, checking her appearance in her mobile. She recently experimented with a fringe. She's growing it out now but it isn't long enough to be tied back. When the wind catches it, her dark locks take on the appearance of a peaked cap.

'Pen,' mumbles Sal, miming a scribble in the air. 'Pen . . .'

Lottie hands her a purple felt tip. Sal looks at it accusingly. Did it *have* to be a purple felt pen? Would a pencil or a blue biro be too much to ask?

'Oh, it's Debate Club after school,' says Nola, scraping some pain au chocolat off her front teeth with a thumbnail and then wiping it on her blue school sweatshirt. 'I'll need picking up at four thirty.'

'Are you not on the bus with me?' asks Lottie, eyes widening. 'Sal, you said, you said I'd never have to . . .'

Sal wonders if this is how it feels to go insane. Whether she is just one more moment of inadequacy from taking off her clothes, goose-stepping down the street and starting a relationship with a traffic cone. She finds madness quite appealing.

'I'm sure we can sort it,' mumbles Sal. 'Maybe Elsie . . .'

The phone buzzes again. Sal glares at it. Flashes angry eyes at the empty fruit bowl. Stares at the fridge door: jolly magnets pinning letters and sketches and overdue bills to its surface. Wonders if there's anything inside that might constitute a nourishing evening meal. Wonders whether saying 'how about pizza?' will be deemed pragmatic parenting, or neglect.

'It's Claire again,' says Lottie, picking up the phone and holding it out. 'Sal, it's Claire . . .'

There's a knock on the front door – three hard thuds with a fist. It's a copper's knock. A bailiff's knock. Sal feels a fist of sickness punch down her gullet to her gut.

'I'll get it,' says Lottie, excited at the unexpected interruption.

'No,' snaps Sal, her voice harder than she intends. She snatches a look at her reflection. Sees her mum's angry eyes, twisted jaw.

Sees the tension in her shoulders; the clenched fists, stiff neck; the haze of gathering malevolence.

'Sorry,' she mutters, trying on a smile for size. 'Sorry, I'll get it.'

She half runs down the corridor. Family photos stare down from the walls. Sal's in none of them. Lewis took them down when he kicked her out last year. It isn't her place to put them back up.

She recognizes the shape of her even through the frosted glass. Knows the dark hair and the suede coat; the paisley and mustard scarf. Knows who's banging on the door.

She nearly turns away. Nearly runs back to the kitchen to hide under the table, the way she and her brothers and sisters did whenever one of Mam's bad lads turned up, shouting for money, for access, for another go on Trina. It's only the nearness of the two girls that stops her. They deserve somebody who can at least pretend to be brave. Her hands feel tingly as she opens the door. She's all fingers and thumbs: all lip-sweat and butterflies. It's all she can do not to void her guts on to Magda Quinn's expensive shoes.

'Morning, sleepyhead,' says Quinn, red lips twisting to reveal perfect teeth: a pink tongue that makes Sal think, instinctively, of a yawning cat.

'Sleepyhead?' asks Sal, fizzing with a nervous energy, head so full of static and fizz that she may as well be underwater.

'You're mine,' says Quinn, brightly. 'Claire said, didn't she? I need a bagman. Somebody who knows the area. Somebody I'm comfortable with. I asked for you personally.'

Sal holds the door handle. Feels her palms ooze sweat. Becomes aware of her own greasy hair, grimy glasses, sweaty, unshaved skin. Imagines Quinn holding a cup to Lewis's lips, a cloth to his brow. Imagines her nursing him the way he wouldn't permit Sal.

'I'm . . . I'm sorry, this is the first I've heard . . .'

Quinn peers past her. Sees Beecher's two girls standing in the doorway. They recognize her at once. Know that she was the lady who was with their dad when he got hurt.

'Oh, they're blooming,' says Quinn, brightly. 'So much of their mum in them, don't you think?'

She fixes her eyes on Sal. 'Shall we?'

'I've got to get them to school,' she says, hand slipping off the doorknob. She can feel her heart thudding. Can hear her own blood. Can hear Jarod.

She's bad, this one. Bad all the way through.

'I'll send a patrol car,' says Quinn. 'Have them arrive in style, eh? Come on now, you've already missed the briefing . . .'

'What briefing? Magda, I don't . . .'

Quinn's smile freezes. Her eyes harden. 'Detective Chief Inspector is a mouthful, Sal. But I'll accept ma'am.'

Sal lowers her eyes. Feels child-like. Weak. Beaten.

'Yes ma'am.'

TEN

Sal's in the back of a shiny black BMW. She's sitting in the middle seat, at Quinn's request. It makes it easy to see her when she's talking. She's angled the mirror so every time she glances at it, Sal's in the centre of the frame. The driver – a young detective constable whom Sal vaguely recognizes from a night out – is at the wheel. He hasn't spoken since Sal got into the back. Hasn't looked her way. Quinn, for all her talk of wanting to be able to brief her en route, has yet to say anything save a few pleasantries about the weather, the view and the house prices.

Sal's holding herself tight, elbows in at her middle. She's too hot in Jarod's old fishtail parka, her black cords and baggy jumper, but she's conscious of her skin, her shape, her scent, and would rather sit and perspire inside folds of greasy fabric than risk having somebody as primped and perfect as Magda Quinn make reference to her sweat patches or stains.

She stares out of the window, making shapes out of the raindrops on the glass. Her therapist has told her she needs to get comfortable with awkwardness; that it is not her responsibility to remove the negative energy from every space. She's a people-pleaser, apparently, though she still contests the diagnosis. She's not sure she's ever really pleased anybody.

She looks down as they pass through Haydon Bridge – gauzy curtains of rain hiding the little town where she and Jarod were members of the youth club known to all as Weardy. It was a place for kids who needed somewhere safe and nurturing in their lives. A place of brief sanctuary, where they could play and create and imagine, free from the violent hands and vicious words of their mother. Dagmara Scrowther was awarded an MBE for her services to young people. Made the papers time and again for her decades of service. It's boarded up, now. Nobody will take on the responsibility.

'Pull in over the way,' says Quinn to the DC. They're a few miles from Hexham, heading east. It takes nearly a full minute to find a gap in the traffic sufficient to let them cross the busy road and into the car park of the Starbuck's that squats in the little dip. Sal has a flash of memory. It had been a Little Chef, when she was a girl. A place where Dagmara would take her for greasy egg and chips, for Coke Floats and pancake stacks with fruit compotes and big hot mugs of tea. She feels a hotness at her chest, her eyes, a prickling sensation in her fingertips. She hears her mother's voice, flabby lips against her ear, spit on her cheek. Feels the rough boards of the kitchen floor against her cheek. Remembers Jarod's gentle fingers, plucking the splinters from her eyelid, her brow, telling her it'll be OK. *It'll be OK, I'll kill her, I swear, one day I'll kill her . . .*

'Cappuccino,' says Quinn, into the mirror.

Sal meets her gaze, colour in her cheeks. 'Sorry?'

'Large. Cappuccino. Skinny. Four shots.' She narrows her eyes. Smiles.

Sal feels her mouth twitch. Hears the DC give a snuffle of laughter.

'Oh, right. Yeah. Um.'

'Oh, right. Yeah. Um,' mimics Quinn, shaking her head. 'Honestly, Sal.' She twists in her seat. Removes a sleek purse from the inside of her long, expensive-looking coat. Hands a credit card to the DC. 'Double espresso,' she says. 'And a blueberry muffin. Sal?'

Sal looks from the passenger seat to the back of the driver's headrest. 'Mocha, please. If that's OK.'

'Skinny, I presume,' says Quinn, angling her head to better evaluate Sal's physique. 'It's the face, isn't it? We get to an age where no matter what you do, the face just goes its own way. The money I spend on formulas, creams, all these lotions and potions – I envy you Sal, honestly. I mean, the way you just don't buy into any of that. You're just like "this is me, matey – you're waking up with the same person you go to bed with"; honestly, it's admirable.'

Sal looks down at herself. Realizes she's wringing her hands together. Sees the loose skin around her nails, the blotches on the backs of her hands. Inside her Doc Martens, she tries to find the seam of her sock with her big toe, to tuck in under the nail. It's a stim, she knows that: a physical tick that provides some modicum of comfort when things are spinning out of control. It's better than its predecessors. She used to pinch her nostrils every few seconds in times of anxiety. Used to work her jaw in circles. Sometimes she'd get a phrase or a sound stuck in her head and would repeat it under her breath until it released some of the pressure building up under the skin.

The DC climbs out of the car without a word. Doesn't look back as he crosses the wet forecourt. He's got longish hair and his checked suit sits nicely on his tall, jointy frame. Sal thinks Lewis would hate him on sight.

'Just us girls, then,' says Quinn, turning fully around in her seat and giving Sal her full attention. She exhales, slowly, through her nostrils. Shakes her head. 'Doesn't have to be awkward, does it?'

Sal's stomach lurches. Her throat feels pinched. She's aware of the dryness of her lips, the fatness of her tongue. She's aware of Quinn's high, heady perfume; her own wet-dog and dying-flowers musk.

'Just happy to be involved, ma'am,' says Sal, snatching a handful of curls behind her ear. She takes off her glasses. Cleans them on her front. Puts them back on dirtier than they were before. They still feel crooked on her face.

'It's a bit of an ambush, isn't it?' says Quinn, looking as if she might be considering the wisdom of her team selection. 'I mean, the gossips at the station will love it, won't they? Can you imagine? They're probably imagining you and me having a fist-fight in a layby even as we speak.'

Sal doesn't reply. Isn't sure what to say.

'Might go the other way, of course,' muses Quinn. 'Some of the lads, I reckon they'll have nastier fantasies. Men's heads – just all filth and tits, isn't it?'

Sal looks away first. Stares out of the window. 'Are we going to the scene?' she asks, at last.

'The scene? Oh, where you found him, you mean? No, I'm not one of those senior investigative officers who needs to micro-manage. I've never seen the need to go and see the scene. You get some dinosaurs who just need to be there, to feel it, as if they're sort of breathing in the sense of a place and sifting the air for clues. All performative bullshit, if you ask me.'

'Lewis always tries to visit the scene.' The words are out of her mouth before she can bite them back. She forces herself to meet Quinn's stare. Something flickers in her expression. Sal thinks of a pike rising to snatch a dragonfly from the surface of a still pond.

'Lewis is a man who makes all manner of peculiar choices,' says Quinn, drily. She gives a tight smile. 'You've heard from him?'

Sal shakes her head. 'From his mother. It's slow going. He's . . . he's not doing what the doctors ask.'

'And you, left holding the babies,' says Quinn, shaking her head, miming concern. 'Must get harder every day. The responsibility alone. And not knowing whether you're building a future, waiting for him to come home and tell you it's all over . . . like last time.'

Sal feels bugs moving under her skin. Feels little spiders moving on her scalp. Looks at the backs of her hands and sees lugworms and slugs pushing through her fat blue veins. Her head thrums – a wire pulled tight.

'Anyhoo,' says Quinn, clapping her hands. 'Can't be spending all day listening to your domestic struggles. Of course, if you'd been at the briefing you'd already be up to speed, but we've got a moment for me to fill in the blanks.'

'I didn't know you'd requested me,' says Sal. She feels her nose begin to run. Dabs at her nostril with the back of her hand.

'Let's not get bogged down with who-knew-what,' says Quinn, removing a hair-tie from her wrist. She takes two fistfuls of her perfect dark hair and scoops them up into a high ponytail, eyes still fixed on Sal's. 'Mahee Gamage. Forty-six years old.'

Sal wonders if she's misheard. Makes a face, not understanding.

'It's a man's name, Sal. You're aware that multi-culturalism is a thing, yes? Not everybody's called Frank Boggins any more.'

'I'm called Salome,' says Sal, with just a touch of edge to her voice. She realizes that she can feel the first stirrings of temper.

'Salami, wasn't it? Your nickname at school? Poor Sal.'

'Mahee Gamage?' asks Sal. 'That's . . . Sri Lankan, I think. There's an academic I read at uni—'

'We know, Sal. Don't waste your brain cells on it. Read the file, like everybody else.'

Beyond the glass, the rain seems to intensify. She watches birds turning circles above the damp green hills; the trees shaking as if rocked by giant hands. Sal tries to focus on the words on the page. Feels the atmosphere in the car settle upon her like brick dust. Tells herself not to try and make friends – not to people-please; not to try and make things better.

'This is our victim?' asks Sal, looking into the dark, hopeful eyes of a portly Asian man. 'Looks kind, doesn't he? I mean, I know you can't really tell, but . . .'

Quinn turns around. Looks at her with absolute loathing.

'*Our* victim, now, is it? On the team for an hour, and . . .'

'I found him, ma'am,' says Sal. 'I held him until the ambulance came.'

Quinn shoots her a hard look. 'Veritable hero of the hour, yes? Of course, we'll never know what forensic material we lost as a result. But yes, *our* victim is Mahee Gamage. Solicitor, up until a couple of years ago.'

'How is he?' asks Sal.

'I believe the prognosis is "fucked",' says Quinn. 'This will be a murder investigation before the day's out. That's how I've recommended we proceed. We'll be able to know more about what's happened to him once he's flatlined – easier to perform a post mortem on a body than a person, in my experience. But even from preliminaries, the lad's been to hell and back.'

Sal's mind fills with pictures of last night's horrors. Sees the terror in those brown eyes; the filth and the blood and the gore upon his skin; the way his mauled finger moved upon the palm of her hand, the skin of her wrist.

'How did you identify him?'

'I sent you the brief five minutes after you got in the car, Sal. You could have been reading up, not staring out of the window like a hungover teenager. Party last night, wasn't it? Good old Elsie. Salt of the earth, that one.'

'The victim?' asks Sal, again. 'ID from fingerprint?'

'Indeed, though I'm told it was a hell of a job to get a usable print. Fingers split like ripe fruit. Lucky to get a usable thumb. Waiting for DNA to confirm, but we're proceeding on the presumption that he's Gamage. Last known address in Norton, outskirts of Middlesbrough. Hadn't been reported missing. No success with an attempt to find a next of kin yet. House used to belong to his grandmother, but she passed away three years back.'

Sal absorbs the information. Tries to fit it into the mental picture of the ragged undead thing that had reached up from the darkness and grabbed her wrist.

'That's where we're going? Home address?' Sal lets her confusion show. 'You said you wanted local knowledge. I've never been to Middlesbrough.'

'Why would you?' asks Quinn, with a smirk. 'You've got everything so perfect just where you are, haven't you? But think of this as a big day for your journal. Middlesbrough – for the very first time! And you get to stand next to me and write down everything his friends and family and work colleagues say, just for good measure.'

'You want me as scribe?'

'Lewis said you do this – the questions, the endless bloody questions . . .'

'Don't,' says Sal, under her breath. She gives a tight shake of her head. Huffs her curls out of her eyes.

'*Don't?*' asks Quinn, widening. 'Did you say "don't", Delaney?' She smiles again, her mouth a cruel, thin line. She glances towards the door of the coffee chain. Sees the DC walking back holding cups and a paper bag. She shoots her gaze back to Sal, narrows her eyes, bares her teeth. 'We'd have had him. Wulfric fucking Hagman. A once-in-a-career case. We'd have put him away. I'd have had my fucking pick. Sky's the fucking limit. But you had to fuck it all up, didn't you? Christ I nearly buckled, didn't I? Nearly lost sight of the bigger picture. Nearly told him to stick what he was offering! Saw sense, of course. It was all going to be . . .' – she mimes a chef's-kiss – 'parfait! But you had to stick your nose in. I had to use the last fucking favour to get a job on a serious crime unit, you know that? I'd made promises . . . and thanks to you, thanks to you . . .'

'He saved your life!' spits Sal, unable to hold it back. 'He didn't kill my mother, didn't kill any of those people . . .'

'And what the fuck does that matter!' demands Quinn. 'Saved my life, did he? You don't know anything, you silly sod. It would have made Lewis's career too. Given him a chance. Given us a chance . . .'

The door opens. The DC slips back into the driving seat. Quinn gives him a welcoming smile, any trace of the fury that had gripped her features now entirely absent. Sal, in the back, is sweating at her temples, her neck. She can smell herself, even over the rich coffee and chocolate aroma.

'There's your mocha,' says Quinn, handing it to the back seat. 'It's hot, now. Be careful. Four pounds eighty, I think. You can settle up when we get there.'

Sal takes the cup. Feels the heat in her fingertips. Thinks again of Mahee Gamage's skin upon hers. What had he been trying to say?

Quinn blows across the lip of her own drink. Finds Sal's eyes in the mirror. Sal feels the heat of her hatred, scorching her flesh, penetrating her bones, cooking the marrow at her very core.

Thinks: *this woman means you harm.*

She forces herself to look away. Pulls out her phone. Calls up the file, and begins to read.

By the time they're past Hexham and heading for the A1, all that matters is the man on the country road, and the unspoken horror in his eyes.

ELEVEN

Bedford Street, Middlesbrough

2.20 p.m.

'Jesus Christ.'

Sal shoots DC Ben Gibbons the kind of look she gives Nola when she's told her little sister to go and stick her face in the air-fryer.

'It's not that bad,' she says, feeling oddly defensive about the network of grimy, run-down streets: all corrugated shutters and potholes. She has memories of places like this – of curtains that don't reach the bottom of the frame; of parents sleeping with baseball bats beneath wide-open windows. Trina took them away from it. Picked a random farmhouse in the countryside and set up home with her wild, barefoot brood. Could have been a pretty story. Could have been inspiring.

'No, look. Jesus Christ,' says Gibbons, again. He nods past her. Sal spots a tall, willowy figure in a white smock and sandals. He's got his hair in curly ringlets and his brown beard is neatly smoothed. He stands in front of the bookie's, having an animated conversation with a West African man clad in swathes of green-black silks.

'And they say multi-culturalism's failed,' says Gibbons shaking his head. 'Preaching to the converted, don't you think?'

'I can't tell if you're being mean,' says Sal, making a face. 'It feels like you are.'

Gibbons smiles. It's warm, friendly. Away from Quinn, he's revealed himself to be perfectly affable company. She's learned that he's originally from Worcester, grew up in a 'normal' household with a younger brother, and has been in a relationship with an old school-friend for three years. They're thinking of getting married in Vegas to avoid having the stress of a traditional wedding. He hasn't asked her yet, but they've talked about it objectively and he's sure she'll see sense. He supports Nottingham Forest. He hasn't slept with Quinn, in case she was wondering. He's heard she's got a reputation.

'You almost done with that?' asks Gibbons, waving a hand towards the wall socket, where he is keeping a proprietorial eye on the phone charger Sal has quietly pleaded to borrow.

They find themselves in the Punk Café, staring through wet windows at the terraced street. From here they can just make out the front door of Terri Down's neat little house, three doors down from the bookie's and five doors down from the shuttered newsagent's.

Quinn met up with her detective sergeant at Mahee Gamage's front door. She'd dismissed her driver and her plaything with the kind of wave a countess might use in the face of a tiresome dinner guest. She'd had enough of them. They were to stay in the car. She'd take it from here.

She'd been gone for fewer than five minutes before Gibbons turned off the radio in the car and asked if it were true that she'd smacked a serial killer in the head with a brick, and that they were in a coma somewhere, and that the bosses had covered it up and struck some sort of a deal that had fucked over DI Lewis Beecher, and if it was true he'd gone off the deep end, mentally speaking, and walked out on his kids, and . . .

Sal, desperately sending text messages to Elsie to double-, triple- and quadruple-check that the girls would be picked up, fed, kept from murder or kidnap or malnutrition – had been grateful for the chance to use the phrase that had never failed her when steering a certain kind of man away from difficult conversational territory. 'Tell me about you . . .'

An hour later, and now fully apprised of Gibbons's arse-clenchingly banal life to date, she'd looked up to see Quinn making her way back to the vehicle. There'd been a purpose to her stride; a little gleam of ice and fire in her striking dark eyes. She was on the phone, reporting in to the head of CID in short, rapid sentences.

'. . . laptop password written on a Post-it note next to where he left it. Still open, yeah. Like he'd just walked out. Email closed and encrypted but he left his website tabs open. Fetish site, though his session had timed out. Lots to play with when the team gets up and running. Pile of post on the mat and the milk blue and rancid in the fridge. But otherwise keeps a nice house, for a bloke. Well-tended, hoovered, dusted. There's a handwritten envelope without a stamp sticking in the letterbox. From a Terri Down – she's here if he's feeling lonely. Worth a punt, certainly . . .'

'Result, ma'am?'

She'd given a laugh at that. Looked for a moment as if she were about to give Gibbons a good-natured punch on the shoulder and a high-five. She smelled something delicious, that much was clear. Sal had sat quiet as a grave, back to feeling like the new girl at a school where her reputation precedes her. She felt the burning gaze on her cheek. On the crown of her head. She wouldn't look up, wouldn't . . . she'd snatched her head up, eyes flashing defiance; the set to her jaw that had made her mum snatch off a shoe and take it to her face.

'Little job for you both,' she'd said, sweetly, readjusting her blouse in the mirror and checking her lipstick with one perfect, blood-red nail. 'Might even be important. No need for a Family Liaison Officer yet, Sal – bit of a wasted journey for you otherwise. Better make use of yourself or people will be wondering what you're doing here . . .'

'That her?' asks Gibbons now, peering through the café's windows. It's misted up with condensation. The handful of customers are all drying out – little clouds of vapour rising from soggy hoods, wet denim, battered trainers. Sal keeps having to shake away the idea that she's a figure in an Edward Hopper painting. Even the rattling of the percolator and the jangle of crockery feels somehow anachronistic. She feels a curious urge to check her skin for brush strokes. She's had too much coffee, not enough food. She's wired. Buzzing. She can feel it all in her back teeth, her fingertips. She wonders whether Gibbons can see her pulse in her neck, in the throb of her temples. Christ how she wants to go home. Home, wherever the fuck that might be. Whoever the fuck it might be with . . .

Sal pinches the skin of her wrist. Feels the clouds clear a little. Looks at the figure making her way towards the front door.

Thinks: *I'm good at this. Show them. Show them what you can do* . . .

Gibbons runs his finger around the inside of his mug and licks the froth off his finger as he makes for the exit. Sal wrinkles her nose, a step behind. Follows him as he steps out of the café and into the cold, gusty air, wincing as the rain scythes in as if from the sea. Watches Gibbons raise his lanyard as he steps into the woman's way. Watches him stand a step too close.

'Terri, is it? We're police. We're going to need a moment of your time.'

Terri stops, one hand on the handle of the blue-painted front door. She's a curvy woman. Anorak and short skirt, chunky calves, big around the middle. She's middle-aged: pink-frothed brunette hair blown into a haphazard wave by the rain. She gives Gibbons a hard look. Gestures at the big bags of shopping in her hands.

'It's up two flights. If you're coming up, you're carrying these.'

'That's not a problem,' says Sal, smiling and reaching out a hand. 'Or we can get you a coffee over the road? The caramel shortcake is so good it should be illegal.'

Terri gives a little smile. Ignores Gibbons and addresses herself to Sal. 'Bloody pricey, though. And they do faff about with the classics. Always putting hibiscus flowers or poppy seeds in the Victoria sponge. Just cheffy shit, isn't it?'

Sal takes Terri's shopping, running her eyes over the contents. Single pint of milk, small loaf, a number of meals-for-one; cheap gin, slimline tonic. They make their way back to the table they just vacated, stepping back into the warm fug as if into a steam room. She sends Gibbons to get the provisions. Sits Terri down and gives her her full attention.

'It's Mahee, is it?' she asks, before Sal can begin. 'Done it, has he? Poor sod.'

Sal takes a breath. Reads the other woman's body language. She's holding herself a little too tight. There's a glassiness to her eyes and a slight twitch to the lines around her mouth, but she isn't about to burst into tears.

'He's in a bad way,' says Sal, gently. 'We're trying to find out what happened to him. Might I ask the nature of your relationship?'

Terri picks up a packet of sugar. Rubs it in her warm, plump palms. Sucks on her lower lip. 'No relationship to speak of, love. Not as you'd mean it. Not even friends, really. I used to clean for him. Barely saw him for months at a time when he was working but, once that all went wrong and he was there in his dressing gown, well, you can't help but talk. Got to know a wee bit about him.'

'You left him a note, yes? Concerned for him?'

Terri plays with the salt cellar. Spills a little. Draws a pattern in the spillage as she talks.

'I've had some problems,' she says, with a shrug. She taps her skull. 'Up here, like. Been through some stuff. You can see it in other people after a while. He was suffering. A year back I found him passed out drunk in front of the laptop. He'd taken all the pills in the house, though thank Christ you can't really off yourself with antihistamines and six ibuprofen. You know how men get when they're pissed and vulnerable. Told me all about what he'd been going through, his regrets – the people who were out to get him. I'm a good listener, I suppose.'

'He said people were out to get him?'

'So he said, though how much was in his head and how much was the excuse he told himself, well, I can't say. He lost his job through it, though. He was a solicitor, did you know that? You will do, course you will. Got sacked and struck off not that long since. Said he was set up – that the stuff on his laptop was there by accident – a file he'd downloaded by mistake, but men will say anything, won't they? To get out of trouble. Either way, they gave him the boot. I don't know what he was doing for money, or whether that was a concern for him, but just after Christmas he said he couldn't afford me any more. Wanted to know if we could maybe go for a coffee or a lunch. He was sweet about it but he's not my type, not really. Hard to get hot for somebody when you clean their toilet and hoover up their toenail clippings. But I called a couple of times. He doesn't do social media. I think he's had some problems in that area – people sending him abuse and such.'

Sal's about to speak when Gibbons places a tray down on the table, slopping his coffee into the saucer. He curses. Sal and Terri exchange a look that says 'men' – their mutual tut unspoken but heard.

'Our boss reckons he was into some pervy stuff, is that right?' asks Gibbons, sitting down and spreading his legs. He looks to Sal as if he's on the toilet.

Terri takes the proffered cake. Picks up her fork. Puts it down again. Shakes her head. 'He's not done himself in, has he? He didn't have much happiness in his life but I didn't think he was serious, not really. It was a cry for help, and I tried to help him, I really did.' She bites her lip. 'Pervy isn't a nice way to say it. He was a big lad and he had his kinks. Nobody would feel good about themselves if the world knew what they liked to get their rocks off to.'

'No,' says Sal, making a face and thinking about her own internet history. 'What was he into?'

'Giantess stuff,' shrugs Terri. 'He was lonely, wasn't he? Mam died when he was young, just him and his grandma most of his life. There is an uncle somewhere, but other than Mahee watering his plants whenever he sodded off back to Sri Lanka . . .'

Sal sits forward – shows Terri that she's listening. That there's no rush.

'I don't know how he got into it – you don't like to ask too much, do you, though some of the things I've seen in the reflection of the microwave would be enough to put you off Barbie for life, I tell you.'

'I can imagine,' says Sal.

'You really can't,' grimaces Terri. 'Anyway, long and the short of it, if you'll excuse that one, well . . . he wants to be swaddled. Cuddled. Maybe crushed a little bit. Good day for Mahee would be spent half an inch tall and pressed between a heel and a shoe. And don't make that face, it's a legit kink. Not to my taste, but who are we to judge? Didn't do any harm, did it? Not until it started blaring out of the laptop during a meeting with his work: some hundred-foot woman telling him she was going to pop him into her mouth and swallow him up.'

'Jesus,' says Gibbons, making a face. 'People are into that?'

Terri picks up her cake. Takes a bite, eyes on Sal. 'Did somebody hurt him? He had enemies, I know that, though whether they were in his head . . .'

Sal chews her lip. Something's tickling the back of her brain. She feels a familiarity, a connection – two frayed threads that she can't quite tie together. She wonders whether she's got enough to avoid any rebukes from Quinn. Realizes that there's no way to win on that score; that her duty is to Mahee and nobody else.

'The uncle. We'll need a name. Also, do you know whether he might have given Mahee access to a vehicle?'

Terri nods, swallowing a forkful of icing. 'Has in the past, yeah. As I say, the uncle's often away, so . . .'

'Tell me about him,' she says, sitting back. 'Help me understand him.'

'Uncle Vijay?'

'No, Mahee. He's more than a kink and a sacking, isn't he? Tell me who he is.'

A slow smile crosses Terri's face. Gibbons sags, already bored.

'You'd like him,' says Terri, and something passes between them. 'Broken people, like him, like me. Like you. We recognize each other, don't we? He'd done wrong. Carried guilt with him like heart disease.'

'He felt he'd done wrong?'

'He felt he deserved whatever he got. Said, calm as you like, that when they caught up with him, he'd take what they dished out. They had him bang to rights.'

'Did he elaborate?'

Terri pauses to take another bite. 'Ulama,' she says, surprised at herself for remembering. 'The Devil Bird. He said he'd heard it. Heard it in his sleep and wide awake. Something was coming for him, that's what he believed. But I've heard so many fanciful stories, love. Maybe I should have paid more attention.'

Beside her, Gibbons wrinkles his nose. 'Aye. Aye, maybe you should.'

Sal kicks the table. Enjoys the look on his face as the coffee spills into his lap.

TWELVE

Hagman's never liked eye contact. Always looks away first. Only manages to maintain an illusion of civility by fixing his gaze on the centre of the brow: a third eye, precise as a bullet hole.

'You'll talk to her, will you? I just . . . I don't have the words.'

Hagman forces himself to meet Theo's gaze. He feels like he's being asked to lift something. There's something so ponderous and unwieldy in the young man's eyes. Hagman finds himself casting around, looking for somebody else to take the weight.

'She's keeping me there, you know? In the past – in that place. I mean, we should – what's that song – accentuate the positive, yes? Eliminate the negative. I mean, it could have been worse.'

Hagman busies himself by the sink, where a spray of bluebells are climbing out of a striped teapot. He's got a little tableau set up: a collection of rural accoutrements assembled in a pleasing rectangle among the unwashed plates and piles of paper that make up the rest of the kitchen counter. He's recently acquainted himself with social media. Is managing to make something close to a living selling his tinctures, salves and herbal poultices to customers who've never thought to ask whether the nice man who makes the potions might happen to be a convicted killer. He picks up his phone. Takes a few more snaps of the gleaming spell bottle, wrapped in a purple ribbon and sealed with good globs of red wax.

'I know she isn't easy to deal with, Wulf, but . . . I want to move on. And she just keeps on – keeps me stuck there, that place . . .' he aims a half-hearted kick at the log pile. Stops himself short before he connects. Crouches down by the fire and gathers up a stick. Pokes, moodily, at the flickering flame. Hagman looks over the long, scarred table-top – papers, books, herbs and weeds leaking green blood on to mountain ranges of legal paper – and wishes he'd learned the art of saying no. What was it Dagmara had called him? A people-pleaser. He'd pointed out, in his own soft-spoken way, that people-pleasers don't tend to go to prison for murder. Dagmara had given that bark of laughter. Shook her head, disappointed in him.

'Alec's not going to put up with it much longer, I don't think.'

Theo turns as he says it. From his position by the fire he looks, again, like a romantic poet: the open-necked shirt, tousled curls; the earnest, beseeching eyes of a man whose pain reaches to the marrow. Hagman wonders what the men on his wing would have done to such a pretty boy. Shakes the image away as soon as it appears, raw and horrifying, in his head.

'I don't know her, Theo,' says Hagman smoothing his beard, then tangling it again with his fingers, the way he does when he's feeling uncomfortable. It's almost white, now. Lottie had told him it looked like a unicorn's tail. He'd smiled at that. Smiled properly, surprising himself with the ease with which his muscles had slipped back into an expression he thought they'd forgotten.

'I thought she'd leave it all behind,' Theo says standing up and turning fully into the dark, low space. He's still holding the smouldering stick – little tufted sigils and calligraphy appearing in the dark air as he jabs it at nothing, everything; at persecutors without and within. 'I mean, I'm out, aren't I? I'm doing OK. I read everything the ladies at the Juris Project sent me and I'll do my bit, like I always do, but . . . I haven't got the – what do you call it? – the righteous fury. That's it. I don't want to be a symbol. I'm not a figurehead of a movement. I'm . . . I'm a bloke, aren't I? Just a person. And something shitty happened to me but maybe that's because I was a shitty person . . .'

'I'm sure that's not true . . .'

'Two people said I killed that man, Wulf. Two people told the police they'd seen me do that . . . that terrible thing. And people believed them. People accepted that I was capable of that.' He stops. Glares at the glowing end of the blackening stick. 'The energy in the house is just so . . . so grey. Like, static. Ash. Once the balloons came down, once she'd put cellophane over the party food, it was like she rubbed her hands together and just went "now what?" Like, getting me home had been what it was all for, and now I was home, and it wasn't enough. Maybe I'm better as a case than a person.'

Hagman fights the urge to put his arms around him. He knows he'll agree to what Theo's asking. Knew before he arrived.

'And Alec? He wants to carry on fighting?'

Theo tosses the stick back in the fire. Picks up a piece of paper from the nearest stack of legal documents and crumples it into a ball, squashing it between his palms. He knows them to be Hagman's preferred kindling. 'He'd do anything to make her feel better but it's like she's in a place where he can't reach her. It's just all . . . where's the justice? Where's the – what's the word? – redress? Like, we don't even need the money. Dad left us OK. But she keeps talking about principle. Bloody principle. She's going to get into trouble, Wulf. She's going to make it worse.'

Hagman gives a tight smile. Decides to fill the kettle, for no other reason than to give his hands something to do. He pulls it down from its hook. Feels the familiar tightening in his throat as he looks upon the lethal-looking curve of black-lacquered metal. The rope mark hides beneath his beard: forget-me-nots of barbed wire.

'You still haven't introduced me to Sal,' says Theo, slumping back down in the rocking chair. He's slouched, his posture sullen, moody. 'Never told me much about Jarod. Never told me much about much, really.'

Hagman glances back. Had there been something accusing in his tone? He lets his confusion show. 'When did you ever ask?'

'To meet Sal? The person you're closest to in the universe? Oh yeah, of course I wouldn't want to meet her.' His voice has a scornful edge. 'I spill my guts to you about every last spit and bloody cough and you just give me this nodding dog routine. You never tell me anything. That's what I've got to look forward to, is it? The ladies at Juris, they said you're the one who's going to help me. Said you've made peace with it all, you're a lesson in how to move forward, find space inside yourself . . .'

Hagman shakes his head. 'I never said I was any of that. They asked me to meet you. To help, if I could. I'm doing my best.'

Theo mimics him, his face pathetic, bottom lip pouting. 'I'm doing my best, I'm doing my best. Jesus, I've done the breathing. I've sat here and drunk your weed-water and pictured the world as I want it using my third fucking eye . . .'

'That's not what we've been doing,' says Hagman, sharply.

'Look,' says Theo, angrily, grabbing for something in the pocket of his tight trousers. He opens his fist. Crystals and shiny pebbles gleam, dully, on his open palm. 'All my charms. I come to you for help and you give me stones.'

'The mahogany obsidian is good for letting go; protecting yourself from the things you don't need . . .'

Theo's face twists into an angry snarl. Then something else seems to grip him, a sudden jerking and twitching, his shoulder spasming, a muscle in his cheek starting to twitch. He drops his head to his hands. Crystals patter on to the concrete flags. 'I'm sorry,' he mumbles, into his palms. His voice is thick with snot and tears. 'Sorry, I just— I just want her to be happy, Wulf. And all she talks about is fucking revenge.'

Hagman fights the urge to rush to the young man's side. He wants to put an arm around him, wipe his nose and tell him it will be fine. For all his fascination with alternative medicines and holistic wellness, he'd like to just go into Dad-mode; to wipe his eyes and make him laugh and tell him if he sorts himself out, he'll take him for a KitKat.

He stays rooted to his position by the sink. Lets the silence lengthen, punctuated with sniffs, the drip of the tap, the rattling of the pipes, the mournful creak of the settling timbers and the crackling hearth.

'I'm sorry,' says Theo, again. 'I shouldn't keep turning up. Shouldn't put it on you. It's just . . . she's been the worst she's ever been, man. Alec can't deal with her. You should have heard them – her screaming at him, over and over; him just taking it, same as always, all calm and reasonable and this-is-what-we're-going-to-do. We don't deserve him, Wulf, I swear.' He raises his head. Stares at Hagman until he has no choice but to meet his gaze. 'Dad didn't see it through, did he? Gave up on me. Gave up on Mam. He let himself off the hook. Just decided he couldn't handle it and offed himself rather than be there for her. Alec's been there from day one. For her, for me. He's taken it as far as he can. We don't need to fight any more, but she's like one of these old generals who doesn't know what to do without a war. I keep hearing Alec on his own, when he thinks I'm at the other side of the house, sitting in his office just sobbing, proper sobbing. He only does it when she's taken her meds and would sleep through a fucking avalanche. It's like a treat for him – a chance to actually show how hard it all is for him too. But I ask . . . I try and think of nice things I can do or say that make him know it will get better and we appreciate him, and . . . he just pretends he's fine.'

'Pick up your crystal,' says Hagman, gently. 'Pick up the amethyst even if you don't want the others. It helps keep the bad thoughts to a background hum. And fine, I'll talk to your mum.'

Theo jerks his head up, eyes sparkling, a hopeful half-smile on his fine features. 'You'll make her see? She'll drop it?'

Hagman spreads his hands. 'I just said I'd speak to her, Theo. She might slam the door in my face.'

'I'll bring her here,' he says, excitedly. 'We could show her what I've been doing on my coursework. She likes old buildings. The old maps. The ones you gave me, she was dead interested in that. It was like before – when I was young, when she was all hyper-focus and we had these adventures: old castles, ruins; hiding from the security guards so we could go and do a brass rubbing of some old graffiti in some boarded-up manor house . . .'

'Theo, I've said I'll help, I just don't want you getting your hopes up that she's suddenly going to make her peace with what's happened.'

Theo closes his eyes. 'It didn't happen to her. It happened to me. And I don't want revenge, Wulf. I'm not like that.'

Hagman listens to the kettle start to rattle and hiss on the Rayburn. He starts looking around for clean mugs. Wonders whether there are still any of the poppy-seed shortbread left in the biscuit tin. Whether he shouldn't offer Theo use of Jarod's room until things calm down a little at home. He likes the idea of being a safe haven. Wonders, again, whether he would ever be permitted to open a place of refuge for the wrongly convicted; a halfway house where those savaged by the system mightn't learn how to be a person again.

'Car,' says Theo, jerking his head.

Both men stiffen, their senses attuned to sudden sounds, changes in the atmosphere.

'They're thrashing it . . .' says Theo, as the rain-speckled window fills with yellow light and a dirty hatchback squeals into the darkening yard. Tips starts barking from her position on sentry outside Jarod's room.

'She looks like one of those toys from the Eighties,' says Theo, standing up and watching as a dumpy, harassed-looking woman climbs out of the driving seat and slams the door as if pursued by angry dogs.

'Sorry?'

'They made a movie a couple of years ago. Big hair. Squishy. Play guitar . . . *Trolls*, that's it.'

'Bloody hell, don't say that, she'll have your arm off.'

'You know her?'

Hagman watches as Elsie Crisp stomps across the yard. Lets himself smile as the doors of the hatchback creak open. A flash of brightly coloured legging. A black hoodie, glittering with buttons and badges.

Nola.

Lottie.

The door opens without a knock. Elsie stands in the doorway, fried-egg eyes, mad smile splitting her rosy cheeks.

'Wulf, I'm so fricking sorry, there's been a mix-up . . .' she stops as she spies Theo. Hagman watches as she works him out; as she puts together the pieces she knows and tries to make them fit with the handsome, blue-eyed young man.

'She's going to go mental,' declares Elsie, looking from one to the other. 'Mental in that quiet way, but mental nevertheless.'

Lottie barges past her, toys spilling out of her rucksack, a yellow-and-black tiger clutched in her arms.

'Uncle Wulf,' she says, radiating delight. 'Sal's out catching a bad man. We've come to play . . .!'

THIRTEEN

Quinn stares at the blank page. It doesn't fill the whole screen. The purple lights of the desktop provide a pleasing backdrop for the glaring, milk-tooth-white brightness. So too the countless little rectangles: policy documents, briefing notes, half-finished witness statements, overtime requests and budget guidelines. She screws up her face. Tries to tease out the one coherent thought from the jumble in her skull.

Concentrate, Magda. Ask yourself what matters.

She closes her eyes. Breathes. Lets her fingers dance over the keys . . .

Her phone rings on the table in front of her. It's so loud and sudden she jerks at the interruption, sploshing the lukewarm green tea into the saucer and smearing a line of jumbled consonants on to her briefing note. She looks at the screen. Her mouth becomes a hard line.

'Salome? I'm sorry, I'd forgotten about you . . .'

She listens for a while. Absorbs the salient points. Once she starts repeating herself, Quinn lets her mind drift. Pictures Lewis. Pictures the utter nothingness in his dark, shark-like eyes. The man he was, who she could help him to become – both had died on that dark, snow-muffled country road last year. His thick skull had saved his life, but the part of him that might have entertained the life she'd planned for him – he'd never woken up. In his desperation to do right by Sal, he had killed the part of himself that was capable of love. Sal did that. Sal! Not her. Not the senior investigating officer. Not the woman who didn't give a damn about Lewis Beecher until he made it clear he didn't want her, would never want her . . .

'Can I stop you there?' asks Quinn, coolly?

'Yes, ma'am.'

She takes a sip of tea. Lets the silence build. 'No, I didn't have a question. I just wanted to stop you there. Are you still with the witness?'

There's a sudden burst of static and noise from the phone. Quinn winces. She hopes Sal's somewhere dreadful. Hopes she's in a phone box, rattled by the storm, inhaling piss fumes and sex-worker business cards and blushing crimson on her round, dimpled cheeks.

'I'm going to need you at the hospital,' says Quinn, feeling more like herself. She looks over the top of the laptop. A bland man in pressed jeans and a tucked-in Coldplay T-shirt is using his cute, trembly puppy as an excuse to chat up the tall, knobbly-limbed young woman who rests her shoeless feet on one chair while slumped into another, cappuccino foam on her round spectacles. Quinn clamps her teeth down on her cheek. Sometimes she hates people so intensely she wonders whether she mightn't be on the wrong side.

'Ma'am, Elsie's having problems and there's nobody else to get the girls, and I—'

'I'm sorry, Sal – we all have problems. You don't just get to knock off early because you've got to burn the fishfingers and get the kiddies into their jim-jams. This is a murder enquiry . . .'

'He's not dead,' says Sal, diplomatically.

'Well, you're only an hour away. Maybe by the time you get there, he will be.'

'And what are you wanting me to do when I get there, ma'am?'

Quinn has to bite back the laugh. What does she want her to do? She wants her to spend time in the room with the dying man. Wants her to breathe in toxic, death-scented air. Wants her to feel the nearness of the grave; to inhale particles of rotting out-breath and watch whatever comes for him at the end.

'You had a way with him, I'm told. Sit with him. Hold his hand. Show what a caring outfit Cumbria Constabulary truly is. Have a heart, Sal.'

'And the children, ma'am?'

A muscle twitches in Quinn's cheek. She thinks of Wulfric Hagman. Thinks of the case she couldn't make. Hates him. Hates him all the way through.

'I'm sure somebody as popular as you has all manner of friends to ask. Lewis never struggled with his responsibilities.'

She can't be sure, but she fancies she hears Sal die a little.

When she hangs up and starts to write, the words flow like blood.

FOURTEEN

Royal Victoria Infirmary, Newcastle

7.04 p.m.

'No.' Sal stands in the harsh yellow light in the pale green corridor, steam rising from her sodden clothes. Her outline shivers like the air above a hot road.

'I've told the last two. And him.'

The nurse nods at the uniformed police officer who sits on the hard chair outside the closed door. He's thick-necked and bullish, a huddled mound of blue polyester and hi-vis. He's working his way through a bag of spicy Nik-Naks. There's a can of Lilt at his feet. He looks entirely at ease with his world.

'It's just, my boss . . . she, she thinks he might respond to my voice, and if I call and say I haven't at least tried, I'm going to get such an earful. If he's unresponsive it doesn't matter either way, does it?'

The nurse is fiftyish. Nigerian, if Sal's any judge. She's got the look of somebody who's heard so many sob-stories she can lip-sync to the new ones.

'I understand, my love. I do. But that's the instruction. No visitors.'

Sal shivers. Looks down at her sodden boots. She's taken two buses and walked half a mile in a downpour to make it to the hospital. Doesn't know how she'll get home. Needs a charge for her phone. Doesn't know where the girls are . . .

She feels suddenly light-headed. Feels like there's a weight pushing against her chest. Feels her pulse, at her wrist, at her neck – beaks jabbing their way out of pale, brittle eggshells. She staggers slightly, a half-step to her left, eyes screw up shut. She smells chemicals and wet wool. Smells burning hair.

'Hey, lovely, hey, hey . . .'

She feels a pressure at her elbow. Opens her eyes into the wide bright ones of the nurse. Feels cool knuckles upon her brow.

'Do you have issues with your blood sugar?' she asks. 'Have you eaten?'

Sal tries to apologize. Feels her cheeks burning. Glances right and sees the PC watching, half-interested. After a moment, he proffers the Nik-Naks. He looks like a child who's been told to share his sweets.

'I'm fine. I'll pop to the vending machine.'

The nurse takes a step back. Casts an expert eye over the bedraggled specimen in front of her. Sal feels as if she's been scanned with a metal detector.

'A lot going on in there,' smiles the nurse, nodding at the centre of Sal's forehead. 'This boss. Proper cow-bag, is she?'

Sal hears herself laugh out loud. 'Proper cow-bag,' she repeats.

'One of my favourites,' smiles the nurse. 'I'm Rose, by the way.'

'Sal,' she says, quietly. 'Salome, actually.'

'Salome?' grins Rose, absurdly pleased. She slaps her on the arm. 'Whose dance so aroused a king that she was granted whatever favour she wished? Who asked for the head of John the Baptist?'

'If I'd been a boy, Mam would have gone with Herod.'

Rose laughs. It's a pleasing sound. From somewhere nearby, she hears the sound of shoes squeaking on the rubber floor. Hears the ding of the elevator doors, the swish and squeak of rubber-bottomed double doors. Far off she fancies she hears crying.

'Your mother is a religious lady?' she asks.

The moment passes. The laughter fades. Sal realizes she's staring into space, a silly embarrassed half-smile on her face. Rose is looking at her, concern written in the lines that appear in her smooth skin.

'Not religious, no,' she says, her throat catching. 'Not . . . not a very well person.' She stops. Sniffs. Realizes that a tear is sitting on her lower lid, swelling, building, yearning to fall. She snatches it away.

'I'll get you some water,' says Rose, after a breath. 'I think there's some cake in the nurses' station. I'll bring you a plate.' She leans in. Jerks her head back over her shoulder. 'It's a two-minute walk.'

Sal has to fight the urge to grab her by the arms and kiss her cheeks. She makes a face instead. 'You couldn't plug my phone in somewhere too, could you?'

Rose grins. Gives her a gentle slap on the arm. 'You not ask for much, eh?'

Sal hands over her mobile, the cracked screen glinting blackly in the gaudy light. 'I'm so grateful.'

Rose waves off the thanks and turns toward the corridor. 'If she faints, don't move her,' she says, over her shoulder, to the seated officer. 'And pick up your rubbish when you clock off. We've only got one cleaner left and she's got better things to do.'

'I never! I . . .'

Sal glances at the suddenly animated PC. He mouths a nasty 'fuck off' at Rose's back as she disappears through the double doors. A sudden burst of temper rises up in Sal's chest and throat. She swallows it down.

Be a good girl, Sal. Don't cause trouble. Keep the mask on, best all round . . .

An echo, deeper-voiced but somehow further off; the echo of her brother.

Show them, Sal. Show them how good you are. You've taken beatings that would kill every one of these bastards. Show them how wrong they are about you. Punch him in his fat face, Sal. Hit the way Mam showed you . . .

She turns away. Opens the door to Mahee's room. Sees wires. Bags of clear fluid. Sees bandages and pinkly glistening skin.

She approaches the bed. There's a rising smell; something foul. She thinks of bad meat. Of the greenish water at the bottom of a vase of lilies.

She says his name. He can't speak. Can't open his eyes. But she says his name because it's the polite thing to do, and because she's cold and wet and she's frightened that she might have totally misread Rose's meaning and is going to be hauled out by the hair and shouted at in front of PC Nik-Nak.

'Mahee?'

She looks down at the notes again. She feels the tingling sensation on the back of her hand as she looks down the bed to where Mahee's arms disappear into polythene bags. His hands have been bagged to protect any evidence that may be beneath his nails. She remembers the feeling of that broken, bloody finger scratching against her cold skin. She tries again to trace the pattern. A name? A number? Why hadn't she scribbled it down while fresh in her mind? Why hadn't . . .?

She leans over him. There's gauze on one cheek, covering the suppurating wound.

'What did they do to you?' she asks, gently. A great surge of pity rolls up from her belly as she looks upon the shrivelled, ruined man. She thinks again of the image of the plump, smiling, well-groomed solicitor.

She starts suddenly as the heart monitor beeps. She realizes she hasn't heard it. Has been so deep inside herself, lost in the aircraft hum of her own panicked thoughts, that she hadn't even been aware of it. Some police officer, she spits at herself. Some fucking hero . . .

She tries to get a hold of herself. Tries to play the role. Wonders, again, if other people think like this. Whether their sense of being an imposter runs so deep that they don't know whether they're even real.

She softens her face. Pushes her wet curls back behind her ear.

'Whoever did this to you . . . we want to catch them. We want to make sure they can't do it to anybody else. And you . . . you deserve justice, Mahee . . .'

His eyes open. Tiny black pupils in rich dark irises; lenses yellow, seamed with red.

'Nurse,' shouts Sal, jumping back and sending the notes clattering to the floor. 'Rose!'

She turns for the door. Sees herself ringing Quinn. He's awake, yes. Told me everything . . .

A bagged hand grabs her wrist. Holds her fast.

She looks back into the wide, fear-filled eyes. His pupils vibrate, his face twisting in hellish paroxysms of pain, terror.

The bag rustles. She feels a pressure against her palm. Shudders, as the twisted, bloodied digit moves upon her skin.

'I don't understand,' she whispers. 'I don't understand . . .'

She snatches up the scattered notes. Grabs the pen from the clipboard.

Starts to draw in tandem with the finger that moves against her.

Only as she's staring at the finished image does she become aware of the high beeping. Only as she's being pushed back from the bed by the half-dozen nurses does she glimpse the twisted figure in the bed, back arched like a bow, eyes staring in terror at the place where it stands.

She pushes herself back against the wall. Looks down at the image she has scribbled on the page.

Nothing. Gibberish. A dying man's last words, daubed in blood and ink.

'What the hell was she doing in here?' demands a doctor from among the press of bodies. 'Get her out. Get her out right now!'

Sal runs from the room, clutching her papers, cheeks burning, eyes stinging; wet fabric against her skin.

She runs past the PC. 'No fire, is there, love?'

She makes it to the toilet by the nurses' station. Throws up into the sink. Keeps going long after she's empty: body bucking and jerking, purging itself; her every sense a miasma of bile and blood.

Only when she's done does she let herself look at her reflection.

It shimmers. She thinks of bubbles. Prisms.

The image splits.

Divides and multiplies like cells.

She picks a face among the multitude. Sees Jarod, looking back. *You can do this. I believe in you. Look again. You'll see.*

She fumbles for the paper. Raises the image to her face and looks again through eyes prismed with bitter tears.

What are you trying to tell me?

FIFTEEN

The stone is gritty against Sal's skin. Damp. She fancies that if she could just keep trundling her brow across the crumbling brickwork, she could work her way into the wall within the year. She wonders if anybody would try and stop her. Whether a crowd would gather to watch – cheer her on as she bloodily moles her way into the masonry.

'Stop it,' she hisses, tongue between her teeth. 'Just stop.'

Sal wouldn't want anybody to think she is hiding. She's made her way into this dark little snicket behind the shops because she wants some time to gather her thoughts – to put herself back together so she can be of some use to the team.

'Bollocks. You're scared. He scared you. They all scare you. Call yourself a police officer? You're a frightened little girl.'

Sal wedges herself behind the big metal bin with its rotting onion reek and its ripped, sauce-splattered bags. Squats down. Rubs the grit from her head with the back of her hand. From here, she can just about make out the car park: wet tarmac bathed in yellows and blues, reflecting off the gleaming bonnets of haphazardly parked cars. She's still at work, after a fashion. Still positioned at the RVI, awaiting further instructions. She's also here, in this little alleyway. She's chugged down two fizzy orange drinks and stuffed a packet of fruity sweets into her mouth. She's devoured two family-sized chocolate bars and a bottle of full-fat milk. Threw her guts up long before she was ready to.

She puts her glasses back on. Wipes the taste of vomit from her lips. Rummages in Jarod's pockets and finds something that might be an old piece of eucalyptus gum. Unwraps it and pops it into her mouth. If it happens to be one of his psilocybin-laced gummy sweets, she doesn't care.

Her phone rings almost as soon as she pulls it from her trouser pocket. She picked it up from the nurses' station before she went out. It's Elsie, ringing to apologize again. Sal's already listened to two voicemails that said pretty much the same thing. She couldn't watch the girls as much. Her hubby was getting tired of being a stepdad and chauffeur-service. He'd lost his temper with Lottie – some song she wouldn't stop singing; her whole repertoire of noises and twitches. He'd put his foot down. Couldn't keep doing this. He'd had a few. She's so sorry – wants to be a better friend . . .

Sal ignores the call. She isn't sure she would know how to reply. The kids are with Wulf, which means she does at least know they are safe and being looked after. It's what social services will have to say that worries her. She's always been prone to little bouts of paranoia but sometimes she wonders just how deep Magda Quinn's hatred for her might go. She's felt herself being watched through the window. Has seen little lights flick randomly on and off when her laptop has been sitting idle. Has heard her pet words and phrases being mirrored in Quinn's speech. She doesn't know what to do with the feeling. She knows it can't be true; that it's her busy little head making trouble for her again. She used to have a boyfriend who told her over and over again that she was delusional: a fantasist – possibly mad. He'd lost patience with her long before she fell out of love with him. Set the tone for every relationship that followed.

She flicks through the messages on her phone. There's a text from Hagman: an apology, and an attempt at reassurance that sounds eerily threatening from a convicted killer.

I've got your girls . . .

She leans back against the wall. Angles her head away from the bin. Watches two teenagers take up sentry outside the entryway to the alley, bodies bisected by the halo of harsh light that spills down from the corner shop. She sees jogging trousers, baseball caps, vapes and bottles of energy drink. Hears nothing of their conversation but finds herself wondering whether she would fare better as a teenager today. Whether she mightn't have been happier had she been born twenty-five years later. Whether she'd get a kinder diagnosis; be declared neurodivergent, perhaps a blip on the autism spectrum radar. Whether they would make allowances for her at school. Whether she'd be entitled to have days off every time it all felt too much. She tugs at her hair, angry with herself. *Is this how it starts*, she asks herself? *Christ, you'll be reading the* Telegraph *next . . .*

She finds herself looking down at her palm. At the grooves and whorls upon her hand – the white scars that peek out from her rolled-up cuff: Endless five-bar gates of perfect whiteness: each one a memory of blood spilled, pain released, trauma exsanguinated. Her therapists have told her she's wrong to miss the feeling.

Again, she feels Mahee's bloodied stump upon her skin. She closes her eyes, hoping she can see a shape. A pattern.

She rubs her palms together. Pushes her hands through her hair. She'll go back soon. She'll give her briefing to whoever Quinn sends. She'll keep her own role in matters small. Quinn has already told her that if Mahee dies while officially under the care of the police, she'll lose more than her job. She'll do time.

God how she wants to call Lewis. Even just to hear him breathe – unload; lighten herself by telling him her fears, her hopes, her insecurities. He's a good listener now he doesn't reply. Doesn't answer back. Doesn't scrutinize. She just wishes he would give her a glimpse of who he used to be. Wishes he would tell her when she's talking shit or getting carried away or being a big soft sod who clings to him like a baby gibbon. She feels tears prick her eyes at the thought: the girls giggling; Lewis trying to make pancakes in the kitchen while she steadfastly clings to him, arms around his neck; her pyjama bottoms bunching up as he wears her like a child in a papoose. She doesn't let herself wonder whether she will ever know such times again. She's good at shutting down unhelpful thoughts; biting them back, swallowing their mass – letting them sink into her gut to become anxiety, heartburn.

'Come on. Show your face. You've done nowt wrong . . .'

Sal hears Jarod's voice. Realizes she's spoken aloud rather than heard it inside her head. Wonders whether she's going mad. Whether Jarod is dead or alive. Whether she's being possessed by her murdered twin.

From the far end of the alley, she hears the faintest clinking sound: bottles resettling inside a dumped bin-liner. Its shiny blackness spills like oil across half of the alleyway; the rest all shadow and blocky, indecipherable shapes. She feels an eerie prickling sensation at the back of her neck, her wrists, behind her knees. She reaches out for the side of the metal bin and pulls herself up, quietly. She realizes she can't be seen from where she has secreted herself. Wonders what she'll say if somebody comes by to drop off the rubbish and spots her burrowed in: a bag lady in a damp parka.

She slips her phone into her pocket. She feels a nearness; a sensation that deeper in the alleyway there is a presence – perhaps a figure. She squints, uncertainly.

She wonders if she should cough. Make a show of emerging from her hiding place. Wonders what the worst thing imaginable would be. Pictures Magda Quinn and Lewis Beecher up against the brickwork, faces kissing like fighting sharks. She feels sick. Feels tears come unbidden to her eyes.

She steps out, soundlessly. Takes two steps deeper into the alley.

'Hello? Hi, my name's Sal . . .'

There is no mistaking the sound this time. Glasses clink, plastic rustles. There's the sound of somebody stumbling – the splash of a hand finding a deep, rubbish-strewn puddle.

'It's OK, I'm police . . .'

She fumbles with her phone, trying to find the torch. Takes her attention away from the darkness just long enough to unlock the device. Looks back up.

She sees the apparition for just a moment. Sees a hooded figure: blackened, fire-licked skin; stitches and slashes and the black eyeholes over milky lenses.

She raises a hand to her mouth. Feels her insides turn to water.

She steps forward, even as her every instinct tells her to run and run. Stumbles in her own vomit. Grabs for the bin and manages to keep her balance.

When she looks up again she is alone. Couldn't say for certain whether she saw anything at all. She feels like she does before a migraine: wet-mouthed, buzzing, strange throbbing zaps at her temples and back teeth. Feels as if she has stood too close to a power station; hair and bones electrified; every extremity on edge.

She turns away from the darkness. Tells herself something pretty, the way she's encouraged Lottie to try when it's all too much. By the time she emerges from the mouth of the alley, she's convinced herself she was just being silly.

In the darkness, Blindworm watches her go. Behind the skin of the mask, a smile.

Thinks: *she's afraid.*

Thinks: *she's as good as ours already.*

Thinks: *you're going to have company, Constance. Won't that be nice?*

PART TWO

SIXTEEN

Hagman's Farm, Alston Moor

11.46 p.m.

'Shout it out – for your ocean animals!'

Hagman doesn't need to look up. Lottie has sung the same snatch of jingle at least fifty times in the last few hours. It emerges from her mouth without seeming to have sent prior notice to her brain. She always seems a little shocked at herself; cheeks pinkening and shooting self-conscious glances at her sister, sitting moodily in the rocking chair by the fire. When she's not belting out the ditty, she makes little trumpeting noises, lips spraying a haze of spittle on to her work as she sits doodling on the rear of Hagman's trial transcripts. She squeezes her nostrils shut too. Works her jaw in circles. He's read that autistic children have something called 'stims', and is trying not to count up the number of odd tics and jerks that seem to briefly soothe her. She deserves better than to be psychoanalysed by a man who lost everything for love of a monster. She's lost her mum. Her dad, too, for all the good he's doing her. He knows he's a hypocrite for thinking unkind thoughts about Lewis Beecher, but he thinks them nonetheless.

'Shout it out – for your—'

'For God's sake, Lottie, will you stop singing that!'

Nola slams the rockers down on the flagstone as she shouts, lifting up the entire chair and thwacking it back down, still seated. 'It's mental! It makes you seem proper, proper . . . mental!'

At the table, Lottie lowers her head, moving her face closer to the page. Her voice is small when she speaks. 'I just like it.'

'If you're doing that when you come to big school, they'll . . . they'll just annihilate you!'

Hagman finally lowers the sheaf of papers he's been hiding behind. Looks up to the shimmering oblongs and blobs; the elongated tadpole in the rocking chair; the multi-coloured gobstopper at the table. He's not wearing his glasses, making the deliberate choice not to be able to fixate on Lottie's twitches. Can't see more than orbs and hazy-edged smudges. His spectacles perch atop his bald head, arms descending behind his ears to caress the rope-burn before it disappears into his thick grey beard, dangling down to where a half-dozen different pendants dangle into his off-white grandad shirt. He has the appearance of both wizard and warrior, though fancies himself as neither. Right now, he's the out-of-his-depth babysitter, counting each tick of the clock. They should have been in bed hours ago, but the thought of bedtime stories and bedclothes and finding a place for them to wash and brush their teeth . . . he isn't sure he can put himself through it. Isn't sure he would survive the flood of memories that would swamp him if the dam were to break.

'I'm sure she'll grow out if it,' says Hagman, awkwardly. 'When I was little I used to have to write out words as I heard them – my finger was like a pencil and I felt all weird if I didn't do it. I don't know why. But I stopped. It's just a thing.'

He can't see Nola, but he feels the air in front of her face shimmer as she gives him what he presumes to be a hard glare. 'And you're an example of good mental health, are you?'

Hagman lowers his head. 'I just mean that if you make her feel self-conscious . . .'

'Oh, me again, what a surprise!' She bangs the chair down hard again. Does it once more for emphasis. 'My fault that she's got Tourette's!'

'I don't have turrets,' says Lottie, confused. She checks her head for ramparts and battlements. Makes a face. 'You're the one saying people have turrets.'

Hagman acquiesces to the silence. Slides his glasses into place. Nola's face comes into immediate focus and it's all he can do not to jerk off his spectacles and throw them in the fire. She's glaring at her little sister's hunched back, eyes shining with something that looks like hatred. Revulsion. 'Nola, she's your little sister – families help each other grow and she's been through such a—'

'She's been through a lot? She's been!' She stands up, arms stiff at her side, fingers curled around the cuffs of her hoody. She takes a step away from the fire, catching her hood in one of the bunches of drying hops that dangle from the low wooden beams. She gives a screech of frustration. A necklace of tears spills from each eye and she all but punches herself with the speed with which she smears them away with her knuckles. She shakes her head at the floor, lips curled far enough back to show the pink of her gums. 'My mam died! My mam! She's only been here five minutes – I'm the one who knew her properly . . . all this "you're doing so well" and "you've got to take care of Lottie" and "you can't bully her cos her mam's been killed" . . .'

'Who's saying that?' asks Hagman, quietly.

'School!' she yells. 'They're all being so nice to me! Even the lads who used to send me horrible messages when she was alive; the popular girls, the sporty lads; the weirdo who used to try and take my bra off whenever he locked me in the music cupboard. They give me these little smiles and look away. I don't get in trouble for anything!'

'I wish I didn't,' mutters Lottie, turning around to better see her sister. 'Why would you want to get into trouble?'

'Because then he might come back!' shouts Nola, grabbing a piece of wood from the stack by the fire and throwing it on the ground at her feet. It bounces under the table. Nola stands and pants, hair falling forward in front of her face. 'How can he just go off? Just not come back? Mam's dead! Dead! And he's what . . . just not able to be a dad any more? Can't deal with it? Deal with what? I don't go out anywhere. I don't have any bad friends. I do my homework. I can even make tea. He just has to be in his chair playing on his phone. That's all. Just be there. I'll do it all!'

Hagman's heart seems to slide around inside his chest. He feels a sudden burst of longing for the life he gave away. Feels the desperate tingle in his fingertips; the urge to throw his arms around a memory and haul it into the light.

'Could Sal still do stories?' asks Lottie.

Nola sits back down. 'This place is so stupid,' she says, with less fire in her voice. 'Your Wi-Fi is so patchy.'

Hagman lets out a breath. He fancies he's back on firmer ground. 'It has good days and bad days. Like we all do.'

'I have both at the same time,' muses Lottie. 'I mean, they're good because of *Elena of Avalor* and *Bluey* and the voices that Sal does when she reads that book about *Our Gags* . . .'

'*Our Gags?*'

'It's a book, I told you. But it's bad because Mam died and I, and I . . .'

She turns back to her drawing. Selects a red crayon and starts colouring in the stick-figure she's sketched out. He lies at the bottom of a staircase, half entangled with a figure drawn in curves of purple. She's smiling, despite the red. School says they shouldn't curtail her efforts to process what she saw. Hagman watches as she wipes her nose with the back of her hand. Reaches out for Happy Tiger and uses one of his faded yellow paws to wipe her eyes.

'Sorry,' mutters Nola, by the fire. 'Sorry for saying you were mental.'

Lottie makes a sound like an elephant with her lips. Nola gives a little laugh. Hagman glances up again at the clock. *Please, Sal. Please* . . .

'What is it you're reading, Uncle Wulf?' asks Lottie, with the air of somebody who wants to make amends. She reaches over to take her hot chocolate from the little nook by the open fire. Takes a slurp. He'd put a couple of drops of valerian in when he was boiling the milk. He'd hoped it would be working by now, but neither girl seems keen on following his suggestion that they go upstairs to Jarod's room and snuggle down with Tips. They find the house spooky. Find the absence of Uncle Jarod a loss too many. They cling to the fire, to Wulf.

'A lad I know – he's got an important interview coming up.'

Lottie keeps looking, her face suggesting that this is in no way an explanation.

Hagman holds up the front of the blue ring binder that's been open in his lap. It has a photocopy of a picture of a castle on the front; some long, hard-to-decipher text along the bottom. 'This is a local history project that was put together for the millennium,' he begins.

'What's a millennium?' ask both girls. They say 'jinx' and laugh, each closing their eyes to make a wish.

'For the new century,' continues Hagman, feeling old. 'The government gave lots of money to good ideas and local communities got to do stuff to celebrate this big date. This lot got some money to put together a sort of report – keeping people's memories safe for future generations. They asked lots of older people for their life stories and then picked out lots of interesting bits to make this.'

'Is it good?' asks Lottie, one eye closed, suspiciously. She squeezes her nostrils shut with finger and thumb.

'I'm not really reading it for that,' he says, glancing again at the clock. He's fed them, so he's done that bit right, but he doesn't believe he'll make it further without doing irreparable damage to the pair of them.

'Why are you reading it then?'

Hagman scratches at his beard. 'My friend. Theo. He wants to make a good impression at his interview tomorrow. Wants to know all the local stories and anecdotes and bits of intrigue.'

'Intrigue means "exciting bits", Lottie,' says Nola, automatically.

'Yeah, the exciting bits. He wants to be a guide at Lumley Castle. Have you been?'

Both girls peer at the grainy image. 'We had afternoon tea there,' says Lottie, brightly. 'With Sal and Dad. I got told off for nearly falling out of a window. There was a suit of armour.'

Hagman smiles, appreciative of the details. 'Grand old place,' he says. 'He wants to be a tour guide so he's asked me to help him find a few little titbits to help him.'

'Titbits means bits and pieces, Lottie,' explains Nola.

'Titbits,' laughs Lottie. 'That's rude.'

'It's important to him,' says Hagman, and feels the weight of it settle in his chest. Theo has a chance at a real life. Has the chance for a new future. He's already done what he can to tip the scales in his favour. Asked the universe to manifest the poor sod some good fortune. He'll never tell him, just as he'll never tell about the rituals he conducts to protect those who matter to him. It's a diminishing number, from which he cannot bring himself to expel Dagmara. For better or worse, he owes her his life.

'Dream job, is it?' asks Nola. 'Is he just out of university?'

Hagman shakes his head. 'No, he's around thirty now, but his life . . . well, he missed out on a lot.'

'Is this the man you're helping?' asks Lottie, brightly. 'Sal told us about him. Said you were always a big soft sod but that it's lovely you're doing something kind for somebody.'

Hagman feels his cheeks twitch. He'd like to give in to the big broad smile but prison taught him to hide any expression of true feeling and he's found it a hard habit to break. 'I don't know about that . . .'

'She said most people would be really bitter that they haven't been enoriated . . .'

'Exonerated,' corrects Nola, retrieving the log from beneath the table and placing it on to the smouldering mound of splinters and ash. She blows on the embers. Picks up the poker and moves a burning splint into the centre of the little hill of glowing dirt. Cocks her head as it bursts into flame.

'He got let off and you should have been, but everybody still thinks you're a baddy, when in fact you're like, the nicest.'

Hagman can't help it. Grins, hugely. His eyes feel hot. He glances down at the folder and has to cough before he can speak again.

'You needn't be having any of that nasty business in your heads,' he says, when he can.

'What do you think our heads are full of?' asks Nola, looking confused.

'Sawdust and mouse turds,' says Lottie, and there's a smile in her voice.

Hope, thinks Wulf, and shakes his head. He wonders when it will die. Reminds himself how to think like a copper. Starts to read.

SEVENTEEN

Sal drills her gaze into the dead coals. Glares so hard that her temples begin to throb. Any onlooker would presume she was practising some new elemental gift – as if one of the crumbled lumps of black ash could momentarily burst back into life.

'I can relight it, if you like.'

Sal turns towards the stairs. She hadn't heard the tell-tale creak of the rickety steps. Can't remember the last thing she heard that wasn't confined to the insides of her skull.

'It's not cold, but I like watching it.'

Sal tries to rearrange her face into something welcoming. To go into Mum-mode. She manages a smile as Nola makes her way through the boxes of paper; the spindly chair; knocking old landscapes askew as she shuffles along, wrapped tight in her quilt.

'I feel like a caterpillar,' says Nola, eyes and nose peeking out through a face-hole in the gathered quilt. Sal waits until she has inserted herself into the low armchair, scattering Hagman's piles of reading, of research, of kindling.

'You look like a maggot, actually,' says Sal, deadpan. 'It's the colour. You're more larval.'

Nola gives her some serious side-eye. Suppresses a smile.

'Do you want me to light it again? He showed me how.'

Sal wonders which 'he' her eldest stepdaughter is referring to. Wonders whether they are ready to talk about Lewis yet. About Mum. Mam. About the future. Whether there is any merit in running at the wall and not stopping until she's very far away.

'Couldn't sleep?' asks Sal, readjusting herself. She's got a green tea on the go somewhere but she'll be damned if she can find the energy to go and look. She knows her posture – legs drawn up, upper body jutting painfully into the hard arm of the chair – is going to lead to aches in her joints when she finally puts herself into a sleeping position. Can't bring herself to care.

'She's unsettled,' says Nola, directing her own gaze towards the joyless hearth. 'I've stroked her nose. I think she's asleep but it's hard to tell.'

Sal feels the urge to reach out and place a hand on the great quilted burrito in the next chair. Makes a fist instead.

'You're a good sister,' she says, at last. 'Better than any of mine. Better than me.'

Nola pulls the quilt around herself. It seems strange to see her without her phone, denuded of the black hoodie. She looks very young. She licks her lips, questions on her tongue. Lowers her eyes before she finds the courage to speak.

'You can ask me anything, you know,' says Sal, grateful for the chance to think about anything other than Mahee Gamage, Magda Quinn. Even if the questions hurt, she'll be indebted for a different kind of sting.

'Do you think he's OK?' she asks, at last. 'That he'll be OK.'

Sal's been preparing for the question. Knows what she wants to say. 'He's tough, your dad. That's one of the things we all love about him. If anybody can come back from what he's been through, it's him, I promise you.'

Her chest clutches as she unspools the lie. Wonders why nobody told her how much of parenting came down to well-intentioned deceits.

'Not Dad,' says Nola, brow furrowing. 'Dad'll be fine. It'll take a while but Dad'll be fine. I mean your brother. Jarod.'

Sal stiffens. She feels the skin of her arms pucker and stiffen, the hairs rising. She suffers a sudden burst of flu-like lethargy, muscular pain, tightness across her chest and back. She makes herself tap her index finger against her chest – to breathe. To breathe, just like Dagmara showed them when she was climbing into their subconscious and unravelling their memories, their minds.

'It's OK,' says Nola, hurriedly. 'Sal, you don't have to tell me . . . it's OK . . .'

'He's alive, yes,' says Sal, and she realizes she means it. 'He is. I don't know if he's doing so well, but I know he's alive. If he wasn't, I'd feel it.'

'Twin thing,' nods Nola, who's always been fascinated with Sal's stories of her intense connection with her slightly older brother. 'You can still feel him.'

'Sometimes I see him too,' says Sal, surprising herself with her honesty. 'In the mirror. Over my shoulder. Little unexpected reflections. It's like he's with me.'

'Is that a nice thing?' asks Nola, sitting forward. Her voice catches. Eyes begin to fill. 'Is it better than the opposite?'

Sal can't stop herself. She reaches out and finds the first part of Nola's shrouded body that she can squeeze. It's a forearm, tense, brittle, even through the quilting.

'Your mum,' says Sal, quietly. 'You know the school has offered to provide somebody to talk to . . . you said no, and I respect that, but maybe . . .'

Nola sits back in the chair. Unwraps the quilt. She's wearing one of Jarod's old shirts and long johns; thick cable-knit socks reaching almost to her knee. She snatches the tears away, angry with herself.

'What are they going to do . . . make me less sad that my mam died? I'm not depressed, Sal. I'm . . . I don't know what the word is . . . I've read all the books, the poems, all the pretty ways of thinking about losing somebody. I don't want to talk it away.'

'That's not what it's about,' says Sal, gently. She stops herself. Closes her eyes and swallows, hard. 'You know you can talk to me, don't you?'

Nola nods, tight-lipped. 'Did you get a therapist? After your mam?'

Sal stretches her back: a pause to find the right words. Takes off her glasses and cleans them on the scratchy wool of the crocheted blanket.

'Dagmara took care of all that,' says Sal, returning her gaze to the fire. 'Took care of everything.'

She feels Nola's gaze on the side of her face. Wonders whether tonight's the night she finally asks for the details. She's read the book and listened to the podcast and Sal has no doubt she'll watch the inevitable Netflix true-crime documentary when it comes out. Violence and blood has stained her young life. Even if she wasn't a copper's daughter, she'd have a morbid fascination with death and injustice.

'The lad before,' says Nola, awkwardly. 'Theo. You've read about it, have you? I didn't mean to be weird when he was here, it's just, I've read loads of stuff online about him and it was a bit weird suddenly having him here, and I could feel my cheeks burning, like, if I was rude or anything . . .'

Sal keeps her expression friendly. Inside, her gut reacts. Nola has a crush. A crush on a man twice her age. A man who lives in the woods. Who's been to prison. Whose name has started to come up in connection with the atrocities inflicted upon Mahee Gamage.

'We got it wrong,' she says, evenly. 'The police, I mean. Prosecution too. It was a mistake, but nobody had the courage to back down and say they got it wrong.'

'It could happen to any of us, couldn't it?' asks Nola, wide-eyed. 'Like, Dad always said that the rules kept us safe and that there had to be punishments for breaking them – that the police were here to make sure the bad people couldn't hurt anybody else.' She chews her lip, eyes glassy. 'It's a fairy-tale, isn't it? Like the tooth fairy or whatever. It's just something we tell little kids. It's all just a mess, really. I mean, Dad couldn't stop Hank, could he? From doing what he was doing. And he's my dad. What chance has anybody got?'

Sal grinds her teeth. She never suffered any misapprehension when she was young: never mistakenly believed that the world was divided up into cops and robbers, rule-breakers and guardians. Her own life never afforded her the luxury. Even so, her chest aches for Nola.

'Nobody knew what Hank was,' she says, gently. 'I didn't know . . .'

'You did,' says Nola, protesting. 'You always looked at him for a second or two longer than anybody else did. We saw you. You knew there was something wrong with him.'

Sal controls her breathing. Turns towards the window as a sudden gust of wind throws a handful of gritty rain against the dirty glass. She has a prickling sensation at her neck, her wrists. She can hear the wasps in her brain; the drone that threatens to become a voice.

'I thought he was a show off,' says Sal, carefully. 'A bit of a prat. I didn't know he was . . . didn't know how much he scared you both. How much he scared your mum.'

'I don't miss her,' says Nola, eyes flashing with a sudden hard rage. 'I'm still too angry to miss her. Do you think I will? Do you think I'll miss her when I stop being angry? I'll remember the good stuff – not her at the bottom of the stairs . . .'

'I sometimes miss my mam,' says Sal, and the words come out in a rush. 'There's no other word for it. I get a smell or a sound or a memory and for a moment I do my thinking with my heart and I just . . . I miss my mam. Then my brain gets involved and I hate myself for it. She was a monster. A true monster. But. Miss her.' She closes her eyes. 'Dagmara too.'

Nola looks as though she is about to reply when some movement at the window gives her pause. Sal watches her as she furrows her brow. Squints. As she raises her hand to her mouth.

'Nola?' asks Sal, twisting in her chair. 'Nola, what's wr—'

She stops, rigid, neck turned at an angle that makes her look as if she has fallen from a height. Beyond the glass, framed by the window, she sees the figure. Sees the same featureless face: eye-slits and patchwork scraps, outlined by a moon that leers down from behind two grimy curtains of diaphanous cloud.

'Sal!'

Sal drags herself from the chair, slipping on the rug by the fire, reaching down to scoop up the wrought-iron poker from the coal scuttle.

'Go to Wulf,' she shouts, pulling on her boots and throwing a glance back towards the glass. 'Three knocks on his door, then two. Prison knock or he won't wake . . .'

'Sal, there was somebody there! Somebody in a mask! That story Wulf told us, the torturer with the dungeon . . .' she stops herself, aware of where her thoughts are taking her. 'Theo. His audition . . .'

Sal doesn't reply. Hauls open the back door and runs into the yard, feet slipping and crunching on the pitted surface; grit, mud, sheep shit. She yelps as she feels something brush her side. Looks down at Tips. Feels the old collie quivering, hackles raised, glaring into the rain and the darkness at her side.

'Easy,' she says, and looks down at her hand. Realizes what she was willing to do. How hard she would fight for what she wants. 'If he was there, he's gone, eh lad?'

She strokes Tips behind the ears. Wishes to God that she be granted the gift of speech for just a moment. She saw what happened to Jarod. Saw whether Dagmara left him alive or dead . . .

'Coward,' says Sal, under her breath. She disgusts herself. Knows that she should be haring through the distant woods, listening for every cracking twig and snagging branch. She doesn't think she can make herself do it. She wants to be near the light. Even a dead hearth gives off the echo of warmth.

'He gone, girl?'

Then: 'Was he there at all?'

She turns. Goes back inside. Closes the door quietly. Nola is only halfway up the stairs. From above, she hears Lottie shriek. Sal's up the stairs in three bounds, shoving Nola aside, yanking open the old wooden door and half falling into the cramped little bedroom. Lottie is sitting up on Jarod's bed, hair wild, cheeks wet, staring at the window.

'A monster,' she mutters. 'Another monster . . .'

Sal holds her until she sleeps. Sits with Nola until she falls asleep in the chair.

By morning, they will have convinced themselves there was nobody there.

EIGHTEEN

Quinn presses herself against the gleaming burgundy leather of the chair. Angles herself so that her neck is hanging over the headrest: a condemned woman facing the guillotine eyes open. She stretches her legs, feeling the tension bite at her calves. Feels one toe crack inside her Giuseppe Zanotti shoes. She stretches out her fingers to their full extent.

'You look like you're in the electric chair.'

Slowly, she lowers her head. Lets her dark hair fall to her shoulders. Smiles, indulgently, at the dumpy figure, half obscured by the thick pleats of the long, burgundy curtains. He's framed by a mahogany bookcase: a drinks cabinet in the shape of an antique globe; a Javanese camphorwood chest, dragons and exotic birds chasing one another across its surface. He suits this space. Looks right, here, at the window, staring through his own reflection at the dark, rain-slicked outline of the elegant grounds. Retired chief superintendent Callum Whitehead.

'I saw myself more as Marie Antoinette,' says Quinn. 'Do you think when she said "let them eat cake" she knew she'd get her wish a couple of centuries down the line. Foresaw the obesity crisis. Quite the seer.'

Whitehead turns away from the window. His silken robe swishes as he moves: a sexy, feminine sound that seems at odds with the figure beneath: amphibian in his curves and bulges, florid and grog-blossomed in complexion. His hair's stuck up a little at the back and thinning on top. His right hand – the one rumoured to have been the one he used to extract information, favours, convictions – is carbuncled with arthritis: a scabbed pink hoof jewelled with red, swollen knuckles. There's been a hole cut in his expensive slippers to permit his swollen toe to protrude unencumbered.

'Time was, you'd know better than to sit like that near me, love. Time was, you'd have got exactly what you were asking for.'

Quinn swills his words around her mouth. Tastes them. Wrinkles her nose. 'I do believe that's the language of the dinosaur, Callum. The unreconstructed neanderthal. I believe it's the kind of language that's got a lot of your types into bother.'

He lowers himself to the arm of the green leather chesterfield. Perches, fatly, bellies clad in swirls of azure and gold. Eyes her for a time – his gaze a tongue upon her skin. 'Can't a chap reminisce?' he says, wiping his fleshy lips on the back of his hand.

'Maybe, in the right circumstances, I could still raise more than a smile.'

He gives what looks like a suggestive leer. To Quinn, he looks like a toad that's eaten a madras. She wonders what he expects her to feel. Wonders how he sees himself. He's not as straight-backed as he wants to be. Not as handsome, or as revered. Not as young. But there's still enough about him to suggest that he's used to having his orders followed. People tend to do what they're told.

'We can't have this rigmarole every time,' says Quinn, coolly. She reaches out to the maritime-style desk. Her brandy wells in the bulb of a deep crystal tumbler. She doesn't really like the stuff, but Whitehead always likes to show off his sophistication. Will force down a cigar he doesn't seem to enjoy if it means he gets to have his assistant bring in a box of fine Monte Cristos midway through a meeting: puffing locomotive chuffs out of the open window. 'I think you know by now, you're not about to turn my head. I can't see me suddenly realizing that this . . .' she waves her hand in Whitehead's direction . . . 'is what I'm crying out for.'

'You're doing pretty well out of it,' he says, licking his lips. He does it again, smile glistening like raw meat. 'Imagine what I'd be willing to do if you really showed some appreciation.'

Quinn takes her brandy. Holds it to her nose and breathes in, collecting herself. She feels fizzy. Wired. Her scalp itches beneath her hair and she can see her pale blue pulse beating in her wrist. She hasn't felt like this since . . . since when? Since before? Before, when she was a rising star, a cop on the up. Before, when her record gleamed with commendations and high-profile convictions. Before, when she was being head-hunted by any CID team that saw the benefits of her reputation for cold, detached efficiency. All gone, now. All those pages of citations, smeared and ripped into confetti and shit by people she wouldn't even have picked for her pub quiz team. Wulfric Hagman. Salome Delaney. Even Lewis. She feels herself grimace as she thinks upon him. Feels saliva flood her mouth. Looks again at her pulse and sees it thudding against her skin: a lunatic trying to drive its skull through the wall of its fragile prison.

'This is what you want to do, is it?' she says, lowering the glass. 'This is how you want to spend our time?'

Whitehead gives a little snuffled laugh. Looks at her with the kind of affection she's never seen him exhibit with his daughters. He speaks of his late wife with both reverence and disdain – extolling the quality of her household management and ability not to ever ask him more than the softest of questions, while sneering, tactlessly, about her dislike of her other wifely duties. 'Like fucking an ironing board,' he'd told Quinn, in the private bar at the castle hotel where they used to conduct their mutually beneficial transactions.

'You've made good progress,' he says, rubbing at one of his swollen, silk-clad knees. 'A fine job, my dear. Prompt, efficient, slightly uninspired leadership – you truly could be the poster girl for the modern police force.'

'Police service,' corrects Quinn, coolly.

'I took a call from Woody an hour before you deigned to pay me a visit.'

Quinn combs her hair with her fingers. She can't quite bring herself to think of Divisional Commander Malcolm Woodford by the nickname employed by his former boss and occasional investment partner.

'He wanted an update,' begins Quinn, sitting forward. 'I can't be bloody everywhere.'

'You can, Magda. You can be where I ask you to be. You can respect the proper way of things.'

Quinn tries to soften her posture. She hates this part of herself – this damnable ability to get men to do exactly what she wants. She knows how to tune them up and play them like fiddles. Knows how to make them feel like they're in control, even as she jerks their strings like so many fleshy marionettes. 'I feel terrible about it,' she says, and looks it. 'But at least he's saved me the job of telling you every last spit and cough. You know all the juicy bits already.'

'So why come? Why visit an old sod at this time of night if you've got nothing new to share.'

'Courtesy,' she replies. 'I wanted to say thanks. Return the favour, so to speak. It'll make a decent case.'

'You're confident you can find out who did this to the sod?'

'I'm confident I can bring about a satisfactory outcome,' says Quinn, with a smile that covers a multitude of sins. 'So to speak.'

'So to speak,' repeats Whitehead. He stares past her, to the big hunting picture on the wall: a murdered stag, leaking red; kilt-wearing hunter standing with their foot on its twisted neck. 'He's a pervert, so I hear.'

'We all have our kinks,' says Quinn, with a shrug. 'Giantism? Macrophilia? That's just a Tuesday for some people.'

'Easy to manipulate somebody with a shameful secret,' says Whitehead, pointedly. 'Somebody knows what he's into . . . tickles his fancy, so to speak. Promises him something he's not able to resist. Overcomes all good sense, doesn't it? Puts himself at risk to scratch an itch. We've seen it enough times.'

'And that's what you think?' asks Quinn, looking at him as if he's an oracle; that she values his insights in the slightest.

'Cut that out,' grunts Whitehead. 'I know you've thought of it already. What I'm telling you, smart-arse, is that you don't know everything. And if you'd just stop the act, you might learn something.'

Quinn presses her lips together. Gives the slightest of nods, chastened.

'Have a read,' says Whitehead, with a slow, sickly smile. He reaches into the pocket of his robe and pulls out a memory stick. He throws it underarm, aiming for her cleavage. Quinn plucks it from the air.

'And this is?'

'The beginnings of a trail, love. A trail we can link to our old friend. I'm trusting your discretion. Don't make me regret it.'

Quinn swallows. Lets herself enjoy the feeling of possibility.

'Hagman?'

'This time, love. This time he's going into a place so deep and dark, he'll never climb out. Him and his little pretty boy.'

Quinn intertwines her fingers. Stretches, cat-like. 'Pretty boy?'

Whitehead stares past her, chewing on his cheek. He'll tell her what he wants and when he wants. Has earned the right to take his time.

'You might want to treat old Sycamore with kid gloves,' says Whitehead, a note of caution in his voice. He turns towards the window, stares out through his own reflection and into the dark. Seems to take a moment for himself, some memory to be savoured, some private delight that hasn't lost its piquancy with the passing of the years. 'His father was something to see, in his pomp. Never lost his taste for high living. I've had to smooth some unfortunate wrinkles for the family, over the years.'

Quinn wonders if he'll offer up more. He gives her his full attention. Seems to make up his mind.

'I'm as honest with you as I've been with anybody in my life, Magda. I tell you as many truths as I can physically force out of my mouth. The ones I can't tell you – it's because I simply can't. You do understand that, yes?'

Quinn feels as though a spider is making its way up her calf. Gives him an appreciative smile.

'You might find out one or two things in the weeks and months ahead – things that might cloud your judgement. I need you to be prepared for the fact that you'll hear about the man I was, and not the man I am.' He sits back in his chair. Steeples his fingers at his belly. Surveys his little empire and the artfully displayed Magda Quinn. Looks, for a moment, like somebody who has it all.

'Sometimes, a decent community copper has to know when to keep their trap shut. Sometimes, what's best for everybody doesn't rightly fit within the law.'

Quinn sits forward a little. She'd really rather like to know how he justifies himself. Whether it's something she might consider mirroring in the future. She studies his pose. Files it away for future replication.

'You know what's happening, don't you Callum . . .'

He holds up a hand. No, he doesn't. But he has the whisperings of an idea, and he wants to cover his arse.

'I may have profited from the Le Gros family,' he says, brushing a crumb from his gown. 'A few minor entanglements, a few contributions to the benevolent fund, you know how it is . . .'

'And you think that your past dealings might be somehow brought to light?'

Whitehead's face loses some of its brief good humour. 'That useless boy. Theo. Good Christ, but he would have cleared himself of any involvement if he'd just kept his trap shut. Had to start believing the bollocks, didn't he? Believed his loving mam and dad when they told him that if he gave the police all he knew, he had nothing to worry about. Silly sod did what a good boy should, didn't he? Gave CID every last spit and cough of what he'd done. Too bloody much. Started spilling out all sorts of stuff that should have stayed on the inside. Started telling them why his dad was so upset, why they were arguing, why he was in the foul mood he admitted to when he left the pub . . .'

'Hang on,' begins Quinn, trying to keep up. 'Theo . . .?'

'Ended up mentioning a name he shouldn't have,' says Whitehead, with a shrug. 'On tape, too! You know, Magda – I gave you the bloody memory stick. God, if I hadn't had a friend in the right place. Interviewing officer had the good sense to call me as well. Wanted me to know that the tape had twisted during the recording so they would be doing it over. A good man – knows how things work. We put things right. Thank Christ for the duty solicitor, eh? Predictable, if nothing else.'

'Callum, I don't think I know what you're—'

'Wasn't a set-up, I swear to you. Just a silly bloody mistake. They happen though, don't they? Can't let a couple of black marks catch the eye of a spotless record, can you? And the poor lad was so bloody innocent, I think he thought it was perfectly normal to start the whole thing over – to record a second interview with better advice; some gentle encouragement not to mention our mutual friend. Called it "take two". And the solicitor – he knew what side his bread was buttered. He'd have shut the lad down in seconds if he'd so much as mentioned that name again.'

Quinn frowns, unsure whether she's meant to understand what he's talking about. 'More on Hagman than me, any road. More his lookout than mine. But I wasn't doing time for murder, was I? I was doing the job I was paid to do. Tidying up.'

Quinn doesn't like the look on his face, eyes piggy, cheeks flushed. Pictures him again, thirty years ago, pounding at Hagman with boots and fists and swearing to God he would see him burn for what he had done. And he'd meant it too. Still does. Still clings to the belief that Hagman killed Trina Delaney and should have been long since dead and buried for his crimes.

Thinks: *this man doesn't forgive. Doesn't relent. Doesn't change his mind.*

Thinks: *he's so much worse than he pretends.*

'Send the bookshop girl to Le Gros,' he says, tapping his lip with his index finger. 'It'll keep him on his toes and keep her busy chasing phantoms. Quite literally, eh? And don't forget, she's a valley girl. She knows how things work. Few decades back, her type would have been cleaning the scullery for a man like Le Gros. Let her see where she stands, eh? Take some pleasure in it, girl.' He licks his lips and nods his head, savouring some delicious private thought. 'There are connections there . . . it might be useful to see what happens when you return to an unlit firework . . .'

'Callum, I—'

'That'll do now,' says Whitehead, taking in a deep breath, as if something has been decided. 'Big day tomorrow. Could be the makings of us.'

Quinn keeps the tight smile on her face. Wonders when he'll ask for his pound of flesh.

He gives her a little leer. 'All this . . . it will be worth it in the end, Magda. The shit you wade through, how it washes off once you reach the clear blue waters. I promise you. People say times change, but they don't, love. People are people. Laws keep people where they're supposed to be. But you and me – we know there's a different way of doing things. We know how to make things right for everybody.'

Quinn keeps her look of warm appreciation on her face.

On the inside, thinks: *you poor old bastard. You've no idea . . .*

Dies a little, as he sits back in the chair and uses his hands to haul his slippered feet up on to the desk.

'Now,' he says, unfastening the robe. 'Let's see if we can't wake the wife . . .'

Extract taken from an article in *Zapow.com* – a premier digital media company for the most diverse, most online, and most socially engaged generation the world has ever seen.

Britain's Most Evil Ghosts

03.09.2015

Blindworm's personal treasure trove of terror included a stretching rack, spiked drum, iron maiden, the infamous expanding metal pears, devil claws, the mangler and a chair of nails. But according to numerous sources, this innovator of violence had a personal favourite: the cage, a metal enclosure shaped like a person that pinned the victim tightly inside while he slowly cooked them over an open fire.

In July of 1298, King Edward I finally located William Wallace and his army and engaged the Scots at the Battle of Falkirk. Although Wallace escaped, the Scottish rebellion was over. King Edward returned south and the supply of victims for John Blindworm dwindled away. In fact, orders came through to release the remaining prisoners. Blindworm dutifully released them into the courtyard where he'd already prepared a massive bonfire. With nowhere to go but the courtyard, the prisoners all died a slow death. The stench was said to be noticed over ten miles away at Corbridge . . .

In time, karma caught up with the sadistic soldier. The terror of Redburn Castle was captured and ironically tortured with his own equipment. Brutalized, maimed and blinded, he was tossed into his own oubliette – a horrifying bottle-dungeon built beneath the castle walls: a place where the king's enemies could be dumped to die of starvation and madness.

The story goes that he haunts the castle and sometimes further away, searching for his missing body parts, and can't join his master in hell until he finds them all. In fact, several guests at nearby Lumley Castle have felt as though they were being strangled by an unseen entity.

NINETEEN

Hagman's Farm, Alston Moor

Tuesday 20 May, 8.06 a.m.

'That's disgusting.'
  'Nola, that's so rude. Don't talk to her like that.'
  'I don't mean *disgusting* disgusting.'
'Sounded like it.'
'She knows what I meant.'
'Well, I didn't care for it.'
  Sal watches the girls play table tennis with words, knocking back pithy rejoinders and cutting accusations as they finish off their breakfast. They sit at opposite sides of the table, barely able to see one another over the mound of papers, files and bottles that have been swept into the centre of the table. She crosses her eyes. Looks down at the piece of thick toast with its greenish, wobbling topping. Wonders if she's allowed to eat it.

'I think it sounds yummy,' says Lottie, enjoying the chance to practise her best 'American child star' impression. 'Shout it out, for your ocean animals.'

'Remember to crush those,' says Hagman, at the sink. He's scrubbing out a saucepan and his words are almost lost beneath the sound of wire scratching metal.

'Crush what?' asks Lottie, looking up from her breakfast. She's in a great mood – the first Sal has seen for an age. She's allowed to stay off school today. Nola too. They had a horrible night and lots of rushing around, and Sal has decided it would have been cruel to get them up for the pre-dawn start they would need to make in order to make it to their different schools on time. She has taken the decision to give them a 'mental well-being' day – a phrase she was careful not to use when she called Nola's rather snotty office manager – preferring instead to use the opaque 'gastric issue' to explain the absence. Lottie slept well on the sofa, snuggled down under a half-clean sheet and a rough blanket. Woke up starving hungry and dived straight into Uncle Wulf's offer of 'a proper breakfast'. She's on to her second boiled egg with toasty soldiers and great steaming bowlfuls of porridge. She preened when Uncle Wulf called her Goldilocks. Sal had seen his mouth twitch under his moustache and beard. Saw a look of genuine happiness on his face as Lottie thanked him for being so lovely and said it was the best egg she'd ever had. Her only query was whether the hen would be OK, having pushed out something so hefty. Sal held back her giggles long enough to tell her it was from a duck.

'Crush what?' shouts Lottie, before making a high trumpeting sound. 'Sorry,' she says, looking at Nola with genuine remorse. 'Just slipped out.'

'Crush the eggshells,' says Hagman, looking back over his shoulder. 'Witches use them as boats and then sail out to sea to brew up a storm.'

Lottie's mouth drops open. 'Honestly,' she says, aghast. 'Is that any way to behave?'

'It's a superstition,' says Sal, mouth full. She'd thought she was at liberty to take a bite of her mint jelly on toast without angering Lottie. She swallows. Takes a swig of tea from the blue mug. 'Probably a good reason for it somewhere back down the line,' she says.

'Or somebody with mental health problems said it once, and somebody else thought it was funny and told somebody else, and then everybody forgot it was a joke and started thinking it was real, and. . .'

'Jesus, Lottie,' says Nola, banging her hand down on the table. 'Enough!'

'Don't,' says Sal, and it's more of a plea than an instruction. 'It's good she wants to know things. You shouldn't really cut her off like that . . .'

'Me!' demands Nola. Her mouth drops open, features twisted with indignation. 'I'm in the wrong, am I? I'm the one who's not behaving the way we should in polite company!'

Sal doesn't get a chance to respond before Nola is jumping out of the chair and pulling up her hood, kicking her way to the door and pushing past her sister's chair. Lottie, ever watchful for an opportunity to perform, throws herself down with fouled-footballer levels of theatricality.

'Nola, please, don't walk off – I've called in, I won't go in, we can do something, eh . . .' says Sal.

'I think it's broken,' sniffs Lottie, from the floor, holding her ankle with one hand and her aching head with the other.

'Just don't!' hisses Nola, one white fist around the black door handle. 'Just don't try so hard. It's . . . it's disgusting!'

'Nola . . .'

She slams the door behind her. They hear footsteps diminishing. Hears the squawk and flap of chickens in the yard as they flee from the hooded black figure who lashes out at the air with knock-off Doc Martens.

'Shout it out, for your—'

'Not now, Lottie,' says Sal, as gently as she can, while slumping back against the knotted wood of the chair. She wants to chase after her. Wants to thrash about blindly in the dark, slashing at the invisible phantoms that tiredness and stress had surely caused her to manifest. *Silly*, she tells herself, again. *Being silly and hysterical. Being a bad, silly girl.*

She closes her eyes. Wonders what a good parent would do. Whether a good parent would even have brought them here; whether a good parent would have accepted responsibility for a task beyond their capabilities.

'What's this?' asks Lottie, pulling herself up. She remembers to wince as she climbs into her chair. She's holding a loose sheaf of paper, covered in different patterns of circles and lines.

'Just silly work stuff,' says Sal, finishing her tea and trying to find the emotional bandwidth to get through the next few minutes. She manages a smile. 'I was trying to make sense of a picture. It's on the other side. I'm trying to see if it was meant to be a letter or a shape or something. I'm none the wiser.'

Lottie turns it over. Moves the image away from her face and back again. 'It's a wheel,' she says. 'Look, like on a . . . horse-and-cart type of cart. Look, you can't tell at first because half the spokes are sticking on its back like a hedgehog, but if you put them in the circle it would be like a wheel, and . . .'

'A wheel?' asks Hagman turning from the sink and pushing his glasses up his nose.

He peers at the page. 'Aye, could be. Clever girl, Goldilocks.'

Lottie gives a little bow. Hands the page to Sal, who considers Lottie's interpretation, eyes screwed up. 'Well, why would he draw a wheel?' she asks absent-mindedly. 'If you're desperately trying to tell somebody something, moments from death . . . I mean that's no time to start playing bloody Pictionary.'

'Moments from death?' asks Lottie, suddenly interested. She picks a piece of eggshell from her fringe. 'Who's this?'

Sal curses herself. Both girls are forever tying her up in those unwinnable areas of parenthood; these places where dissembling is preferable to truth and concealment a kinder gesture than honesty. 'A man has been hurt,' she says busying herself by drawing a circle, and spokes, in the spilled sugar by her side plate. 'It's possible that somebody kept him somewhere he didn't want to be. He couldn't speak to us, so he drew this. I don't know why.'

'Will they cope without you today?' asks Lottie, concerned. 'I mean, whoever did that needs to be caught, don't they? We can't have people running around doing that to one another.'

Sal sees Hagman turn away, covering his laughter with a cough. She finds herself wanting to rush to her youngest stepdaughter and squeeze her in a great bear-hug. Wants to preserve her as she is; keep her good heart in aspic. Her sincerity is a gift Sal isn't sure she could ever emulate.

'I was only there to . . .' Sal stops herself. She's conscious of her face and the way it might betray her if she talks with Lottie about Magda Quinn. Forces herself to stay bright; to keep the mask on a little longer. 'I wasn't really needed. I'll be back at work as usual on Wednesday. Just boring old car crashes for me, I promise.'

At the table, Lottie is scratching at the neck of her uniform, trying to look down her own top for evidence of flea-bites. She stops as a thought seems to make her catch her breath.

'Were you in danger? You weren't in danger, were you? You said you wouldn't. You know you said that . . .'

Sal rises in tandem with the volume of Lottie's panic. She's licking her lips, tongue in and out, in and out, breathing hard, rocking back and forth. Her eyes are glassy, face pale. Sal tries to gather her into her arms, but she holds out one arm, palm open, elbow locked. Sal forces herself to obey her wishes; to not touch her, despite her every impulse.

'You can't . . . you can't too, you can't . . .'

'Do the thing,' says Hagman, recoiling. 'The song. The ocean animals thing!'

'Lottie, I'm safe. I was never in danger. I'm here. I'm not going away . . .'

Lottie throws herself forward, arms encircling Sal's neck, trapping her curls, yanking at her hair as she snuffles against her scalp. 'You can't . . . you can't . . .'

Sal feels like she's suffocating – their mingled hair bunched around her mouth and nose, wet tears spilling into her ear. She holds on tight, nostrils full of their blended scents; all charcoal and wet dog, hospitals and damp.

'Lottie,' says Sal, and she can barely hear her own voice. 'Lottie, if you want to talk about it . . . about what happened – what you saw . . .'

Lottie sniffs against her neck. 'Sal . . . door.'

Sal looks up just as the door opens inwards. She looks up, expecting to see Nola, features twisted in fresh disgust. Instead, she's confronted by the sight of a young man, dark-haired and strangely pretty, like a rendering of one of the romantic poets by an artist with a taste for cheekbones and ringlets. He's wearing a polka-dot scarf, tucked into an open-necked shirt, dark jeans and open, unlaced boots – the ensemble topped with a long grey military-style coat. He has the look of an arts student from the Seventies.

'Oh bugger it, Theo, I forgot!'

Lottie raises her head. Narrows an eye. 'Are you a pirate?'

Theo stands in the doorway, letting a cold, rain-speckled wind gust across the threshold. He makes a hook with his index finger. Closes one eye. Gives a good-natured 'garrrr' that Lottie allows herself to giggle at, snot popping in one nostril. Sal gives her another hug. Stands up. Puts on her formal smile.

'Theo, yes?' she says, and decides not to proffer a hand. 'I'm . . .'

'Sal, yes,' says Theo, brightly. 'Salome. Salami, ha ha. Never Sally. Cool necklace.'

Hagman makes a noise, clearing his throat and raising his eyebrows at the handsome young man.

'Sorry, sorry – not that I've been asking. Wulf here – doesn't give much away, does he? I've had to boil him for weeks just to get a juicy piece of meat off the bone. Anyway, enchanted.' He gives a theatrical bow as he says it, his eyes never leaving Sal's as he lowers his head.

He throws an apologetic glance at Hagman. 'She wouldn't come,' he says, wincing. 'One of her clubs.' Theo makes a show of reminding himself that not everybody knows what he's talking about. 'Mum,' he adds. 'I'd hoped Wulf could magic her better. Quite the charmer, our Wulf, in the "magical charms" sense of the word. Done me the power of good, though she won't agree. Reckons I've given up. Rolled over. Shown them my belly and throat and nuts all at once, and . . .'

'Rude word,' says Lottie, reaching up to take Sal's hand.

'She's right,' says Sal, grateful for a reason to break eye contact. There's something intense about his stare. Something that makes the hairs on her arms stand up beneath her borrowed, baggy shirt.

'Apologies, little miss,' says Theo, bowing again and directing his words at Lottie. 'For giving offence, I give you this vow. Shall you ever require the services of a knight errant, I do humbly offer my sword. Just trumpet three times, and I shall gather my bannermen and ride for your side. I shall . . .'

'You're weird,' says Lottie, appreciatively.

Theo grins, a flash of white in the gloom of the poorly lit room. It's a practised gesture, Sal thinks. His whole nature seems like a series of artistic choices; his personality and comportment shoplifted from a rail of character traits and idiosyncrasies. She wonders how much of himself died in prison. What he's going to use to fill the void.

'We can rearrange,' says Hagman, wiping his hands on his cords. 'Or not. Whatever you think. Or she thinks.'

'And what do you think, Wulf?' asks Theo, teasing.

'I'm happy with what's best for everybody,' says Hagman, sagging a little.

'That's our Wulf,' says Theo, clapping his hands. 'Not a wish for himself, this man. If he found a genie, he'd set it free on the first wish.'

'I'd wish for more wishes,' says Lottie 'Or more genies. I've thought about this and I think it's watertight.'

'Watertight?' asks Hagman, from the sink.

From outside there's the sound of a horn, honking. 'Alec,' explains Theo, apologetically. 'Škoda Fabia. Only had it a few weeks. Doesn't want to risk the paint job by driving over your potholes and gravel. That probably sounds rude but he won't mean it like that. He knows he's being a big baby but it's his pride and joy.'

'Who's Alec?' asks Lottie, now fully recovered.

'My mum's husband,' he says. 'The reason I'm standing here, in all my glory.'

'I think my sister would fancy you,' says Lottie, closing one eye and assessing the specimen.

'Nola!' says Sal, trying not to laugh. She's almost forgotten about Magda Quinn.

About Mahee Gamage. About dying men on country roads and people not staying put. Had become herself for a moment – a girl who wanted to work in a bookshop and became a police officer by mistake.

'It's my audition,' he explains, to Sal, this time. 'Interview, might be better. Here, do you like this . . .' he alters his posture. Causes one lip to curl, to drool; face contorting into a twisted mask of pure, hate-filled malevolence. Sal feels Lottie stiffen; she presses her face into Sal's hip.

'Too scary, too scary,' says Sal, widening her eyes and nodding at Lottie. 'We don't need more nightmares.'

'Oh shit, I'm so sorry,' says Theo, springing back upright and knocking his head on the iron grille. 'Shit, I didn't think!' He shoots a desperate glance at Hagman. 'Shit, that's my bad. Totally. I was being the character I'm going to be, that's all. As a tour guide. Wulf's been helping me. Alec too. I think they'll go for it. Was it scary, yeah? Proper scary?'

There's another honk from the little lane behind the bower. Louder. Longer. Theo crouches down in front of Lottie. Waits until she looks up, then pulls another face, a silly one this time: protruding tongue and gargoyle mouth. Lottie splutters a laugh and Theo lets out a breath. As he rises, Sal notices his eyes take in the piece of paper that she's still clutching in her hand. Sees a moment's confusion twist his features before they settle back into place. He gives her a smile.

'Out of practice with kids,' he says. 'Like them, though. You never know, eh? Mam has it that it's all over for me – that they've taken the best years. Not the thing you want to hear when you're trying to look forward. But Mams are to be listened to, aren't they? Why else would they make so much noise? You listen to yours eh, little one. Looks like a decent sort.'

Sal gets a whiff of him as he rises. Deodorant, air-freshener; a trace of selenium shampoo. Was that dandelion, perhaps, in the place where his sculpted jaw met his delicate neck. Wood sorrel? Loam?

Up close, she can't help admire his appearance. She chides herself. Thinks of what he's been through at the hands of brother and sister officers whom she would gladly disown. Thinks, for a moment, what prison might be like for a beautiful boy.

'And there's the third one,' he says, as his stepfather honks the horn with purpose.

'Wish me luck, eh? Ooh fuck, no, don't do that – it's break a leg, isn't it?'

'Rude word,' says Lottie, a little brow-beaten by the strange man's energy. 'Shout it out . . .'

'. . . for your ocean animals!' finishes Theo, and Lottie beams. 'Anyway, Wulf, whatever happens, you did good with me. Not the end of the world if it goes wrong, is it? A fella's got to make a living.'

Sal wonders if the words are thrown with a hint of accusation. She believes he deserves his compensation. Believes that Wulf does too. Knows, in her bones, that nothing is fair and that life is meant to hurt. Mam taught her that. Taught them all.

'Give it your best,' says Wulf, earnestly. 'They'll be proud of you whatever happens.'

Theo looks at him for a moment too long. Shakes his head. Fixes Lottie with one last look as he pulls open the door. 'Ask Uncle Wulf to tell you all about Blindworm. Kids love horrible stuff, right? I swear, I've dug so deep into this guy I feel like he's in the room some of the time. Like he's telling me how to play the role! Awesome bit of heraldry, by the way,' he says, nodding at the paper in Sal's hand. 'De Creasy's coat of arms had two, I think.'

'A what?' asks Sal. 'What did you say it was?'

'It's a Breaking Wheel. Looks like it to me, at least, though my head is all full of Redburn and Blindworm, so God only knows if I'm right. It was a symbol of martyrdom, in tribute to St Catherine. De Creasy, Lord of Redburn, the one who gave Blindworm to the mob when his usefulness was over – he had it carved at the openings and exits of his keep, for all the good it did. Ruin now. It's . . . well, it's a place that means a lot to me. Dad and I, well – nobody wants to hear a sad story. Not much left now. Just a few rocks and a wall with a tree growing out of it . . .'

There's a fourth honk on the horn. 'Get my number off Wulf,' he smiles. 'We can meet up again. I'll tell you all about it.'

'And you are?'

Theo steps back as Nola stamps across the room past the fire, and up the small wooden staircase. The whole house creaks. Dust falls from the timbers. A door slams.

'She seemed nice,' says Theo, on his way out. 'Lovely to meet you all. And Nola . . .'

Sal walks to the back door. Looks across the yard to where a gleaming white Škoda is tucked in against a hawthorn edge. It's idling, engine running. She hears a whisper of Radio Four as Theo opens the door and climbs inside without a backwards glance.

She wonders, as she retreats to the warmth of the kitchen, whether she had imagined it. As he crossed the pitted, sodden farmyard, it had been as if his whole manner was changing; his stance, his walk, the air around him.

'Sal! Sal, your phone's ringing. Somebody called Magda . . .'

She shivers. Wraps her arm around herself but feels no warmth. The chill has gone to her bones.

TWENTY

'Salami,' says Quinn, then makes a little *tssk* of disapproval at herself. 'I'm so sorry, that just rather slipped out. You know how it is – you try so hard not to say something and then it's just there.'

Sal takes the phone out into the cold little corridor that leads to the outhouse and wood store. Wraps her arms around herself. Opens the back door with her elbow and stands in the cold, blustery air. Watches Tips nosing at a feather that stands proud, white-tipped, end sunk in the churned-up mud.

'Sorry, lost you there,' says Sal, leaning against the door frame. 'Is something wrong? I'm not in. I cleared it with Claire . . .'

'Yes, well, that may or may not be the case, Sal – rather a big investigation going on, in case you weren't aware. I had personally requested your secondment, even with a view to a more permanent move. I mean, can you imagine? How jolly it could be, all girls together?'

Sal wonders whether Quinn is holding a mirror as she talks. Whether she's admiring her perfect red lips and basking in her own reflection. She sounds like a wicked stepmum in a Disney film.

'It was very late when I got . . . home,' begins Sal, weakly. 'And the girls are, well . . . it's been unsettling, and . . .'

She hears Quinn huff out a blast of dissatisfied air. Hears her take a sip of something. 'Thing is, Sal, there have been one or two questions asked about my judgement – not least because you, well – how do I put this? – nearly killed the victim . . .'

'No,' says Sal, straightening up. 'No, I'm sorry, you don't get to joke about that—'

'From a certain point of view, it does rather look as if you snook into the room, put pressure on a critically ill man, and that it was only by the grace of God that he didn't slip away from the sheer trauma.'

Sal can't help herself. 'Sneaked,' she breathes. 'Not snook.'

'So really, the very fact that I'm disappointed you've taken the easy option . . . it's remarkable.'

Sal turns as Hagman appears in the door to the kitchen. Sees Lottie at the fire, toasting bread on the low flame.

He jerks his head at her. Everything all right?

She shrugs. Mimes hanging herself then winces, apologetically. He has the grace to smile as he turns away.

'I haven't got transport,' she admits, weakly. 'Had to get a train and a taxi back last night.'

Quinn laughs, seeming to enjoy the thought. Sal hears the rasp of a vape, spottily inhaled. 'The nurse says he gave you something,' she says, after a pause. 'Tried to scribble something down.'

Sal's mind fills with the shaky lines, the misshapen circle. 'I put that in the report,' she says, stepping out into the rain. She looks up at the skies. Wonders whether her hair could cope with a lightning bolt.

'I understand you've got a personal connection with a certain Theo Myers,' she continues, coolly. 'Good friend of the family, I understand.'

'I don't know him myself,' says Sal, sounding tired. She feels the previous day's exertions at her shoulders, the nape of her neck, the backs of her thighs. Feels it in her bad hand.

'Our mutual friend. Uncle Wulf . . .'

'The Wulfric Hagman who saved your life, you mean,' asks Sal, unable to help herself. 'That Wulfric Hagman, yeah? Saved you and Lewis both.'

Quinn's voice hardens, a nerve clearly struck. 'There are always two ways to view any occurrence, Sal,' she says, without humour. 'Any narrative can be woven around a set of circumstances. For all I know, he caused that car accident. Christ knows what he would have done with me if she hadn't turned up – or what we could have learned if you hadn't bashed her brains in with a rock . . .'

Sal shrinks from the blows. Flinches into herself. Feels her throat begin to close. 'That's not . . . you can't . . .'

'I've got a use for you,' she says, and springs creak as she throws herself back on to wherever she is seated. 'I don't want to hear any whining about it. Think of it as an opportunity. Show everybody that you know what you're doing and haven't just been riding Lewis's coat-tails—'

'No,' says Sal, straightening up. 'No, don't you dare!'

'Sycamore Le Gros,' says Quinn, seeming to pluck the name out of nowhere. 'I understand you know him too. Took something approximating a witness statement at the scene. Rather cursory, I feel. You're the nearest. Go and give him a poke. See if he can remember a direction he may have come from . . .'

'I asked that! He's answered that!'

'And it must be said that the assistant chief made a rather useful point at this morning's briefing – that perhaps we might want to begin a search of nearby buildings, barns – says there might be mine workings in the area; some sites of archaeological interest where a person like Mahee could've been kept without being noticed . . .'

'That hasn't been done?' asks Sal. 'What are you asking me – just go and start tramping about the valley peering into barns looking for a man who's no longer there?'

'It's a tick-box exercise, Sal,' says Quinn, sighing at the very petulance of her subordinate. 'Two birds, one stone. Oh, and then you can go and use your Family Liaison skills. It was a fortnight that course, wasn't it? Go and sweet-talk the family.'

'Which family?' asks Sal, voice rising. A chicken clucks its way across the muddy ground, shivering in the rain. It looks at Sal, and Sal experiences the bewildering sensation of being actively pitied by a wet hen.

'The Myers boy,' she says, sweetly. '"Devlin" I think the name is now.'

'No, Mag – ma'am, they've suffered enough, been through so much – we can't just wade in, and . . .'

'Thank you,' says Quinn. Then adds: 'Shower and shampoo before you go round, yeah? They don't think much of the police. Let's not play into their hands . . .'

'You fu—'

Quinn ends the call before she reaches the end of the gasped, half-strangled expletive. Sal wraps her arms around herself. Scratches until she breaks the skin.

Oh Sal, look what you've done, you silly girl. Let me take care of you, you poor thing. Let's make it all better . . .

Tears spark in her eyes as she thinks of Dagmara. Bile rises as she remembers the crunch of the rock upon that hairless skull.

Whispers: 'I'm so sorry.'

In her head: *I know love, I know.*

TWENTY-ONE

Coatham Stob, Middlesbrough

'You're quite sure?'
Quinn's sure. She's had three coffees already. The pulse at her neck is fluttering as if beneath warm, wet kisses. She can feel sweat oozing through her palms, behind her knees, across her brow.

'No bugger ever wants the complicated stuff.'
'No?'
'Bought every bloody variety of pod. They all say "flat white".'
'Perhaps you should have become a barrister rather than an amateur barista.'
'Oh, that's very good. I wish you were the first to have thought of it.'

Quinn and Detective Constable Lorena Worth find themselves in the low, slightly grubby conservatory at the rear of Alain Southey's home: a modern, Scandinavian-flavoured construction veiled by a line of cypress and pine. The rain is coming down hard on the glass roof. Quinn finds herself thinking of hard peas rolling around on the skin of a snare drum. Wonders when she ever heard such a sound.

'It really is a lovely spot,' says DC Worth, agreeing with her own earlier contention, repeated for emphasis. Worth talks a lot when she's nervous. Quinn's instruction to keep her mouth shut isn't helping with the anxiety. Worth, in her yellow raincoat and soggy, mustard-coloured bobble hat, is all but shaking with suppressed conversation.

'This is what it's all about really, isn't it? You work hard, put some money away and then get to kick back and enjoy it. Too many people, well, they work and work and fight for every penny and then they drop dead of a massive heart attack three weeks after their retirement party. Not for me. Few chickens and a campervan, that's the way forward – not that I wouldn't love something like this. Maybe if I stop all the expensive coffees and avocado bagels, eh? That seems to be the advice.'

In the wicker armchair, Southey gives her an indulgent smile. 'I'm pleased you approve. I fear your generation won't be permitted the same path.'

'Oh I don't know,' continues Worth. 'I've nearly got the deposit together. And my boyfriend has an aunt who might not be around much longer and always liked him, which probably makes me sound awful, now I think about it . . .'

'Sounds like a glorious future,' says Southey, sliding the box of elaborate coffee pods back into the sleek black box and putting them away in the drawer beneath his chair. As he opens it, Quinn spies crosswords, word searches, a packet of humbugs. Thinks, for a moment, about her own far-off retirement and hopes to God that she's done something sufficiently significant during her working life to make up for the abject pointlessness of old age.

'You don't miss it?' asks Quinn, peering through the smears of rain to the neat gardens beyond: a summer house sitting by the stand of trees. Mrs Southey is within, fingers moving over the keys of a laptop. She doesn't know they're here. Alain Southey answered the door himself – a tall, knotty figure with a luxurious crop of white hair. He's still dressed with the same crisp creases and spotless neatness that he exhibited during his four decades as a criminal lawyer, the only concession to retirement being the big green cardigan that he wears over his pink shirt. 'You had quite the reputation, so I hear.'

Southey moves around uncomfortably on the chair, as if trying to scratch a hard-to-reach spot. He purses his lips. Takes the pause he so frequently employed during his many decades appearing as legal representation for half of Teesside's criminal fraternity. Sucks on the thought like a humbug.

'I think the good times have rolled,' he says, with the slightest of shrugs. 'The legal profession as it was – it's a thing of the past. I think I saw the best of it and got out just before the worst. I keep myself busy enough, and God knows, my wife is never short of suggestions as to how to occupy my time.'

Quinn makes a show of rummaging in her bag. Opens a file at random and squints at the words on the page as if searching for a specific detail. She wants him to think they have more details than they do; that anything he tells them will just reaffirm existing intelligence.

'Mahee came to work for you in 2008, yes? In the June?'

Southey winces as the rain redoubles its efforts to smash through the glass. He looks as though he's going to suggest they enter a different room – to gather instead in the living room they had passed through on their way in. She has a memory of teal walls. Bare floors; huge canvas prints of bullfights and flamenco dancers covering the walls.

'I've no reason to doubt you,' says Southey, whose green tea and honey is sitting untouched on the low table at his side. 'Mrs Barnfather was responsible for paperwork, records – keeping us bona fide and shipshape.' He looks momentarily wistful at the mention of the absent, long-deceased office manager. 'Of course, it's all findable, if that's a word you'll accept. Just not at hand, as it were.'

'But you do want to help us, Mr Southey. I'm right about that, yes? It'll make it easier to process things in my own mind if I can underline your name and put a big star next to it. A big "this guy did all he could" sticker, yes?'

Southey's mouth twitches, his smile one of genuine amusement. 'I'm sorry you and I never got the chance to cross swords before the bench,' he says, running his finger around the collar of his shirt. 'I'm sure we could have had some grand old ding-dongs.'

'Ding-dongs,' muses Quinn, turning her back on Southey and glaring through the glass, the rain puddling and gathering in ways that make the panes seem frosted. 'You haven't asked what happened to him.'

'To Mahee?' asks Southey. 'I'm au fait with the known details.'

'Au fait?'

'I know you found him in a field by a country road somewhere near Hexham. I know he's unlikely to survive much longer. I know that you've had a couple of road bumps on your career path and that a case like this, if handled right, could be your ticket back to wherever it is you feel you've been wrongfully removed from.'

Quinn finds herself smiling. She likes the old solicitor. Likes the playful, gently combative way he conducts himself. She doesn't think he has anything to hide, but old habits die hard.

'I'm informed that you let Mr Gamage go from the firm in October of 2022,' she says, coupling her hands at the wrist.

'Sounds about right,' says Mr Southey, with a level of exactitude that strikes her as deliberately unlawyerly. 'Can't have been more than a few weeks before my big retirement shindig. Brazilian meat buffet, if you can believe it. Lovely place near the university but a chap can only eat so many steaks before he feels like a pillowcase full of bricks.'

'We understand there were allegations of inappropriate conduct,' says Quinn, directing a hard stare at the young, curly-blonde DC who has talked them both into a state of mental numbness on the drive back to Teesside from Cumbria.

'I rather felt for him, to be honest,' says Southey, shaking his head. 'He swore blind he'd been hacked but he had form for it. Lonely chap, I think. A career can bounce back from a lot but not watching porn in the office. Not during a briefing. Not when you're linked to the projector and you've got six colleagues and a community campaigner sitting in the boardroom. To be fair, I think he was almost glad to be shot of us. At least the blasted screeching stopped.'

'Screeching?'

'Goes with the territory,' says Southey. 'We get unhappy customers – people who think they've been mistreated or badly advised. And Mahee had a couple of higher-profile cases. You know about Theo Myers, I shouldn't wonder. Half of his problems came from that night. Duty solicitor and he gave this frightened young lad the right advice – say nothing, don't drop yourself in it. It was the right thing to say but – as things panned out – the advice got skewed. It formed a central pillar of the campaign. Somebody decided to make life as unpleasant for Mahee as they could. Persecuted him with this damn screeching bird. Just an effect, obviously, but somebody had done their homework. It's a Sri Lankan myth. Something that would scare him and him alone, even if he didn't know what the hell it was until one of the cleaners had a panic attack after hearing it on the answerphone.'

'You blamed Myers' supporters?'

'It would be nice to think that a criminal lawyer might only have one enemy, Magdalena. Would that it were so.' He stops himself, sucking on a thought. 'You're Callum's protégée, as I understand it? Stick with him. He'll see you right. He knows where the bodies are buried, after all. This is helpful, yes? I know it's quite the drive.'

Quinn knows that there will be questions asked about her own need to attend Southey's home, a few miles inland of Middlesbrough. She's senior investigating officer. She presently has a team of fifteen officers under her command. She should be back at headquarters, directing things from behind a laptop screen and making sure all her budgets add up. But there's something about her that needs to be here; to oversee – keep her purview panoramic. Lewis used to tell her she was a control freak. She'd preferred 'enthusiast'.

'Theo's father,' she says, quietly. 'He hanged himself, am I right? While Theo was inside. And his mum got together with the guy who led the campaign?'

'Adores her, God love him,' says Southey. 'Upright fellow, is Alec. Spent his life fighting the good fight. There are pubs in Belfast where he'll never have to buy a drink, I'll tell you that. Freed more wrongly imprisoned bombers than can be considered seemly. God bless him, I'm pleased he's letting himself enjoy a proper retirement with Tara. It's the real thing. Paul . . . he was never really involved in the campaign. Killed himself in stages, really. Drank himself away. Didn't help that he was the reason Theo was even in Middlesbrough that night. Never forgave himself for telling him to do what the solicitor advised. Couldn't quite believe that it was all happening. As far as I remember, he hanged himself at some pretty spot out Hexham way. I shouldn't wonder that they can't see it from their new place.'

Quinn feels her heart start to race. Her thoughts turn to Callum – to the old connections between the men who could trace their links to the valley for generations. She wonders how much of this has been stage-managed. Whether she's leading from the front or half a dozen steps behind.

'Don't talk to Alec without knowing what you're after,' says Southey, carefully. 'Don't be fooled, neither. He might look like a Greenpeace campaigner but he's got a mind like a whip. As for Tara, I've never had the pleasure. I hope she's thriving. Fallen on her feet with Alec, that much I'll tell you for free.'

Quinn doesn't register the comment. She already knows that this is all coming at a high price. Knows she'll pay it, if she can make a case that sticks. Clean up two blots on her employers' copybook: Myers, and Hagman.

'Softly, softly,' says Quinn, under her breath. 'Of course.'

In her head, she can already feel the chief constable's palm in hers. Can feel the soft leather of her new office seat beneath her arse. Can see herself on true crime documentaries, talking about how she got her man.

'Who else?' she asks, at last. 'Theoretically. Who else would be on Theo's hit list?'

Southey smiles, enjoying watching her mind work. 'Callum's chosen well, I see.'

TWENTY-TWO

'Something pretty,' Sal mutters, crunching through the gears with her left hand and snatching her other across the steamy, rain-slicked glass. Jarod's old Land Rover wheezes, coughs, backfires gunshot loud. 'Think of something pretty . . .'

It was Lottie's advice – a desperate bid to offer some practical advice. *Whenever I feel like I want to smash people . . . I think of something pretty. Something nice. Like, a dragonfly, or something. Or a necklace with that pink stone on it . . . the one you put in the spell-bag, to keep me safe . . .*

Sal had stormed out while Lottie was still talking. Closed the door behind her with a bang. She's hated herself for the past five miles. Already sent a dozen different texts to Wulfric's phone, under strict instruction to pass them on to the girls.

She tries to think of something pretty. Wonders what she's looking forward to. That had been one of Dagmara's favourite questions. *What's on the horizon, then? What you got your sights set on?*

She stares out into the hazy grey. Thinks of still-damp watercolours, liminal greens and greys, blurring as if the whole valley was being viewed through a cigarette paper.

A mile back she'd seen a barn owl erupt from a branch like white fire. Swerved two wheels into a ditch in her lunge to watch its perfect white outline against leaden sky. She'd grinned. Yelled 'look, look at that!' and felt her heart constrict as she realized there was nobody around to share it with. She tried to drink it in for them, to absorb every detail so as to better regale the kids, Wulf, Lewis. She pictures its magnesium feathers shimmering in the headlights: talons like knives, eyes like halogen bulbs.

Thinks: *Lewis.*

She works her jaw in circles, refusing to let herself get upset. Not now. Things to do. Important things. Take solace in purpose, wasn't that what somebody had said on Instagram? Some white-toothed, bright-eyed beauty, telling her she could be anything she wanted to be – to go for her goals; to know her worth. She swallows, wincing as her throat rasps. Her lunch is sitting uncomfortably in her chest. She can half convince herself the lump in her throat is indigestion.

She glances at her phone. It would be so easy. She could pull over, take a breath, make the call. Tell him, we miss you. We need you. We'll be with you every step. Just come home, please. I can't do this any more.

She glances out the window. Looks down to the ruined remains of the farm where Mam died; where Trina Delaney bled to death on the kitchen floor. The farm is a sagging shape on the landscape now. A place of fallen slates and rotten timber. Crooked skeletons of sunken, crumpled outbuildings; lumpen skulls rising from the soil.

Thinks: *Dagmara*.

She knows she can't outrun it forever. She needs to see for herself. Could she truly not remember? Could somebody wipe their every sin from their own memory? If that were so, surely it would be a cruelty to persecute the empty shell. Three doctors have declared her amnesia to be entirely genuine, albeit a mental response rather than a physical one. She just sits, most days. Sits there in her waterproof chair, slippers on, blanket around her shoulders. Watches the telly mostly. Doesn't mind an extra helping at mealtimes. Worries about people, according to the undercover cop who spent five weeks masquerading as a care assistant in order to verify the validity of her condition. He'd been convinced. She remembered nothing. Could give them nothing.

Sal doesn't know what she wants to be true. Isn't truly sure what to feel. Her instinct is to ask questions. She wants to sit across from her and request an explanation. She wants to know how much was real and what was a carefully curated cover. She wants to know if she killed those people because she enjoyed it, or because she truly believed she was serving a noble purpose. She's got herself halfway there twice already. Never made it beyond Edinburgh. Always turned back long before the road bridge, tears streaking her cheek, throat hoarse with swallowed shrieks of indecision.

She shakes her head, trying to focus. The police cordon is a little way ahead and she could do without talking to anybody if she can help it. She doesn't trust herself not to come apart if anybody is so much as slightly nice to her. She slows to a halt in a little layby, just around the curve from where Mahee Gamage's broken body landed. She rummages in her phone and pulls up the Ordnance

Survey app. Expands the image and uses her finger as a stylus to draw a red circle around the point. Were the kids here, she would mime looking up, recoiling from a giant finger in the sky.

'Right, so I'm there, I mean here, and . . .'

She mumbles to herself for a moment, scowling through the rain in the direction of the stone pillars that stand outside the driveway of Sycamore Le Gros's home. She pulls a sheet of paper from her inside pocket. Unfolds it and compares the two images. Le Gros owns both fields, according to the Land Registry. Owns another handful of random acres further back towards Hexham. He used to own more. Has sold off assets with enough regularity to suggest concerted downsizing, or money troubles. Quinn believes he's worth a quiet chat. She'd said it in that way of hers. Wonders, unbidden, what Mam would make of her. *She'd kill her*, she thinks. She would. Anybody else touched us, she'd cut them into pieces. No, we were hers to torment. She was our mam, right. She'd made us. She had the right to break us if she needed to . . .

Sal snatches her glasses off, pressing her hands to her face.

'Stop it! Stop it!'

She looks up, red-eyed. Glares at herself in the mirror. Sees Jarod and shakes him away.

The wind blows around her in irritating circles as she steps from the car and trudges, damply, over the pitted tarmac. She starts to make her way up the slope, one foot in front of the other, gripping with her toes as she tries not to slip on the slick carpet of grasses, brambles, cow shit.

She glares up at the familiar slopes, thinking her way up and over the tumbledown walls, the barbed wire strings; up and into the valley beyond, to the rugged wilderness of trenches, scars. She thinks her way on to the snaking roads, slews left around pine forests and rusting mining gear. She climbs the mountains in her mind, their sides steep and treacherous like waterless tarns or quarries consumed by nature. She lets her imagination drift skywards. Summons up a panorama of the valley where she was raised, where part of her died. Stares down, God-like, at the threadbare rag-rug of earth and grass and mud – carelessly tossed over a floor of rock and holes and ore, of subterranean relics from the industrial past. Here and there, abandoned farms stand mute, rain-soaked and eyeless. Trees grow in some of these excavations, trunks bent against the ceaseless gale.

She keeps on tramping. Controls her racing thoughts.

Tries to concentrate on breathing. What had the guidance counsellor said? Name five things you can see, four things you can feel, three things you can . . . what, what else was it? She sees spots dance in her vision. It feels as though there are bricks being laid out on her chest. The world tilts. She feels like she's falling off the edge of the world. Desperately, she tries to unball her fists.

'Woah there, old girl. Hold hard!'

She turns into the rain, raising a hand to shield her glasses. The bulk of Sycamore Le Gros is marching hard in her direction: long woollen socks, tweed plus-fours, Barbour jacket open to reveal a splendidly waistcoated belly. She glances at his arm, at the shotgun broken in the crook. He gives a grin, waving with one broad, muddy hand.

'Looking for me, I presume!' he yells, while still several feet away. 'Saw you on the eye in the sky. Thought I'd spare you the walk.'

'Eye in the sky?' asks Sal, trying to find her professional mode. She softens her manner. Realizes just how much she had tensed at the sight of the weapon. How much she suddenly despises being on her own.

'One of the young men working on the solar panels yonder – has a gadget you people would give your right arm for. Drone, he calls it. Like the verb. Like the worker bee, one supposes. Sends it up like one would a . . . well. A helicopter, I suppose. Shows the whole farm if you go high enough, though God knows the weather isn't co-operating.' He rubs his hands. Puts them on his hips. Turns to face the rain, red cheeks turning redder as the cold, rainy gale strikes the little squares of unbearded cheek. 'Popped it, has he?' asks Le Gros, lowering his voice. Some of the bombast seems to leave him. 'The man I hit. Died, one presumes.'

Sal notices herself reaching out to put a reassuring hand on his arm. Stops herself. Tells herself that she's good at this. That she's done it before.

'The gentleman in question is . . . well, he's hanging in there,' says Sal, making sure she meets his eyes. 'He's critical. But people have come back from critical.'

'Haven't stopped thinking about it, poor sod,' says Le Gros, stuffing his spare hand in his pocket. 'Poor fellow. You'll know him by now, one presumes. DNA and whatnot.'

'We're pursuing several lines of enquiry,' says Sal, turning away from the wind as her hood starts slapping her face.

'And I'm one of them?'

Sal gives a polite smile. Decides to try honesty as a policy. 'My boss,' she says. 'We don't get on. She's sent me up here to mess me around. To mess up my day. So she can sit and think about me being miserable, I suppose.' She scowls. Shakes her head at the general shittiness of it all. 'It's just like bloody school.'

Le Gros seems taken aback for a moment. Recovers himself. With a broad grin, laughing like a cartoon butcher, belly wobbling and chops jiggling.

'Oh they're the worst, aren't they?' he says. 'Not had many, proud to say, but my God my father was a hard taskmaster. Didn't start out at the top, y'know. Not even the middle. It was ground up for me, just like any other hand. Some of the hardest days of work I've ever done. You'd be weeping with exhaustion, blood on your fingers, on your face, lambs bleating so loud you'd swear you were in hell . . . come back to me some days. Strange times. Strange smells. Puts me back there with the old names. Big men. Farm men. Men like Myers.'

Sal keeps her expression even. 'Myers?'

'Paul. His father before him. Grandfather too. Worked this farm for as long as there's been the name Le Gros over the gate.' He looks away. 'Theo's welcome, of course. Would love to have him here, but, well . . . haven't had the conversation, as it were. Not sure how one makes the approach.'

'Theo's working in a warehouse, I understand. His mother wants him to continue fighting for compensation . . .' she stops herself, making sure she looks embarrassed at her indiscretion; making herself seem dippy, trustworthy, easy to manipulate. Wonders if it's an affectation or a bone-deep truth. 'So I'm told,' she adds.

'I did hear Alec made a little faux pas back in the autumn,' he says, giving her a little elbow in the ribs. 'Bought them a little holiday place. Turkey, I believe. Presented it to darling Tara – he'd had a video done and everything – a proper my-darling-I-did-this-for-you moment. Went berserk. Heard it from a pal at the golf club. Couldn't believe he was trying to get her to stop fighting. Said they wouldn't be swanning off to sunbathe until she'd got compensation for all the poor lad had lost. Timing wasn't the best, of course. I do feel for the boy, but honestly, they've already landed on their feet. Not short of a penny, old Devlin. Money goes back longer than most of the old surnames in these parts. Le Gros – well, that's a cross I bear with good humour.'

'He's done a lot of good, I understand,' says Sal. 'Made fools of the police and prosecution once or twice.'

'Freed more IRA bombers than the Good Friday agreement,' laughs Le Gros. 'Nice to have the freedom to pursue one's passions, to fight the good fight. Didn't even finish his Law degree but he's run rings around some of you buggers over the years. Don't know if Daddy was proud; he wasn't the sort to say. He'd wanted him to stick at it, but Alec went and got in with the beret-wearers or the flower-power bunch or whoever it is that takes sober, sensible men and turns them into people with ideas of their own. It was all peace convoys and *Socialist Worker* and taking on the man – right up until his father dropped dead and he saw the benefits of honouring his wishes. Running the family business, such as it was. Sold off the bits he didn't want and invested the proceeds. Played the markets. Did very well.'

Sal looks back down towards the road. Sees the yellow-jacketed officers huddling together in groups around the white van; the two patrol cars.

'Very well,' adds Le Gros. 'Gave him the space to do what he was good at. Poke the bear, one might say. Hates an injustice, does Alec. Swear to God, he's a man of principle. Anybody who says they were already at it when Paul offed himself . . . they'd have me to answer to.'

Sal follows Le Gros's gaze. She can make out the tip of the ruined tower. Redrum? Redriver? Redburn? She remembers some story that Hagman had told them when she was small. Remembers Mam, taking the piss. Telling her it was bollocks. That Hagman would tell her owt if it meant she'd go to sleep quicker and he could have his end away.

She pushes down her feelings. Gives Le Gros her full attention. Hopes she can wrap this up. Go back to the farm. Apologize properly. Do some good . . .

'In the ruin,' says Le Gros. 'Swinging there, from the roof joist. Couldn't take any more, so they say.'

'And who are they?'

Le Gros gives her a puzzled look. Coughs. Turns and spits.

'He used to go there with Theo,' he wheezes. 'Their special place. Not so sure it's anybody's special place now.'

Sal runs out of things to say.

'That enough for your boss?' asks Le Gros. 'You came back. Grilled me. Honestly, I'll talk to you here and now about anything you like but my solicitor, well, he's already said that if this gets official, we just go no comment. Easiest way. Why incriminate oneself, that's the thrust of it. Bit mercenary, but he has a point. You'll understand, I hope. But really, if you do come to talk about anything that threatens our association, well – proper channels, yes?'

Sal considers him. She suffers a familiar twinge across her neck. Feels the headache start to climb.

'You'll call me, yes?' she asks, fumbling for her card and putting it into his waistcoat pocket. 'Anything crops up. Anything jogs your memory. I wouldn't ask, but . . . I would love to come in with something useful. Show her I'm not a waste of space.'

Le Gros smiles down. Looks past her at the land he owns, which he's selling off, probably with each new red letter.

'Of course, dear lady.'

She waits for him to bow. To swan off in character.

She's disappointed. He walks away like a man with a lot on his mind.

Article from *Goodlawbadlaw.com*

How English law believes you're guilty – even when declaring you innocent!

By Alec Devlin
03.09.2022

You've seen it enough times on TV. You know what the chap in the robe and the curls is going to say even before they do. It is for the jury to decide the facts of the case; they must follow the judge's directions of law. Guilt must be proven. Some judges like to reassure anxious juries. A favourite cliché of many is then to say, 'If I am wrong on the law, a higher court will put it right.'

'*That's a relief,* the jurors are meant to think, *we can trust that even if this old duffer has got the law wrong, no real harm will come of it because that "higher court" will make everything right again.*'

Theo Myers learned last week what they must have guessed already: the promise that a higher court will put wrongful convictions right is hollow. There may be statutory provision for the state to atone with compensation for subjecting innocent people to wrongful convictions and imprisonment but it is worded in such a way that compensation can virtually never be paid. So it is for the Theo Myers Campaign.

When Theo was discharged from Frankland Prison – a category A prison for the most dangerous men – he was given, like any discharged prisoner, £46.00. That was the only recompense His Majesty's Government was prepared to make . . .

TWENTY-THREE

Sal stops reading. Takes off her glasses and rubs her eyes. She realizes it's been raining; that her printouts and notebook are sitting soggily on the picnic table at her side, her laptop speckled with countless spots of rain.

'We can bring it inside for you, if you're getting chilly.'

Sal focuses on the speaker. She's in her twenties. Pretty. Good eye make-up and an expensive-looking necklace at her thin, spray-tanned throat. She manages to ground herself. Manages a smile.

'I think that ship's sailed,' she says, looking at her stone-cold cappuccino.

'Bacon sandwich went down OK though, yeah?'

Sal glances at the plate. Wonders whether a bird snaffled the last little scrap of crisp rind. Whether it would give it back if she chased it into the undergrowth.

'Another?' asks the waitress, clearing her things and shivering as the wind picks up the chill of the fishing lake and wraps them both inside a bitter gust. Sal makes a face.

'It was a nice idea, in theory.'

She likes it here, at the little fishing lake, with its glamping pods and its neat little footpaths, its zooming dragonflies and raucous wildfowl. Likes the sizes of the portions at the café too.

'You're police?' asks the woman, unable to ignore the sodden briefing documents that she carefully hands over as she cleans the table. 'You're dealing with what happened?'

Sal nods. Reaches out for her stone-cold coffee and takes a swig. Grimaces.

'Come on, I'll do you another. On me.'

Sal can't find the strength to protest. Takes another glance up at the violet-tinged sky, at the band of yellowish storm cloud that seems to draw outline upon the horizon. Follows the waitress inside the warm little coffee shop. Two big men in jogging suits and gilets, fat necks and big shoulders, raise their heads in greeting. They're devouring all-day breakfasts, a bag of sliced white bread open on the table between them.

'Regulars,' says the woman, darting behind the counter and setting to work with dials and brushes and the frothing of milk. Sal lets her eyes linger on the cake. Wonders whether Caramel Apple Betty would be a good name for a burlesque act. Wishes Jarod were here to say it to.

Sal takes a seat at a Formica-topped table. There are angling trophies in a case by the door. A tired-looking Plummer terrier noses her foot.

'Shackleton,' says the woman, with an audible tut. 'Retired rat-catcher. Served his time.'

'We have Tips,' says Sal, giving the dog a stroke behind his ears. He has scars on his muzzle, across his brow. 'Been in the wars, has he?'

'Only bloody ratter we've had that will chase a squirrel up a tree. Mental bugger. Lovely nature, but if he thinks there's a threat . . . instinct, I suppose.'

Sal fishes out her phone as the sketchy Wi-Fi serves up a brief moment of connectivity. She realizes she's missed a call from Elsie. Calls it back without listening to the message.

'Speak of the devil,' says Elsie, as she answers, a little breathlessly. She sounds stuffy, as if she's coming down with a cold. 'You OK? I can kill her for you. Like, no problem at all.'

Sal smiles, tiredly, grateful for a friend. 'Just throwing her weight around, really. Letting me know what she thinks of me, as if I didn't know. Water off a duck's back, really. Just wish I knew what I was doing.'

'Seems like you know damn well, girl,' chides Elsie. 'Collision investigator, Family Liaison Officer, bagman to the boss, and now you get the chance to go and pick up all the slack. Fill in the gaps, and such.'

'Fill in the gaps?'

'Gone off like a hare, of course,' says Elsie, withering. 'Doing things her way – acting like she knows what's going on when in fact she's just making it up as she goes. You should have been in the briefing. Claire tried to get you a bit of credit but she shut her down. What are you up to now?'

'Snacking,' smiles Sal. 'Heavily. Got some apologies to make when I get back so I'm stretching it out a little. Doing some reading.'

'That's where your problems started, girl.'

'I feel like my head's a bit rattled, and . . . look, I know sometimes

I get the wrong end of the stick and I wouldn't want anybody to start anything based just on my half a suspicion, but . . .'

'Get on with it, love, we've got turkey dippers and spaghetti hoops cooking here. I was just seeing you were OK.'

'Theo Myers,' she says, before she can help herself.

'Wulf's friend?' asks Elsie, her voice becoming less devil-may-care. She's a good detective sergeant when she has time to be.

'It's just, Mahee . . . it's too random, isn't it? Maybe he's into kinky stuff and he'll drive miles and take risks for the chance of a hook-up, but . . . the screeching bird? That's a bit theatrical, isn't it? And . . . look, there's some kind of link – I just can't make sense of it, or . . .' she rattles to a close. 'I'm going to send you some names,' she says, at last. 'I'm sure Quinn has the analysts running this stuff, but on the off-chance it's slipped through . . . well, I'll send you it. See what you think. A couple of articles too.' Her fingers move over the keys. She hears the ping as the message arrives on Elsie's phone.

'Who's Blindworm?' she asks, reading the attached headlines. 'And Alec Devlin?' There's something in her tone that suggests a familiarity. 'The campaigner? Freed the Guildford Twenty-Seven, or whoever. Made tits of the lot of us and rightly so? Aye, the lad who got done for kicking that tramp to death . . .'

'Is that how you categorize it?' asks Sal, stroking the dog's scarred head. 'Random attacker. Theo was wrongly identified. Gamage, well – he gave the advice that, with hindsight, might have contributed to Theo's time inside. And those names? They're witnesses who have been actively named in the dozens of press clippings about the whole debacle.'

'You've checked on their welfare?'

'I've run a Police National Computer check and sifted on social media. Found a vehicle of that night which belongs to Didier Mabuse. Posing with it in a picture taken in October last year. Can't be sure it's the same guy but he's posted links to Theo's recent disappointment.'

'He's not getting compensation, last I heard. Would be enough to persuade me to lose my temper, I think. Perhaps a little bit of revenge is understandable.'

'You didn't see Mahee,' says Sal, quietly. She takes a sip of her fresh coffee, smiling gratefully at the young woman. Hears Elsie make all her little noises as she speed-reads.

'I'll talk to Claire,' she says, at last. 'Keep your name off it, just in case it makes Quinn put the blinkers on. No harm with the softly-softly-askee-monkey approach, though, eh?' Her voice takes on a new timbre. 'You could ask Wulf . . .'

Sal stares into the froth of her coffee. Wonders what she's doing. Whether she's taking a risk, or just pratting around in the background and making a balls-up of everything. She's felt the same way most of her forty years.

She strikes ahead, hoping that Elsie is sufficiently intrigued to read all the articles. Takes a breath before sending her a link to a website that had caused her coffee to get cold.

'All right,' mumbles Elsie, getting comfortable and opening the last link. She growls. 'What the fuck is an oubliette?'

Article from *parliamentofowlz.com*: a site created by educators and experts on topics related to education as a place to share expertise and knowledge about all things academic.

The Oubliette: A Chamber of Horrors

By Daphne Ogle
11.01.2022

So . . . What is an oubliette?

Oubliette (pronounced 'oo-blee-ett') is a French term from the verb 'oublier' (which means 'to forget'). It was so named because a prisoner was thrown down into one and then forgotten. An oubliette was a unique type of dungeon, with the only entrance a trap door at the top – out of reach of the prisoner.

Often, this horrible prison was shaped like a very narrow passage, not wide enough for the prisoner to sit down or even get down on his knees. He was forced to stand or lie prone as he starved to death. He could tilt his head back to see the grate, far above his head and out of reach, but that was all.

Oubliettes were sometimes built within the walls of the upper floors of a castle rather than in the dungeon, so that victims could hear and smell the life of the castle as they slowly died of deprivation in unspeakable conditions. Corpses were left to be consumed by vermin, and many oubliettes were discovered centuries later to be strewn with human bones.

At the bottom of Leap Castle's oubliette were several sharpened wooden spikes pointing menacingly up from the floor, eight feet below the trap door. So many skeletons were discovered in the oubliette in the Twenties that it took three cartloads to transport them from the premises.

Warwick Castle's oubliette is horizontal, long, narrow, and paved with jagged stones that jut up from the floor. In this case, the prisoner lies prone on the stones, the ceiling of his tiny prison inches above him so that he cannot move away from his agony. In addition to the inescapable physical pain, the prisoner might easily lose his sanity in the clammy, claustrophobic conditions.

The long-demolished Redburn Castle in Northumberland is rumoured to contain the bones of its final prisoner – the notorious torturer and executioner Blindworm, who served King Edward I with astonishing barbarism and cruelty. Rumours persist that the entrance to the dungeon lies hidden somewhere in the vicinity – still containing the mouldering bones of one of history's worst sadists.

TWENTY-FOUR

The dazzling spotlights of Lumley Castle capture perfect circles of mizzling rain: the droplets suspended like bubbles in a wand. Sal finds herself staring, transfixed. She's seen the castle before – even stayed here a couple of times with different suitors trying to show her the same good time. She's not impressed any more. It's the lights that hold her attention, shining back in endless reflective prisms on the wet lenses of her spectacles.

'Going in there, actually, love.'

Sal turns at the sound of the voice. Realizes she's standing in a reserved parking space, staring at the sky like she's trying to stop a nosebleed.

'Sorry, sorry – miles away.'

She hurries out of the space and listens to the smooth purr of the big engine, the top-of-the-range tyres gliding smoothly over the gravel that rings the tall, sturdy tower.

'Stop it,' she tells herself. Then: 'Don't get all bloody Tony Benn.'

She giggles, surprising herself. The familiar admonition had arrived in her head in a perfect recreation of Lewis's voice. She feels her stomach knot. Remembers, unbidden, the time he had bought a beret for her birthday, complete with matching raincoat. He'd told her to get herself on marches and start handing out *Socialist Worker* to commuters. Her initial crime was to purchase a Che Guevara T-shirt. Lewis took the prompt and really ran with it.

Sal glances up as she crunches her way towards the imposing double doors. It looks suitably grand, all lit-up and towering above the darkening countryside. Inside, the walls are four feet thick, the dark panelling and plush tapestries giving the narrow reception area a gloomy air. Sal spies the suits of armour in the entrance and can't help herself. They give off a metallic chink as she taps them.

'Everyone does that,' comes a voice from an open door behind the check-in desk.

Sal turns, guiltily, holding her offending hand as if burned. 'Sorry. I didn't see the sign.'

A man emerges from the little room. Closes it behind him and stands behind the solitary seat at the dark wood desk. He's older than Sal. Smart, in his three-piece suit and neatly parted dark hair. He's got one of those beards that isn't quite a goatee – just a rough patch of dusty stubble that Sal would love to rasp a match-head against.

'No sign, no problem,' smiles the man, wiping his mouth. 'Just snaffling down a bite to eat. Do excuse me.'

Sal smiles. She likes the way the lines crinkle around his eyes as he talks. Likes the slight impishness to the smile. Hears Jarod, in her head: *Impish? He's nigh-on fifty* . . .

'You're staying with us?' asks the man. Sal crosses to the desk. Reads his name badge. He's Adam.

'I wish,' says Sal, looking around at the silver plates and gleaming goblets that stare down from display cases mounted on the bare brick. 'I have done. Afternoon tea voucher as well, a while back. Very nice.'

Adam doesn't look in any rush to resume his seat. Doesn't seem as though he's going to ask her any more questions.

'I'm Sal,' she says, hands still in her pockets, hunched into her parka. 'Cumbria Police, actually.'

Adam's eyes widen just a fraction. She gets a better look at his brown eyes. Likes the energy he emits, the vibration around him. She's never thought of herself much of a judge of character, but he seems a decent sort.

'Adam Marshall,' he says, without removing his big, hairy-knuckled hands from the back of the leather chair. 'Manager, as it happens, but at the moment I'm manning reception, abet poorly. I'll have to have a word with myself. Give myself a verbal warning.'

Sal returns his smile. 'What were you having?' she asks.

'Ravioli and toast with grated cheese,' he says, miming ecstasy. 'From a tin. I swear, I have to sneak around this place like a poltergeist just to avoid upsetting Chef. I've told him, I'm a man of simple tastes. You can give me all the foie-gras blinis on pig-snout shavings but I'm going to be pining for an egg sandwich.'

Sal puts her elbow on the desk as if taking a seat at a bar. 'You'll have seen all the goings-on, I presume. I was raised not far from here and I know how the rumours blow in on the wind.'

He seems about to speak. Stops himself as two guests make their way noisily down the wooden stairs – red carpeting failing to muffle the deathly creaks from the timbers. Adam makes pleasantries. Tells them there's a nice pub called The Cart's Bog Inn if they didn't fancy trying the hotel's à la carte menu. They assured him they would think about it.

His voice changes when he speaks to the toffs, thinks Sal. *He went straight into BBC newsreader mode. Didn't even try that with you, did he? What was it that somebody wise had called poverty? A stain that won't wash off?*

'You're Jarod's sister,' says Adam, when they're alone again. 'Delaney, isn't it?'

Sal closes her eyes. It had been going so well

'You know Jarod?'

'Not well, but . . . well enough, I suppose. He's all right, is he? Haven't seen him in for an age.'

'In here?' asks Sal, astonished at the thought. Jarod would hate it here more than she does.

'No, Lion at Allendale. My local. Aye, he described you well enough.'

'What did he say?' asks Sal, feeling her pulse quicken. *Don't,* she tells herself. *Not now* . . .

'Oh, just a general picture,' smiles Adam, waving his hand in her general direction. 'Mad hair, bit scatty – usually looks out of place . . .'

'That could be construed as mean,' says Sal, feeling the tension bleed out of her as she gives in to the grin. 'I do not have mad hair.'

'Not Medusa mad,' says Adam, giving her mess of unmanageable curls an expert once-over. 'Suits the name, anyway. Salome, isn't it? Isn't she the one who danced for Herod? Asked for the head of John the Baptist as a reward?'

Sal sucks her lip. Wonders if she's flirting.

'Very good,' she says clapping her hands. It's not a familiar gesture and she hates herself for it at once. 'Sorry, I went a little bit high school cheerleader there. Forgive me.'

'He's all right though, yeah? There was some bother, wasn't there? After he took in that bloke who . . .' he tails off, clearly unsure how to proceed. 'He didn't talk about it much, not what happened. But he lost friends trying to prove he was innocent. Man of principle, that one. Tell him I'm asking after him.'

Sal nods, unsure how else to move things along. Points again towards the distant road, shielded by the high bank of trees. She tries to imagine the great and the good at the riotous banquets held here in the Seventies: knights and jesters and maids – jousting tournaments with French sticks used as lances; suits of armour goosing every woman who passed them on the stairs.

'I wanted to talk to you about something else, as it goes,' she says, in the voice she used to use on her boss at the bookshop. She goes a little coy. Softens herself a little. 'Theo Myers,' she says, and the name catches in her throat. *What are you doing? Making it real! Letting your paranoid delusion out into the world . . .*

'Alec's lad?' asks Adam, brightly. He nods, enthused. 'The one who had the . . .' he tails off, clearly unsure how best to express himself. 'You're not giving him grief again, are you? Poor lad's been through enough. I mean, you're only doing your job, but . . .'

'I understand Theo's being considered for a position here? One of the tour guides?'

Adam makes a face. Lowers himself into his chair. He moves his fingers over the keypad, a little distracted. 'Only in his own head, I'm afraid,' he says, and it seems to pain him to say it. 'I mean, he scared the life out of us, but can you imagine? Honestly? I told Alec he could come and show us what he had but, honestly, when I said we'd give him a job I was thinking more on the maintenance staff or in the kitchen. Even if he didn't have all those nasty headlines behind him, we couldn't let him near the guests with that bloody get-up on. I mean, it was genuinely sinister.'

Sal takes a moment to get her thoughts in order.

'My friend has seen the performance,' she says. 'Said it was a bit over the top.'

'This place can be spooky enough after dark,' he says, glancing at his screen. 'We're not the Lindon Dungeons, you know what I mean? We do well out of all the history buffs, the people with beards and walking boots and a guidebook. Local history tours are always fully booked. The Blindworm story – I mean, it's bollocks, but that doesn't stop us playing up to it. Not that he's ours to claim.'

'I'm a bit hazy on the history,' says Sal, apologetically. She remembers one of her foster mums telling her the gory details then chiding herself for being so insensitive. She seems to recall an extra half-hour of reading time, a glass of milk and a Trio. She'd have been in paradise, if not for the nightmares – for Jarod's absence; Uncle Wulf on trial for her mother's murder . . .

'Torturer and jailer of Redburn Castle,' he says, with the practised smoothness of somebody who knows his subject inside and out.

'Only a wall and some old masonry there now. Burned to the ground centuries ago. More significant historically than this place ever was, but historical significance doesn't do much against fire, does it? Anyway, when the last owners bought this place, they sort of co-opted Blindworm into our story. Cobbled together a bit of nonsense about it being here where he met his end. Fleeing from the hordes, apparently. Banged on our door for shelter and the lord of the manor turned him away. They dragged him back to Redburn. Cut bits off, broke his limbs, tossed him into his own pit. Horrible story, though whether there's a grain of truth in it . . .'

'So Theo's not got the job?'

'I don't think it quite sank in,' says Adam. 'I'm expecting a call from Alec later, so maybe I'll find a way to make it a bit clearer. He'll probably talk me into giving him a second audition, soft sod that I am. Dotes on that lad, though.' He stops himself, drawing a sudden connection in his mind. 'You know his real dad killed himself down at the ruins of Redburn, don't you? I mean, not my place to say, but Christ, that makes it even creepier. I'm surprised Alec encouraged it, to be honest, but maybe it's what Tara wants.' He laughs, shaking his head. 'Hard work, that one.'

Sal keeps her face neutral. Doesn't react the way she wants to at the casually tossed misogyny grenade. 'Oh yes?'

'Well, you'll have seen the worst of it when she was campaigning for her son – giving you lot short shrift. Couldn't turn the telly on without seeing her face.'

'You don't sound impressed. She was fighting to free her son.'

Adam looks at her a little awkwardly, clearly trying to select the right words. 'There were some who said she didn't have much interest in him before he was locked up. That it was his dad who did the heavy lifting, so to speak. She was always, well, I don't know what she was doing but it was Paul doing the drop-offs and pick-ups and taking him to drama clubs. At least, that's how I heard it.'

'Heard it from?'

Adam shrugs. 'You know this place, you said so yourself. Everybody knows everything, or at least, some version of it. But it was Alec, as you're asking. Last time he was in.'

Sal doesn't reply. Hopes he'll feel uncomfortable and fill the gap with something useful.

'Been a tough time for them all,' he says, obligingly. 'Alec's had enough of it all, between you and me. He's been poorly, I think. Wants to just put his feet up for a while – enjoy the birds and the books, finish writing his story. She's still wearing a tin hat and manning the machine guns. Theo seems caught in the middle of it all. I liked the lad, honestly. Can't imagine him in prison, can you – sweet lad like that.'

Sal grimaces as her phone starts to buzz in her coat pocket. She holds up a hand in apology and walks away from the desk, taking up sentry beside the suit of armour. She sees herself momentarily reflected in the bulbous breastplate; puffing out her cheeks, narrowing her eyes, pulling down her cheeks. She feels her legs give way as she becomes her mother. Turns away, steadying herself on the metal arm. Answers, breathless, dizzy.

'Claire,' she manages. 'I'm just . . .'

'I know you are, sugarplum, but I'm hiding in a cubicle with my tights around my ankles and I've only got a sec myself, yeah?'

Sal feels herself relax at the sound of the familiar voice. Claire's her boss, on paper. In reality, they're both oarsmen aboard the same leaking longboat and their relationship exists largely on bartered favours and agreed-upon white lies.

'The briefing was brutal, love,' confides Claire, her voice echoing. 'You weren't so much as bloody mentioned, though I made sure every bugger knew it was you who got the cleaner talking and provided the preliminary intel on the crash site. Quinn's face was a picture. Fucking cow-bag.'

'I don't care,' says Sal, wishing she meant it. 'It's not important. But, look, I'm talking to somebody now about . . . well, I don't want to say suspect, but I do have a suspicion, and it's one that I don't like having, and . . .'

'Breathe, babes, yeah? Do the tappity-tap thing on your chest. It'll be OK. You're one of the good ones so you've got to trust yourself.'

'Lewis isn't here to make my fuck-ups go away any more, Claire,' says Sal, and the words come out of her in a rush that leaves her seeing stars. 'God, I hate saying that but it's true. I'd have been in a cell by now if not for him. They'd have got Dagmara. I mean, the deals that were done just for me – it's no wonder Quinn hates me.'

'Stop being a people-pleaser, yeah? She's a bitch. She's vile. Get on board with the zeitgeist, babes. Would be daft if we all hated her on your behalf and you're privately thinking she's awesome, yeah?'

'I wouldn't go that far,' says Sal, with a sudden smile. 'What was it you wanted?'

'Automatic Number Plate Recognition on the car you asked me about,' she says, her voice changing as she pulls up the file on her phone. 'Didier's a hell of a name to be lumbered with. Anyway, clocked by the police van near Brockbushes Farm, Corbridge way on 3 January, 11.06 p.m. Nothing since. Is that connected to this?'

Sal closes her eyes. She thinks she's starting to see it. Hates the picture she's painting. Wonders whether she can bring herself to tell Quinn.

'You there, babes?'

'I appreciate it,' says Sal, suddenly feeing the weight of the day. 'I'll call you when I know what I'm doing.'

'You still at Wulf's?'

'I prefer it somehow. The girls too. It's . . . it's kind of normal, I suppose, but it's not ever been a normal we've experienced. I can't explain it. I just like being there.'

'And social services?'

Sal doesn't want to think about it. Not yet. 'I think they owe me a little leeway, don't you? Anyway, I'm finishing up then going to get warm. Thanks.'

She hangs up. Returns to Adam, who's placing a steaming latte on the desk. It looks creamy and delicious in its red china mug. 'Thought you might need a boost,' says Adam, warmly. 'You're a latte girl, yeah?'

Sal takes the mug. 'You're a legend,' she says, gratefully. Scalds her lip on a swig of milky caffeine. Savours it, the taste and the sting.

'You look like you're carrying the weight of the world,' says Adam. 'Helps to tell a barman, sometimes.'

'Is that a line that ever works?'

'You'd be surprised. But, look, if you're involved with what happened down on the road, what Sycamore saw . . .'

'You know Mr Le Gros?'

'Know him? Bloody hell, most people reckon that half the kids in the valley were conceived on those stairs during the Seventies. His dad died here. Aye, Sycamore's a regular. He and Alec can put the brandy away, I can tell you that much. Why do you think I said we'd give Theo a try-out? And that's no easy house for the lad. Mother's not good on the drink. Alec's nigh-on had it. Honestly, if you'd seen the way she reacted when Paul told her about the villa . . . and the bust-up at Ladies' Day.'

'Yeah, I heard,' says Sal, trying to loosen an already flopping tongue.

'Don't know much meself, but she was on the Pimm's and didn't like the way some woman in the county stand was looking at her. Went for her like something feral, according to the mum of one of our waitresses. Proper trying to tear her hair off, she was. Only thing the woman had said to her was that she was sure she recognized her from somewhere, and that proper set it off. Alec had to smooth it all out but the poor sod was mortified. I think she's in a lot of pain, but, well, you can't be doing that, can you?'

Sal lets it all sink into the mulch. Plants a seed. Hopes to God it doesn't grow.

'You said he's writing a book?' asks Sal, always interested in people brave enough to get their words down on paper. 'All the cases he's been involved with, is it? A memoir?'

'Local history,' says Adam. 'Writes some of it in the bar upstairs. Really quiet place. Nobody in there now, as it goes. If you wanted to bring your coffee, I could give you the grand tour.'

Sal meets his hopeful gaze. She experiences only the faintest flicker of regret as she declines the offer with a wrinkle of her nose.

'Duty calls,' she says, and means it. 'My girls.' She raises her hand to her mouth as soon as she says it. Her girls. She feels her cheeks pinken.

'I can give you my card,' he says, a little crestfallen. 'If you do decide . . .'

Sal finishes her coffee. Gives a nod of thanks and makes for the door. She stops before she pushes it open. Looks back at him over the rim of her glasses.

'I know where to find you when I need you,' she says, and enjoys his answering grin.

Pushes at the door, feeling cool.

It won't open.

Pulls it.

Scuttles out, pulling up her hood.

You are a liability, girl . . .

Out loud: 'I know.'

TWENTY-FIVE

Wulfric Hagman, ducking briers, pushing through hawthorns, brambles; cobwebs in his face and beard, clinging like caul.

He glances back over his shoulder, squinting through the grey air and the steam that rises from the sodden, boggy earth. He thinks of old horror movies: gothic churches and slanting headstones rising from an ethereal mist. Thinks of skeletal hands punching through from the wet earth.

Leave off, lad – you'll scare yourself.

Hagman doesn't really know why he's feeling apprehensive. This is his land, albeit in Jarod's name. He supposes it's what Sal calls 'generalized anxiety'. He hadn't known the condition existed when he was a lad. It was always easier to believe the bullies in their alternative diagnoses: wimp, bum-boy, gaylord; all the things that Cumbria's adolescents could fling at the sensitive, unsporty lad who'd drifted into their orbit. He'd always just thought himself fiercely shy; had thought himself awkward and gawkish rather than showing signs of Autism Spectrum Disorder, as suggested by his defending counsel at trial and by a number of prison psychologists since. Nola and Lottie, better versed in the subtle nuances of the neurodivergent, had told him it wasn't anything to be ashamed of and was, in fact, a superpower. He hadn't asked for further clarification, which, if the literature were to be believed, could be viewed as irrefutable proof that he was as neurotypical as the next man. Follow-up questions were rarely his forte, even as a police officer. He'd never had the gift of hyperfocus, save one romantic infatuation that had enslaved him so entirely that he was willing to give his life to end it. It hadn't worked. Instead he gave twenty-three years.

He turns up the volume on his Sony Walkman: a piece of black-and-orange retro that he traded his cigarettes for while inside, and which the girls had looked at with a mixture of horror and fascination. When he'd pressed down 'record' and 'pause' at the same time, Nola had asked if he was taking a screenshot.

He pushes forward through the trees, thinking of Lennon. Thinking of Fairport Convention and Creedence Clearwater Revival. Thinking of Dusty Springfield. Of 'Lily the Pink'. He'd adored his records when he was a youngster. Loved being the first to find a new band. He'd listen to albums over and over, trapping himself in the same loop of electric guitar and folksy warbling. There was something soothing about it; a way of controlling things beyond his reach. He was the same with foods. With books. He always sought comfort rather than distraction; sought something nurturing instead of entertainment. He thinks upon Jarod. Screws up his eyes as the hurt hits too deep. Flinches from the thought, grabbing for a mossy branch. He feels it squelch beneath his fingers. Feels mud beneath his nails.

He slips the headphones off. Stops the tape. Stands still. The woods chime with birdsong. Hears whitethroats, blackbirds: the angry twittering of vicious robins, butchering one another in the hedgerows. Theo had said he'd made an inroad on the grey squirrels; that there would be more songbirds this year because there were no predators eating their eggs. From the cacophony in the dark branches overhead, he wonders if the lad has perhaps gone overboard. He knows it's very much in keeping with what he knows of him. There's something a little off about Theo, even by Hagman's standards. The lad seems to be all 'transmit' rather than 'receive'. He doesn't feel like a fully realized person. Seems too much of a performance for Hagman's liking, much as he's warmed to the lad. He doesn't judge him for it. Pretty boys like Theo do hard time. Hagman has no doubt that his bravado is a suit of armour; his eagerness to please a way of keeping the stronger lads on side. Hagman wonders what parts of himself he buried when he went inside. He remembers he used to laugh a lot. Used to sing when he was walking. Used to whistle, now and again.

Whistled this morning, lad. Whistled while you were making breakfast for the girls.

He finds himself smiling. Thinks upon Sal and the girls, in the kitchen, by the fire. Thinks upon family. Upon love.

Soft sod. Just do what you came to do . . .

Theo's encampment is in a little clearing two thirds of the way into the wood. It's camouflaged so perfectly that Hagman had been forced to ring Theo for directions the first time he had tried to find the spot, his heart almost stopping when he heard the ringing coming from behind the big elm six feet away. Theo doesn't like to use modern accessories. Likes to make his own little den from fallen timbers and strategically placed sticks. Doesn't believe in leaving a footprint upon the earth. Won't erect anything that the wind won't scatter upon the next storm. The only concession to modernity is the string of solar-powered fairy lights, winking dimly in the gloom. They're suspended from the two big trees which bookend his camp.

Hagman sniffs the air. Theo always lights a fire in the little pit outside the opening of the low, leaf-strewn sleeping quarters. Likes to cook up whatever he's nabbed with his ball-bearing catapult. Buries the bloody skins so as not to attract foxes. The camp usually carries a greasy, butcher's-block air but here, now, Hagman can only smell the wet earth and the bog-water reek of rotting wood.

'Theo?' he shouts. 'Theo . . .'

He half hopes he answers him. He doesn't want to be able to do what he came here to do. Wants to be stopped. Wants his hand to be forced.

Get on it, lad. It's there or it's not.

Hagman ducks down at the open entrance to the camp. Spies the damp bed-roll and the green rucksack, the flap hanging open, disgorging its litter of clean and dirty underwear, unopened tins of convenience food, crumpled, soggy-looking paperback books. Hagman opens the bag to its full extent. Rummages inside. Plum tomatoes. Baked beans. Heinz ravioli. He thinks of Tara Myers, of Mam, making sure her precious baby has all he needs.

Focus, lad.

He opens each of the books in turn, glancing at the titles as he does so. *Grisly Tales of Northumberland. North East Folk Tales. Blindworm: The King's Favourite Torturer.* He picks that up and squints through the grey air at the blurb on the back. Scans the testimonials. 'Sick and twisted'. 'Unreal violence'. 'A gory romp'. Hagman wrinkles his nose. He isn't sure he's ever enjoyed a book that could be described as a 'romp'. Isn't sure it sits neatly with the subject matter: Theo's sadistic killer.

The book falls open at a page that has been marked with a postcard. It shows an old pen-and-ink drawing of the ruined Redburn Castle. It shows the battlements and grounds; a line of yew trees cresting the low hills, down past the cattle-dotted fields with the tumbledown outbuildings, to give a sweeping grandeur to the imposing bulk of the four-storey castle, topped off with ramparts and proudly unfurled flags. He peers at the date. 1841. It's by a D. Matheson. He turns it over. Reads the simple message.

> Son,
> I did my best. I just wasn't strong enough. Don't forget what I've taught you. Don't let them win.
> Dad.

Hagman swallows. It's Theo's dad's suicide note. It's addressed to Theo's wing at HMP Frankland. From the files, Hagman knows that the poor bastard had already been dead three days before it made its way to Theo's cell. Knows that Theo spent time in the hospital wing after that; that he was tranquillized for months that followed, first with prescription drugs and then with whatever he could barter on the wing.

Everything was available to a pretty boy like Theo, if he was willing to pay up.

He replaces the card. Ducks back out from under the wet, leafy covering of the low roof. Something stops him. Urges him to check beneath the bed-roll for the one thing he hopes not to find.

The little glass bottle looks just as it did when Hagman made him a gift of it. Two inches tall, stoppered with wax, a sigil of an oak tree embossed in the red seal.

Do it, lad. Do it or don't.

Hagman thinks of Sal. Of the girls. Of what they stand to lose if his suspicions are confirmed.

He looks around for a stone. Finds one with a pleasing heft and brings it down neatly on the glass. It doesn't make a sound as it cracks and splinters.

He rummages through the pieces. Picks up the three leaves. Brings them to his face.

Reads: *Mahee Gamage. Didier Mabuse. Constance Andrysiak.*

His stomach roils and twists, acid rising up his throat to burn his larynx and wet his eyes. He'd so hoped he was wrong.

He looks down at the shards of glass that litter the mulch on the floor by the fire pit.

Looks at the leaves in his hand. He realizes too late that in trying to exonerate Theo, he's also incriminated himself. He's destroyed evidence. He's withheld vital information.

He starts scooping up the bits of glass, nicking his fingers on the jagged shards.

Stuffs it all back under the bed-roll, the mud and the leaves and the glass. Snatches up some printouts and stuffs them in his pocket. Steps away.

Fucked that up, son. What are you going to tell her? You've got her a suspect, but you've destroyed the bloody evidence? Call yourself a police officer? Thirty years to reflect on why you were so shit at it the first time, and you're still a liability.

Hagman lashes out as something catches him on the shoulder. Turns around to see the lowering mass of the great oak; trunk moss-slimed, carbuncled with scars and rings. In this light, in this place, it could almost have a face – could almost be a leering gargoyle, hook-backed, white-eyed.

He walks away from the camp faster than he came. Pushes through leaves and trees as if being pursued. He's gasping hard, sweat soaking his clothes, when he emerges from the treeline at the lower lip of the farm. Sees the warm yellow glow of the kitchen, the trio of heads lowered as if in prayer, pencils moving over coloured paper. Uncle Wulf is going to judge the art contest when he gets back. There's a hot bath for the winner. The loser has to stand under the broken gutter for twenty seconds. Lottie had made up the rules at breakfast and Hagman, too distracted by his own grumbling worries, had agreed without thinking. Hagman fancies he'll have to join in with the game, just so he can pick somebody to undergo the forfeit.

There's a knocking on the window. Lottie's waving, holding up a picture of a squirrel riding a bicycle. She's smiling in a way he hasn't seen in a long time. For a moment she's a kid again, eager to show the nice police officer her drawings, her writings, her poetry. He's telling her about his own favourite authors; favourite musicians. He's promising to bring her some tapes and she's saying they only have a CD player, and he's promising he'll change that, at her next birthday. He'll get her whatever he wants.

He feels sick all the way through. Feels like there's something rotten inside of him; something fetid and black. Thinks of the character he has created: the lisping, sadistic torturer, imprisoned in some hellish tomb beneath the earth. Thinks of the darkness of such a place; the chasm of filth and bones and hopelessness, and wishes that they'd just damn well thrown him in there when they'd had the chance. Wishes to God he'd let them do away with him long before he had the chance to ruin so many lives with his own selfishness, weakness, need.

He gives her a thumbs-up. Nods, appreciatively.

'Grand, that,' he mouths, through the window.

From *LangleyandDistrictHistoricalSociety.com*

By Dr P. D. Horobin
13.04.2018

In 1966 an excavator being used in the process of laying foundations for a new brick outbuilding on a field above Langley Dam, fell through the earth into a cavity which – on further inspection – turned out to be a man-made chamber. This find was reported in the (long-defunct) *Evening World* newspaper under the headline 'Secret Passage at Hexham, Torturers' Lair Unearthed'. The newspaper story said that the underground room, which had been hewn out of solid rock, was over five feet deep by two feet wide and was overlaid with eight inches of thick stone slabs. It appeared to be bottle shaped originally, and workmen reported being able to see down into a deeper pit beyond. They could make out the shape of an iron grille and what appeared to be human remains.

Landowner Barnaby Le Gros told the newspaper: 'It's a damn nuisance. The excavator was just biting in when suddenly a great lump of earth gave way and all but ate itself up. It's a pretty gloomy spot there and the rain had been coming down for days and the next thing there's a great hole in the earth and we're all staring down into what looks for all the world like a dungeon. Goodness knows when it last saw the light of day. It's not more than a hundred yards from the earthworks of Redburn Castle, so perhaps it's from the same time or, heaven forbid, they could even be connected. We're hoping we'll get the permits to fill it back in and get on with the build, but we may be up to our eyes in archaeologists and whatnot if they get themselves in a flap.'

Mr Le Gros went on to outline the local legend of Edward I's favourite torturer: a terrifying creation known by his hated nickname, Blindworm, and who personally oversaw the execution of thousands of Scots. Blindworm is said to have worn a hood made from the skins of his victims and was eventually thrown into his oubliette – an underground chamber into which prisoners were thrown to die of hunger and starvation. The word comes from the French word 'forgetting'.

Realistically the tunnel may be no more than old mine workings, although there is certainly the possibility that the area containing the table may have been used in the sixteenth century for religious services during the period when Catholic services were banned.

TWENTY-SIX

'And you're sure?'

'No. I've made this repeatedly clear, Magda – we aren't sure.'

'But sure as you can be without being sure?'

'No. No I can't say what you want me to say . . .'

Quinn watches herself in the darkened, rain-dotted glass. Watches herself change.

Sees the way her likeness softens its pose, tilts its head. She's talking into her mobile, but every inch of her posture suggests she should be twirling a curly telephone cord around her finger, twisting and tightening, reeling in the man who protests and simpers at the end of the line.

'Gerald, you and I have always understood one another. We have that telepathy. I know what you can and can't say, so I have to do a little interpretation. Translation, if you will . . .'

'Magda, I've already said, if I could, I would.'

'But you can't rule it out,' continues Quinn. 'Indeed, it's more likely than not.'

'Any defence barrister will have a field day with "more likely than not".'

Quinn stops. Flicks the switch inside herself and returns to her usual pose: stiff-backed, anxious, shoulders up by her ears.

'I can't take that to the press,' she says, shutting her eyes. 'I can't say that it's "likely" he had human remains in his stomach, Gerald.'

'Of course you can. They'll eat that up.'

Quinn swallows, feeling a little queasy. She's not eaten since shoving down a quinoa and edamame bean salad at lunchtime. Walked past the RVI vending machines without letting her eyes linger on the Monster Munch.

'You must have something for me, Gerald.'

At the other end of the line, she hears Gerald Cribbens rustling his papers and clicking on his keypad. She used up her favours just getting Mahee's stomach contents to the front of the queue. He'd rung with optimism in his voice, pleased to report that his very expensive forensic specialists had analysed the unidentified meat that Sal had bagged up at the crime scene, and were able to report back that it was almost certainly human flesh. Because it was already in an advanced state of decay when consumed, it's so far proven impossible to retrieve any DNA samples or to confirm its make-up. Even so, Cribbens had expected an 'attaboy' for giving her something suitably grisly to take to the chief superintendent. It could, he opined, be a career-maker.

Quinn shoots a look at Mahee, at the stick-thin, blotched and bandaged figure; all tubes and blankets, bleeps and bags. She tries to make sense of the picture. She has to give a briefing in fifteen minutes and what she has to report back sounds almost surreal. Sounds a little too familiar. Sounds like the same story she took to the top brass last year about a suspected serial killer she had identified; the same Wulfric Hagman who had done two decades for murder was her prime suspect in a series of murders made to look like accidents and suicides. She had the goods on him. Could place him at each scene and had independent witnesses who'd heard him bragging while inside about having offed a couple of 'really bad men'. She'd been given permission. Given approval. Given Lewis Beecher. And she'd ended the investigation covered in blood and snow – her life saved by the man she had tried to put away for ever.

But Theo Myers could be different, she thinks. Could be a real redemption story, for her, if not for him. She hasn't got anywhere near enough to arrest him and would tear strips off a junior officer who suggested showing their hand at such an early stage in the investigation. They need to perform due diligence on his movements, his relationships, his state of mind. Need to know about the real lad, not just the headlines. She has two analysts working up a precis of his dealings with police and knows that, viewed through the right lens, she can make him seem highly attractive to the Crown Prosecution Service. They don't like getting it wrong. Don't like looking foolish. They'd love the chance to redress that balance and have another crack at him. And she can make it happen.

She realizes Cribbens is still talking. Ends the call. Mashes her lips together into a thin, bloodless line.

Gives her attention to the half-dead thing in the bed. She hadn't wanted it to come to this. Would truly have been content to wait, were things any different.

She takes the vial from inside her coat. Pictures Callum, raising his glass and toasting her health by the light of the flickering fire. Breaks the seal and recoils at the sudden, heady, ammonia reek, blood rushing to her head in a way she hasn't experienced since sniffing amyl nitrate while undercover. She feels her pupils diminish to pinpricks. Hears, deep inside herself, a voice dormant since she went through the car windscreen on that whited-out country road.

Don't, Magda. This isn't what you want. You're not this person . . .

She holds the bottle under his bandaged nostrils.

Waits.

Watches, as the half-dead thing opens its eyes: hell dancing on the yellow irises; lenses seamed with blood.

A cry; strangled, squawked; the breathing tube causing him to choke, gag; machines beeping, beeping . . .

Push! Don't let me fall! I'm nearly there! Nearly . . . no!

His voice, the cry of the devil bird.

TWENTY-SEVEN

Going to be worse, Wulf. Every second you keep your mouth shut . . .

Hagman is trying to ignore the voice. Trying to concentrate on the here, the now, the precious idyll that he's maintaining through pretence, deceit.

'I think that's her,' says Nola, her voice a little muffled. She's making an attempt at de-cluttering the kitchen. Hagman is trying not to feel mothered by the teenager. She's always been quiet with him; always kept their interactions polite, if not overtly aloof. She's trying, at least. Wants to at least get the table cleared and some of the detritus mounded into more visually appealing shapes. 'Did you know there's a ring in this floor, by the way? Found it under the little sideboard.'

'Do we have a sideboard?' asks Hagman.

'Keep still,' says Lottie, her face looming in front of his: deadly serious and tongue sticking out with concentration. 'Purple or pink?'

'You choose,' mumbles Hagman, trying not to wince as Lottie pulls at his beard and continues to twist it into braids.

'This is all Theo's stuff, is it?' asks Nola, straightening up and trying to put some of the folders and books and papers into a neater pile. She finds a new pile of dirty dishes and keeps her smile fixed in place as she takes another trip to the big Belfast sink.

'I'm thinking we'll use lavender for decoration, so pink might be quite complementary,' says Lottie. Her breath is warm on his face: all pork casserole and freshly warmed bread. They should have waited for Sal. Should have got all this done sooner. Should have put down a gingham tablecloth and a posy and had the girls scrubbed behind their ears.

Tell her, Wulf. Tell her as soon as she comes in.

He's been fighting with himself. The less he tries to think about Theo, the more his suspicions keep jumping up and down for his attention. And every time he realizes that the younger man has questions to answer, he finds himself flooded with a huge surge of guilt. All day she's been driving around the valley; the shire, trying to play her part in the hunt for Mahee Gamage's tormentor, and all the while, he's been keeping his own counsel about the inscriptions on the little spell he had kept among his meagre possessions.

The door opens. In front of the fire, Tips raises her head.

Sal looks cold and wind-blown, cheeks chapped. She's wet almost up to the knees of her flared black cords and both boots are rusted with thick mud. When she smiles in greeting, it's automatic – a trained response.

'Sal! Oh God, we've already eaten . . . I said we should wait, but Nola was rummaging in the cupboards and acting like she was about to die so we just sort of had to go for it, and . . .'

Hagman enjoys watching the warmth flood Sal's features. Watches as Sal wraps her damp arms around the youngest girl, taking care not to jerk her hands lest she lose purchase on Hagman's beard. He gets a whiff of her as she rises: rain, mud, strong coffee.

'You OK Nola?' she asks the older girl. The table is between them, sparing them both the indignity of the awkward hug. 'Made progress, I see. Looks almost immaculate.'

'It looks less like a skip, at least,' says Nola, pleased.

By the fire, Hagman looks a little hurt. 'A skip?'

'Take no notice,' says Lottie, weaving two braids together to form a small hammock beneath his chin. 'I think it's cosy.'

'Did it go OK?' asks Hagman, raising his gaze and letting it settle on Sal as she begins filling the kettle and picking through the crusts that litter the breadboard.

Sal gives a tired shrug. 'Brain's fizzing and tired at the same time. Don't know what I'm doing, if I'm honest.' She taps her forehead. Makes a face. 'Theo didn't get the job, by the way. I was up at the castle. Said it was never going to happen, no matter what he did.'

'That's a shame,' says Nola, hand resting on the stack of papers and books. 'He worked really hard.'

'Something else will come along, I'm sure,' says Sal, and seems disappointed with herself that she can't think of anything more useful than a banal platitude. 'Maybe he could do tours in Hexham or something. Same character. They do them in York and Edinburgh . . .' she tails off, remembering something else.

'You didn't text me,' she says to Hagman. 'Are the Myerses going to open the door to me?'

Hagman keeps his face neutral – a task made more difficult when Lottie begins trying to untangle an uncooperative braid.

'I've been a bit, preoccupied,' he begins, trying to keep it light. 'Thought we might want to have a . . . a chinwag, before anything else . . .'

'You haven't called them?' asks Sal, looking pained. 'Wulf, I told you – Quinn won't just let it slide. She's slapdash in some things, but if she's asked me to do something and I don't do it . . .'

'There are things you should know,' says Hagman, awkwardly. He shoots a pained glance at the girls. 'Shall we have a stroll, maybe? Talk it through . . .'

'You're starting to think he did it,' says Sal, and lowers herself into one of the dining chairs.

'Did what?' asks Nola. 'This thing you're doing – the man who got hit by the car. You're not saying that was Theo, are you? I thought you knew who was driving.'

'Somebody had kept him somewhere, we think,' says Sal, picking her words. 'There's a connection between him and Theo. He was his solicitor. Gave him what might be considered bad advice.'

Nola frowns. She begins rummaging through one of the piles of paper. Finds it between two battered hardbacks. 'No comment isn't always your friend,' reads Nola. 'He printed it out.'

Sal looks suddenly intrigued. 'Is there an author's name?'

Nola shakes her head. 'Some stuff ringed in red pen. Can't be that important if he just left it. Anyway, you're not saying Theo would take some sort of revenge, are you?'

The room falls silent. Both adults, both children, begin to think of Theo Myers. Of his lovingly crafted character. Of the vengeful torturer and executioner, Blindworm – his eerie habitation of the role.

'Will you call them now, please?' asks Sal. 'I only came back because I hadn't heard from you and I wasn't far away.'

'Can't somebody else do it?' asks Lottie, and Hagman is grateful she's asked the question that's nagging at him. 'You've been so busy.'

'Yeah, leave it until the morning,' says Hagman. 'There's casserole. I can put another loaf in . . .'

'Wulf, I've got to go and knock on the door at least – I only held off because it made sense for you to grease the wheels. I mean, they owe you, don't they? All that you're doing for him . . .'

Hagman feels his cheeks flush. Suddenly feels played with. Picked at. Fiddled with. He makes a face. Lottie seems to understand. Steps away from him and lets him rise. He feels dizzy. Feels sick.

'I'm the one balancing the books,' he says, quietly. 'I . . . well, I owe her.'

'Owe whom? Tara? The mum?'

Hagman looks pained. Decides to get it all over with at once. 'I don't want you going there on your own,' he says. 'I think . . . think maybe he's not very well.'

Sal's giving him her full attention now. Is waiting for more.

'They don't . . . they don't think very much of me either, Sal,' he says, trying not to sound self-pitying. 'Or at least, they shouldn't.'

'You're losing me, Wulf.'

He throws another anguished glance at the girls, desperately unsure how much they should be allowed to hear. But they have known violence. Known blood. They've already witnessed how cruel the world can be. Perhaps treating them as adults might be a more respectful act than ushering them away while the adults shout at each other.

'I found something,' says Hagman, and leaves a pause, expecting to hear the voice in his head give him a telling off. Hears nothing. Wonders where she's gone.

Sal turns away from the girls. Hagman starts scratching at his beard and Lottie makes a grab for his wrists. 'No, it looks brilliant!'

'He asked me for a way to . . . to let go of the things that were holding him back. Asked for my help in letting go. Making sure that things can't catch up with him. Most people want to let go of hate or shame or self-loathing . . . I didn't think it could do any harm.'

'And what does Theo want to let go of?' asks Sal, pulling off her glasses and wiping them furiously on her front. He realizes that they're misting up. That her eyes are already prickling. That she knows he's been keeping things from her. Wonders, for a terrible moment, if he shouldn't just tell her all of it. Tell her why he owes the family. And who they owe in return. Wishes to God he'd waited a little longer before he'd put that damn rope around his neck. Wishes he'd dealt with one last job as a police officer. Whether Tara will tell her what she told her ex-community police officer when he was already up on murder charges. She'd told Callum Whitehead as well. And Callum had made the situation go away. He wonders whether Theo knows. Whether Paul ever told him. Whether he killed himself before he was forced to have the conversation. Whether he killed himself at all . . .

'Wulf, just tell me what you know.'

He tells her. Tells her what happened to the little glass vial. Tells her when it happened. Tells her he'll make it right, he's sorry, he'll make it right . . .

As she glares through him, as she bangs past him and out the door and into the rain, he keeps his face pointed at the floor. Doesn't raise it again until the cold, blustery air cools his burning cheeks.

Fucked that up, lad.

Breathes: 'Aye.'

TWENTY-EIGHT

Quinn can see herself in the mirror above the little dressing table. Can see the smudges of darkness beneath her eyes, the pores across her nose; in the deep lines carved down to the red batwings of her mouth. Can see herself getting smaller. Older. Less. Can feel her stomach acid bubbling like lava; grit on her skin, in her hair, beneath her nails.

'There's nothing here, Magda. It's wishful thinking. Pure speculation.'

Quinn locks eyes with her own reflection. Mouths insults. Takes another swig of the Corona that she's permitting herself to swig straight from the bottle. She found it in Constance Andrysiak's fridge within five minutes of breaking in.

'Nothing there?'

The hard-faced woman on the other side of the line gives a sigh that seems to start at her toes. 'It's been a hard few months, Magda. And goodness knows we're pleased to have you. Any protégée of good old Callum's; well, we're all grateful he's taken an interest. Obviously it's my honour to be able to keep him in the loop and well, show my gratitude for all he did, but . . . he's deep into retirement, Magda. And his heyday was a long time ago. My fear is that you're hitching your wagon to the wrong horse. This fanciful theory you've cooked up – it isn't even worth taking forward to the CPS. You know that. You must know that.'

Quinn doesn't reply. She hasn't got anything to say. Detective Superintendent Emma James is sounding increasingly exasperated: sounding as though she's having to use a lot of self-control to conduct herself with something close to decorum. Sounds like a frazzled mum on the sixth week of the summer holidays. There's going to be trouble before the day is out. And she isn't asking much. She wants to be briefed properly. Wants a full breakdown of the first thirty-six hours of the investigation. Wants a cost–benefit analysis of Quinn's decision to proceed as if the victim were already dead. Wants to know whether Mahee Gamage is ever going to add his name to this year's murder stats. Whether welfare checks have been made on other ex-members of staff at Gamage's old legal practice. Wants her to do nothing until they've spoken with the legal department about the potentially catastrophic fallout of talking to Theo Myers.

'There'll be questions, Magda. It will pay to have answers.'

'He can't speak,' says Quinn, drowsily. She shakes her head and watches her dark hair shimmer. She thinks of Sal. Of Lewis. Closes her eyes and rests her head on the soft, silver-grey velour of the headboard. Feels lighter than air.

'We can find a way around that. One way or another he's going to tell us what happened to him. And there's a part of me that is deathly frightened that he's going to say he fell down a mineshaft and we've pressed the nuclear button on something that could have been nowt more than a funny pub story. But on the off chance he's a victim of a very serious crime, the information he gives us will be used to make a proper arrest plan. To build the intelligence we need . . .'

'To alert him to the fact that we're on to him, you mean. Let him slip through the net.'

Quinn grinds her teeth as James sighs, theatrically, into the phone. 'Magda, do you know how close we came to having to pay this kid millions? He didn't do it. It was a mistake. You don't go and arrest somebody who's just been declared innocent; somebody who's had their life ripped away from them. You don't go after that poor sod without a lot of evidence. And what have you got?'

Quinn readjusts herself. Reaches under her damp coat for her notebook. Leafs through, damply, to the most recent page of jottings.

'Didier Mabuse,' says Quinn, holding her own gaze. 'Last seen four months ago. Last social media activity four months ago. Last text messages sent four months ago . . .'

'You've requested phone records?'

'Phone died not far off Kielder Water – little place called Chipchase Castle. Less than an hour from where Mahee was found.'

'Hang on, let me mark this down . . .'

'Constance Andrysiak,' she says, smoothly. 'She's signed to Chester Sylvester Talents. Spends months of the year away on cruise ships and gigging. Decent voice. Very Joan Armatrading, according to Chester.'

'She hasn't been reported missing,' begins James.

'No, but that's because she's got a pretty bloody perfect life. Last week of February she got back from a seventeen-day tour singing aboard the SS *Lagertha* in the Norwegian fjords. Two shows a day. Was due to come home for a recharge then get back in touch with Chester for her next dates. I've spoken with him. He's still waiting.'

'And where's home for Constance?'

'Norton,' replies Quinn. 'Not far from Middlesbrough. Good old way from Kielder.'

There's another pause as James digests it. 'The samples under the nails?'

'We don't have a sample of Constance's DNA, but we could source one, I'm sure.' As she speaks, Quinn lets her eyes roam across the chaos of the madly patterned carpet. Sees glitzy dresses and abandoned espadrilles; make-up brushes and dejected-looking wigs; empty junk-food wrappers; hairbrushes taffled up with platinum-blonde twists.

'Still not enough,' says James, chewing on her lip. 'Not nearly. Mahee will give us chapter and verse once he's well enough. If he points the finger at Theo then we can make a move, provided everything is above board. But with a case as potentially high-profile as this, well . . .'

'He's running to Wulfric Hagman,' says Quinn, and the room seems to blur and tilt, a strange zapping sensation in the meat of her brain. 'If Hagman helped him . . .'

'No,' says James, sternly, as if Quinn is a bad dog. 'No, no more of that, Magda. You don't think it would look a little suspect if the two men who embarrassed the police and lost years of their lives through our incompetence . . . if they suddenly became prime suspects in an attempted murder.'

'Murder,' says Quinn, coolly. 'You've seen what was in his stomach. She's dead.'

'She's not even a missing person!'

Quinn looks around her. Makes herself a little comfier on Constance's bed. She doesn't doubt she's done the right thing, albeit within the parameters she sets herself. She doesn't just want to nail a killer – she wants to do so with such panache that nobody will ever think of her as the fuck-up who became obsessed with Wulfric Hagman and Lewis Beecher, and lost out on both.

'What's this about you utilizing one of the collision investigators as your personal bagman?' asks James, and Quinn is sure she can hear somebody else relaying instructions at the far end of the phone. 'Salome Delaney?' There's a pause. 'Jesus, that's Lewis's ex, isn't it? The one who's raising his kids while he puts himself back together. Elsie's been texting all day but I've had no chance to . . . Jesus, Quinn!'

'They're not together,' spits Quinn. She squeezes her hands together. Holds the Corona bottle and grips until her knuckles are white. 'I needed expert knowledge. And she had a bond with Mr Gamage.'

'You mean you saw a chance to fuck her around and have some fun.'

Quinn watches herself in the mirror. One cheek starts to tic: a muscle spasm high up beside her eye. It seems to pull at the corner of her mouth. She can taste her own sour emptiness, the acid pile of suppressed hunger. She would quite like to stay here, in this little flat, with its mirrors and sparkle and chocolate-brown cushions, its imitation sheepskin rug. Would like to flick on the wall-mounted TV and snuggle down in Constance's paisley pyjamas. She hasn't got a sense of her yet. The bedroom is decorated like a tastefully bland hotel room: William Morris fabrics on the drapes and upholstery; pale tartan carpet and chipboard furniture clothes in real-wood veneers. None of it sits correctly with the zanily scattered luggage and the exotic, sequinned dresses. Quinn knows that for the past three and a half years, Constance has had her name down as tenant on the electoral register. If Quinn had done things properly, she'd have uniforms knocking on doors, asking questions, going through the bins and the paperwork, sifting for anything linking her to Mahee Gamage and Theo Myers. She's no time for that now. If she doesn't get Theo into an interview room soon, she's going to miss out on the biggest opportunity of her career. She can put things right. She can make it all worthwhile. She can win.

'And this Mabuse bloke . . . you believe he's been taken by Theo as well, do you? All part of the big revenge plot?'

Quinn drains her bottle of lager. Makes sure James hears her glug.

'Mabuse hasn't posted anything on social media since the sixteenth of January. Want to know what that was?' Quinn watches her lip curl in the mirror. Watches her face twist. 'One word: Justice.'

'Justice regarding what?'

Quinn holds her phone in front of her and navigates to the Facebook page belonging to the Tunisian waiter. 'Regarding the headlines about Theo losing out on his bid for compensation.'

'The European thing?'

Quinn readjusts herself. Rests her head upon the soft headboard of Constance's cold, unmade bed again. 'He did this. And if he didn't, he's got nothing to worry about. He'd have legal counsel.'

'Just like before,' mutters James.

'Well, he might give it the old no-comment again, he might not. He might confess to having done a very bad thing, in which case we've just righted a very significant wrong, and regained a bit of credibility over his release.'

Quinn hears James thinking. It had seemed much simpler when she and Callum had talked it over. They both understood, instinctively, how to maximize opportunities. Neither would ever ask themselves whether they believed Theo to be guilty. What mattered was how they could make the most of it for personal advancement.

'I can't authorize this, Magda,' says James. 'Not at this stage. Not without a lot, lot more.'

Magda's lips become a thin, white line. She'd hoped it wasn't going to come to this. She reaches into her damp coat and retrieves the small burner phone. Calls a number. Holds the two phones together as if they are kissing.

She hears the conversation, tinny whispers and short, tense pauses. She finds herself smiling, as if she's just watched her dad beat up a playground bully. Listens to the artfulness with which Callum explains to James the way things work. Drops names like bombs. She can't wait to tell him what James said about him. Wonders whether she mightn't like her job.

She lifts the phones apart. Listens to Whitehead.

'Don't let me down, lass,' he says, and she finds herself feeling strange, in her gut, her throat, her pulse points. Realizes that she's suddenly nervous. Thinks, for just a moment, that she might be about to make things so much worse.

'You can trust me,' she says, and wonders how many times she has made a lie of the statement. How long she'll have to hitch her wagon to Whitehead before she can trundle over him and on to the next one.

She realizes she's ended both calls. That she's staring into empty air. Realizes how much she wants to call Lewis. Wants to do the doting wife bit: mop his brow and hold his hand and feed him crumble, or whatever the fuck it is you're supposed to do with somebody who woke up from a coma without any recollection of the burning passion that had been building between them before they were both left for dead in the snow. She'll help him remember. Will even pretend to like kids if it means she doesn't lose him to a simpering little bookworm who looks like they should be working in HMV and coming to work in a Hufflepuff scarf.

Magda slides off the bed. Takes the empty bottle from the table. Looks around. Lifts the mattress. Looks, tentatively, through the bags. Eventually, she finds a suitable pocket. She takes the polythene bag from the pocket of her blouse. Hopes it retains a whisper of her scent, just for the sheer damn decadence of it. Slips Wulfric Hagman's blood-and-grease-dotted chamois leather into the warm, dark space.

Nods, as if in agreement with some unspoken voice.

Closes the door without a backwards glance, phone already at her ear.

'We're arresting Theo Myers,' she says, as the call connects with Cumbria Police control room. 'We've got the OK.'

The words give her an adrenaline rush that makes her skin tingle. She feels like she's been nettled all over; like she's taken too much of something delicious.

Then, on impulse: 'Take Wulfric Hagman too.'

TWENTY-NINE

A body in a bed. Bandages. Sheets stained pink. Liquids pumping in and squirting out: skin like uncooked pork.

Behind his eyes, Mahee Gamage falls . . .

For a moment, he feels the bone-jarring impact afresh. Feels himself smash into something hard; sodden, pinwheeling away to crunch against the bare brick. He feels again the splash of the fetid water – the desperate fight to breathe.

He lives again the horror of coming to in the pitch dark. Feels again his rising panic, the surge of agony at his hip, his back. Tries to stand and slips back into the filth, reaching out a slimed hand and clutching, desperately, at the bare brick.

He bites down on the memory as if to kill it. Sees, before his image turns black, the pale hand reaching out towards his own; the last kiss of the dying moon serving to wash her marble skin in a golden light.

Hears the snuffled voice, at his ear.

'He won't wake up . . . he won't wake up . . .'

And now he is remembering afresh those desperate, terrifying days and nights, of screeching and begging: hate and rage and threats rising from his open mouth like a swarm of flies.

Remembers her, decreasing in increments; becoming less, descending into the terrors of the dark.

Again, he hears her whispering, the voice strangled, rasping. Hears her talking to somebody else; some figure in the dark.

Mahee tries to wake. Tries to pull himself out of this endless, merciless horror. Searches, desperately, for another memory into which he can burrow.

Sees the face, peering down – a sliver of blackened, ruined skin. Thinks of the pictures on cigarette packaging: blackened, cancerous lungs.

Thinks: *you will die here.*

Thinks: *you will die, and nobody will even notice you're gone . . .*

Tastes again the stinking mud upon his lips, his tongue, in his hair. Feels the creatures upon him, scuttling upon his skin, stalking over the sopping strips of fabric he has wrapped around his bleeding wounds. He's smelling himself. Smelling himself rot; his voice bouncing back from the curving walls of the chamber and rising almost to the distant peep-hole far above. He's feeling himself diminish. Feeling his body begin to feast upon itself, digest itself; organs turning as foul as the leaking, reeking lesions in his skin.

And now the girl is lost in her madness, thrashing, kicking, hurling her fragile cones at the brick wall. She's screeching, as some buried danger skewers her calf; some piece of rusted metal rising in a sudden surge of filthy mud and swirling water. She's kicking out at something beneath her, looking up in sudden terror as torrents of blackish water pour down the narrow opening above, splashing into the chamber like slurry from a pipe.

And now he, too, is hurling himself at the brick. He, too, is hearing the mad chattering and skittering as the creatures that have hidden in the shadows begin to slither and slip from the spaces between the stones; their terror tangible as the sudden burst of floodwater begins to spill from above as quickly as it rises from the floor.

Starving, dying, half-made, he is surging again the brickwork that he has probed so many times with his numb fingertips; saturated skin bursting like unpricked sausages with every contact with the rough stone; the crucifixion nails and crumbled timbers; the bones and the skulls and the teeth and . . .

He's following the screeching. Reaching out for her, trying to pull her towards himself through the rippling, screeching tide.

He's feeling again the slime and mulch and bones beneath his feet, reaching out, feeling sleek fur, twitching whiskers at his cheek. Sees it. Sees where they're coming from; the broken curve of wall, barely bigger than a cat-flap.

Behind his eyes, Mahee swallows the endless mouthfuls, retches and gags and fights for a desperate breath of air. Wriggles and writhes and screams in the dark: a maggot burrowing into rotting flesh.

Remembers her voice, rising: a moment of clarity as she thrashes against the rising water, feet barely touching the floor now, rising, rising on a squeaking, biting tide . . .

Sees himself inching deeper into darkness. Pulling himself through packed clay, wet earth; the sudden blessed moment as his hand found the world from which he had been snatched . . .

Sees his desperate, tumbling run across the flooded field, the glance back at the great burned wall of the ruined castle; splashing through boggy puddles and free-flowing streams on legs that buckled and slipped and refused to support his weight.

Again, he fights to keep going. To raise help. To save himself. Save her.

Sees the blinding yellow lights. Feels the brutal impact; the agony in his hip as he's thrown down the glittering tarmac, tumbling in an orgy of shattering bone and flailing limbs; sharp branches, barbed wire, clawing at him, clinging to him, shredding him as he pulls himself desperately on, one arm dragging him into the darkness by his fingertips, and . . .

Mahee Gamage fights his way out. Beats on his own closed eyelids. Begs to be set free.

The monitor at his bedside doesn't change. The doctor at the foot of the bed doesn't look up from the charts.

Upon his lifeless tongue, the name he wants to scream:
Constance!

THIRTY

Sal turns up the volume on the stereo – feels the bass line from some mid-Nineties guitar anthem right in the centre of her chest. She remembers festivals. Gigs at stone circles and cloaked in forest. Remembers bongos and weed and dancing way past dawn. Wonders where the fuck that girl went. Whether she's still her mother's agent – sabotaging herself, hurting herself, letting herself down. Wonders when she'll fucking learn.

'Prick,' she spits, wrenching the steering wheel and taking the left turn with a spray of muddy gravel. Through the darkness, she eyes the mucky white coats of a dozen sheep, turning away and bolting as Jarod's battered Land Rover bangs and scrapes along the rutted surface of the road. Then, meekly, even in the sanctity of her own skull: *Sorry. That's not fair, Wulf. Not your fault you're softer than I am, and I'm nowt but feathers and slime . . .*

She bangs the steering wheel with the heel of her hand. What had he been thinking? Rummaging at a potential crime scene; destroying evidence, keeping secrets. She can't help but let a picture of his big sad face flash into her head.

She hits the steering wheel again. Glances at the passenger seat where her phone is bouncing around on the soggy, dog-stinking leather. The screen is blue, lit up with a number she can't make out. She knows all the statistics about accidents involving telephone use at the wheel. Can't seem to find it in herself to follow the rules.

'Hello? This is Sal . . .'

'Sycamore Le Gros,' comes the booming voice. 'Apologies for calling so late. Is this a good time?'

Sal can't seem to focus on his words. Can't seem to distinguish between the sounds in her skull and the words in her ear; the spotty, squeaking rain on the glass; the darkness fractured by the splinter-cracks in the windscreen.

'. . . not an ideal time,' says Sal, weakly. 'Might I be able to get back to you.'

'Certainly, certainly,' says Le Gros, sounding relieved. 'Probably a nothing. Beyond ambition lies lack of cognition. Not a bad ditty, that. Might I ask that you make it rather, erm, higher on the list of priorities than . . .'

'I'm losing you,' says Sal, wishing it were true.

'Phoned the old boy, too. Wulf. Must have an old number for the fellow. Rather . . . rather pressing, as it were.'

Sal turns the music down. 'What's happened?'

'I think, perhaps – I could use some advice, I think. Statutes of limitations, and such. My solicitor hasn't been very helpful. Then, he's removed from it, isn't he? Not living it every bastard day for thirty years . . .'

Sal pulls over. Gives him her full attention. 'I want to help, Mr Le Gros. I'm rarely successful, but I do try.'

'Dashed grateful to Callum, you know. Bastard of a man, but one always rather thought of him as one's *own* bastard, if you see what I mean. But, he's had his pound of flesh and more, don't you think? I can't keep . . . I'm too old to keep doing this. I mean, I'd rather it just came out.'

Sal doesn't reply. Doesn't want to tip him the wrong way as he stalks along the rope-wire of his conscience.

'Straight as a die, was Wulf. He'd have done it properly, I think. Luckiest night of my life when he put that rope around his neck.' She hears him take a sip of whatever liquid courage he is imbibing straight from the bottle. 'God, that's a vile thing to say. Meant Callum could handle it, if nothing else. But maybe if he hadn't . . .' he sighs. Claps his hands and then curses as liquid sloshes. 'I've wasted enough of your time,' he says, with a loud sniff. Tries to cough some bluster back into his voice. 'Wasn't a bad stick, Daddy. Different times, weren't they?'

'Your father, Mr Le Gros?'

She hears him give a low groan as he descends back into whatever private torment prompted him to make a partial attempt at the right thing.

Before he rings off, Sal says a name. 'Whitehead,' she says, cautiously. 'What does he have on you?'

Le Gros doesn't answer. Just breathes, transfixed by whatever memory is playing in his mind. 'If I could . . . if it were possible. But he's always known how to . . . how to make people do what he wants. Makes you feel like he's doing you a favour even as he's got his knee in your balls. Or in my case, enough shame to bury me.'

'Mr Le Gros, we can talk things through. You and me. Wulf, even, if . . .'

He ends the call.

Sal sits for a time trying to work things out. Thinks of the people who have mentioned Le Gros's father. Rum old boy, apparently. Ever-present at the raucous parties at Lumley Castle in the Seventies. There'd been a reunion hadn't there? Mid-Nineties. Just when it was all turning to shit for her and Wulf. Just before Mam died and Hagman put the noose around his throat.

She squints through the darkness to the little gap in the fence where the gritty road disappears between two old, crumbling pillars. Hagman had described it perfectly for her, all hangdog and maudlin. He hadn't wanted to think the worst. He didn't want to judge Theo the way everybody else did, not with their shared histories. He still can't be sure what he thinks, but he knows that Sal can do things right.

'She'll find a way to tie you to it,' mutters Sal, warning herself, lurching as she turns the battered car on to the track. 'This is what she's wanted. She'll tie you to it . . .'

She turns the music down, aware of an irregular squeaking sound beyond the song. Winds the window down and feels the cold, gritty rain upon her face, on her glasses, flapping at the collar of her too-big overshirt and parka. She hears birdsong so loud and bright and full it feels unnatural, uncanny. She's lived in the countryside most of her life and never heard such an ever-building crescendo of song.

Sal thinks of Hitchcock. Of talons on her face, beaks at her eyes, her neck. She cranks the window closed. Forces the protesting Land Rover up the track, sloping away in parallel with a low farm wall strung with barbed wire.

The doubts start as soon as the understatedly grand barn conversion comes into view. It's a warm, soft space. Sal knows what she's bringing with her. Knows what shit she's about to spray into the lives they've been trying so damn hard to rebuild.

'What are you doing?' she mutters. 'Tell Quinn. Take your punishment. Tell her to fuck off if you have to. Tell the whole lot of them to fuck off. You can . . . you can go back to a bookshop. You could write a book, for fuck's sake.' She realizes her eyes are crying, disobeying a direct instruction. Shakes the drops off, smearing a hand across her nose. 'This isn't how it's done, Sal. Isn't how it's done . . .'

Security lights flash into life. She raises a hand to shield her eyes. Squints through the rash white light and sees two figures stalking through the garish brightness. Sees a small figure. Slight. Overcoat and pyjamas, flat cap and wellies; something solid in their right hand.

The second figure stalks ahead, one foot dragging behind, the limb turning inward.

Light reflects off a leather jerkin.

'Mask,' she breathes. 'That's a mask . . .'

She fumbles for the keys. She wants to stamp on the accelerator. Her hand slips as she reaches for the handle. Manages to click it open at the second attempt.

'Sal Delaney, Cumbria Police,' she says, her voice sounding weak. She says it again, louder this time, as if to reassure herself . . .

The figure in the leather mask steps forward. Up close, she realizes how extravagant his costume is: the craftsmanship that has gone into the assemblage of so many swatches of mismatched leather; the stitches dainty, precise.

'Mantle?' asks Sal, needing to say the word, unable to help herself, staring at the leathery material that is wrapped around his head and part of his face. 'Is that the word?'

'No. that's more of a cloak,' comes the voice behind the mask. It remains static: a collage of different skin tones woven into something like a balaclava. There are no eye-holes: just a Rorschach ink-blot that changes form with every minute alteration of the light.

'You gave me a start. I didn't . . . didn't want to turn up uninvited, but . . .'

'You're Wulf's friend,' comes a voice. It's soft, local; cultured even. She peers at the second figure. Glasses, neat beard. There's nothing to him, really, save the lethal-looking club he holds in his right hand.

'What were you going to do with that?' asks Sal. 'Not really the way we encourage people to deal with intruders.'

'You're right,' he says, and as he steps into the light she recognizes the drawn, gaunt face. Sees Alec Devlin transformed into a fragile, fading old man. 'Worth a mint, this,' he says, staring at the metal-headed object. 'German. Mace, is the word you're looking for,' he mumbles, dropping it as if it were hot. 'Lord, I'm shaking like a leaf. We've had . . . had one or two silly sausages popping by to make a nuisance of themselves. Some funny business. Some . . . shenanigans. I don't know what we were thinking.'

'I was doing it for Mam,' comes a petulant voice from behind the mask. It's so incongruous that Sal finds an absurd desire to laugh.

'You had an interview,' says Sal, rubbing her temples. 'How did it go?'

'Call back tomorrow,' says Theo, from under the mask. 'They have some things to mull over.'

A thin, reedy voice warbles across from the bulk of the house. 'He didn't do it, y'know. Never did none of it. Weren't even there. You're picking on an innocent man – again.'

Theo takes a fistful of his face and pulls it off, hair plastered across his sweaty face.

'It's the police, Mam. Wulf's friend. She's all right.'

'None of them are all right, Theo. Not a one of them!'

Sal reaches back inside the car. Turns off the engine. Tries to get a hold of herself. To tell the lie she came here to.

'Theo, look . . . there's been some developments. With your case. I'm a Family Liaison Officer and, well, after all you've been through it seemed like the least we could do to ensure you have our support in what's sure to be a difficult time.'

Theo makes a face. Looks at Alec. 'Sorry Sal, I didn't get much of that. Alec? Did you get that?'

Sal has to raise her voice as the birdsong rises from the dark canopy of the trees.

'Mahee Gamage,' she says, quietly.

Theo looks at her expectantly. Looks at his stepfather and back again. 'Aye? None of my favourite people but I'm trying to move on, y'know? Trying to make up for all the lost time. Look forward, not back.'

Alec moves to his side. Takes him gently by the arm. Looks at Sal through dirty bi-focals, spotted with rain.

'What's happening, Ms Delaney? I can't imagine that any dealings with Theo would be conducted at this hour, this way. And not by an officer of . . .' he tails off, looking pained. 'That sounded awful. I'm so dreadfully sorry. It's just . . . you can imagine.'

'Have they said who did it?' asks Theo.

The security lights flicker off. Flash back on a moment later. Mrs Myers-Devlin is walking across the grass. She's stick-thin; her bare legs not much more than knotted rope, bone-white between the hem of her well-worn dressing gown, and her slouchy slippered feet. She holds herself as if in pain, one hand at her belly.

Sal wants to turn and run. Doesn't want to bring any more pain into this quiet, pretty place. But Theo is a viable suspect. Moreover, he's a headline-grabber. And Magda Quinn will take whatever pieces she finds and string them on a necklace until the picture looks right. Theo might have done something terrible. Might have hurt people. If he has, he deserves to at least be dealt with as a human being rather than the symbol that Quinn will try and turn him into. The damage she could do – one exonerated prisoner brought back to prison and everything the Juris Project is trying to do will be left redundant. She could restore faith to a system that Sal knows to be broken.

Sal realizes she's staring at Theo too hard; that the situation is becoming awkward. She wants to ask him so many questions. About the bottle at his camp. The names on the leaves. His dad. Wants to ask him why the hell he's so obsessed with a medieval torturer. When he decided to take a horribly appropriate revenge.

'You'll come in, will you?'

She realizes that Devlin has crossed to his wife's side. He has an arm around her, all but holding her up. Sal tries to find the two passionate campaigners from the press clippings and sees only their echoes. Something has drained them. Slurped them of their life.

Thinks: *they know* . . .

'Oh,' begins Sal, and realizes she doesn't really want to be here. That the girls are at home. That she has apologies to make.

Devlin leans down to his wife. Whispers something in her ear. Sal watches her stiffen. Twist her pale, wrinkled face into a knife-slash smile.

'Would rather get it over with,' she says, breathless. 'At least it's a friendly face.'

Sal isn't sure what to say. How to respond. She was just meant to arrange an interview. Can't help wondering whether Theo will go no comment.

'Only if you've got a moment,' says Sal, placing her hand in her pocket and fumbling with her phone. 'That's OK, is it Theo? I'd love to pick your brains about a couple of things.' She gives Devlin a glance. 'Yours too, as it goes.' She pushes on, making her say the name before she loses her nerve. 'Blindworm. Redburn.'

'Redburn?' asks Theo, gripping the mask tight. 'That's where Dad, well . . . but Blindworm. I've been living him, I swear it. Never prepared so hard for a role in my life. I can show you, if you like.'

Sal looks at the boy's happy, puppyish features.
Thinks: *I don't know what you are.*

'You've heard about my little history project then?' asks Devlin, quietly. 'Very much of a family fascination. Rather hope I get to finish it.' He squeezes his wife. Coughs, frilly, grimacing as a pain stabs at him. 'Anyway – we're getting wet. Would rather get the old bones somewhere dry.'

'We've got so many artefacts,' says Theo, awe in his voice. 'Me and Dad found a piece of bone there, when I was small. We're sure it was a knee joint, calcified around an iron nail. Pride of place in the collection. Alec, well . . .' he slows down. Stops. 'Mahee,' he says, as if remembering why she's here. 'I want to know everything.'

Sal makes sure she looks away first. Curses herself, as she hears herself speak.

'Sure, let's go in.'

In her head: *you silly, silly girl.*

THIRTY-ONE

'She seemed really cross, Uncle Wulf.'
'I know.'
'I mean, Sal doesn't get cross. Not really. Not like Mam used to.'
'She thinks I've been keeping secrets from her.'
'And have you?'
'I don't know.'

Lottie gives him a look, eyebrows raised, one eye enlarged. She has her hands on her hips for extra emphasis. The light of the low, flickering fire projects her shadow on to the barn wall; hair rippling like snakes. Lottie herself, up close, is no less daunting. She's wearing a coat over dressing gown and pyjamas and her feet are stuffed into huge wellington boots – the tops so high they look more like fishing waders.

'It's my friend,' says Hagman, putting his foot on a length of dried timber and wrenching off one of the branches. He snaps it over his knee. Snaps it again. Tosses them into the smouldering pit. 'Theo.'

'The actor?' asks Lottie, her demeanour changing. She smiles, remembering the handsome, funny, silly man. 'Is he OK? Have you done something bad to him?'

Hagman straightens his back. God, he's feeling his age. He's beginning to feel uncomfortable in his own skin again, his senses over-stimulated by every infinitesimal contact. The rain has brought midges, brought mud and slurry, and he keeps feeling tiny creatures moving upon his skin. Each trickle of sweat makes him shudder. He's spoken to a succession of therapists about the times when his skin feels . . . what was the word . . . ?

Wulf, lad, go on spit it out . . .

. . . feels scratchy. Feels wrong. Scribbly, perhaps.

And when did you feel that, eh? What were you doing when the world was all scribbly-scratchy, Wulf, lad?

He screws up his eyes until the voice fades. Wonders, again, whether mad people know they're mad. Whether he mightn't in fact be the voice in somebody else's head.

'He's going to have to answer some questions about somebody he knew,' says Hagman, selecting a good-sized hunk of chopped wood and standing it on the old stump. 'Somebody Theo doesn't like very much . . . he's been hurt. A lot.'

'And the rozzers think Theo did it, 'cause he's got form, yeah?'

Hagman grins behind his moustache, enjoying the note-perfect Cockney geezer persona she is currently inhabiting. 'Something like that. And he hasn't got form. There's no blemish on his character. He's innocent.'

'Like you,' says Lottie, arms out, turning a slow pirouette and humming a tune from her mum's jewellery box. 'You were in prison for like, ever, and you didn't do it.'

Hagman feels a stiffness slide icily into his joints, stiffening his shoulders, elbows, knees. Feels himself tensing in every tendon. 'It's complicated,' he says, tiredly. 'I'm free. But I was never found not guilty. I'm a convicted . . .' he stops himself, aware he shouldn't be talking with Sal's girls about anything sensitive. Sal had said so. It had been one of the last things she said as she slammed out of the house, colour and tears on her cheeks.

Ballsed that one up, didn't you, lad? Playing Happy Families and you're sitting on evidence . . .

Hagman brings the axe down, cleaving the wood perfectly in two.

'Cleft in twain,' he mutters, the way he often does when words pop into his head and demand to be allowed out of his mouth. He sometimes gets stuck on little phrases, little noises. He wonders whether that's why he and Lottie get along.

'It's so dark,' says Lottie, looking up at the inky sky. Hagman follows her gaze. Sees battles raging in the sky: grey-coated legions thundering their hells down upon one another; veiled in grey cannon fire; flashes of sabre steel. He swallows drily. Tastes his own blood. Hears his mobile ringing.

'That'll be Sal,' says Lottie, chewing on her lower lip. 'I'll get Nola. She promised. She said.'

Hagman's grateful for the respite. He rubs a dirty hand over his sweaty face and gags at the feeling of grit and bark rasping against his skin. Taps at his chest with his index finger.

Missing Dagmara, aren't you, lad? Missing her medicines and the way she could soothe your busy brain. Missing the murdering bitch who set you up and left you to fucking rot . . .

He can't see the screen without his reading glasses. Answers with a neutral hello.

'Wulf? Oh I'm so pleased you picked up, thank you – I know many wouldn't, given the situation, but look, big apols, yeah? Like, proper oodles of apols with a great big I'm-sorry ribbon on top, yeah?'

Hagman recognizes the voice of Jacqueline Cho, the freelance public relations officer brought in by the Juris Project to manage media enquiries and ensure its cases remain in the public mind and gaze. She's good, usually, even if Hagman suspects her girls' school accent and over-enunciated vowels are an affectation.

'Jacqueline, yes, hello.' He lets out a breath. Sits down on a log, the gathering fire wafting smoke into his face. He screws up his eyes. Hopes to God things aren't any worse.

'You'll have seen, of course. I mean, I know you're like, literally in the back of beyond, but, Theo will have rung, yes? I mean, I'd be livid. Livid.'

Hagman rummages in the pockets of his padded shirt. He's got some bay leaves somewhere. Marker pens, too. Lottie's demanding they try out 'something witchy' and he can't see the harm in casting a basic protection spell and perhaps letting go of some bad habits or excess guilt. He checks the back of his work trousers: all zips and pockets and patches designed to stop him sawing his leg off while coppicing. He always wears them to make a fire, safer in the knowledge that – in the event of a sudden flare – only his top half will be flammable.

'I don't know what's happening, Jacqueline. Last I heard, somebody suggested it was Mahee Gamage who'd been hurt on the road, but . . .'

'Livid,' repeats Jacqueline, before pausing to suck on a vape. 'Alec read the riot act, natch. I don't think I've ever had such a telling off in such a lovely way. Patience of a saint, that man.'

'Jacqueline, I'm sorry, but I don't know what you're talking about.'

'The posting, Wulf. On X. Twitter, if you're a geriatric. Silly, really, but it's been taken down and I don't think there should be too much of a rumpus.'

Hagman glances up to see Lottie dragging Nola through the treeline and into the little clearing. Against the dark slashes of the slim trunks, she's barely detectable in her black hoodie and camouflage trousers.

'What did you, erm . . . X?'

'Oh God, that's precious, Wulf, really. What did you X? Well, we X'd or reposted a line from a spokesman, natch – furious that police were again attempting to ruin the life of an innocent man, cooking up some spurious case about injuries suffered by somebody with whom he had an apparent vendetta . . .'

'That's not what's happening,' says Hagman, bringing the axe down in the stump. 'Jacqueline, you know about the other names, don't you? The other two people he blames . . .'

'In the loop, Wulf, clued up and clued in.' She sounds like a radio DJ as she says it.

'That'll be why they're not calling back,' she adds, distantly. 'The suits. Lots of activity in the cube.'

'The cube?'

'The meeting room where they go when they want to feel like they're in a legal drama, you know.'

Hagman feels Lottie poke him in the ribs. Looks again for the bay leaves. Tries the back pocket of his trousers. His hands close around a sheaf of paper.

'Good opportunity for Juris, as you can imagine. I mean, why copy me in to the email unless they wanted me to do something with it. Poor Theo, though. Alec called me direct, that's how upset he was. I said the same thing I've said so many times before . . . we have to use every opportunity to make sure people don't forget about the Juris Project; about Theo and people like him . . . Alec said I'd just handed Theo's enemies a loaded gun; they could have ridden this out, and now their own bloody side was weighing in. He did, you know. Really said "bloody".'

Hagman hands the papers to Lottie. Finds his marker pens in his shirt pocket and passes them to the girls. He looks in his pocket for something to wipe his inky fingers on. Can't seem to find the rag he keeps in the back pocket of his work trousers. Wonders if a bird took it from the windowsill when it was drying, then chides himself for thinking like a Disney princess. Uses his shirt front instead. 'Draw,' he instructs, feeling useless, wanting the call to end.

'You took it down, yes?'

'Of course! Alec is a thoroughly good egg. There wouldn't be a Juris Project without him. Least we could do, though I did say that we would have to comment officially when the first journalist starts sniffing, which won't be long now we've rather tipped them the wink.'

'And why are you ringing me, Jacqueline?'

Jacqueline sucks on her vape. She sounds congested as she talks. 'Hoping for an update, as it happens. Jarod. Dagmara. It's all been rather an awkward pause, in terms of what we can and can't say, things being rather stymied with ourselves and Cumbria Police. We know and they know, and nobody quite knows what to do about any of it, but what it means is that an innocent man – that would be you – is still being labelled a killer and people like Callum Whitehead can say such vile, hurtful things unchallenged.'

Hagman flinches at the name. Jacqueline continues, 'The documentary that's just been picked up by Netflix. Produced by Wagtail, who are so good at this kind of thing. I've seen some of the clips, Wulf. He lays it on with a trowel. Everything that Quinn thought she had on you, he's laying it all at your door. They've thrown in a couple of "Hagman maintains his innocence" but it's open season, really. And Whitehead, well, it's like you're the devil himself. I wasn't personally consulted about the decision to buddy you and Theo up, but with hindsight, well . . .'

Hagman swallows. He feels like there are fingers at his throat.

'I'm not writing on this one, it's too good.'

Hagman realizes Nola is talking. There's no adolescent sneer in her voice. She's just sitting by the fire, holding the piece of paper that Hagman had handed her, angling it to better read the script by the light of the fire.

'Oh is Sal there?' asks Jacqueline, a little shrill. 'The girls? Gosh, they must miss Jarod terribly. What have you told them? I mean, that's so much to carry, isn't it . . .?'

Hagman's grateful that the call crackles and cuts off. He tries not to put his hand across his chest, even as he feels his heart pounding against his ribcage like a lunatic trying to break out of a cell.

'Did Theo write this?' asks Nola, looking up, a little smile playing at the corners of her lips. 'He's good, isn't he? Is this not important? I can't draw on it – this bit looks old.'

Hagman gives himself a shake. Rubs his sweat into his beard. Grips for the shard of selenite on its cord about his neck.

'I'll get you something else,' he mutters, trying not to wheeze. He can feel the hard thumbs of a suddenly flaring headache, pushing against his eyes.

'Have you read it? He's really worked hard. Is this all for that job interview?'

Hagman reaches out. Takes the pages from Nola's fingertips. Turns it over. Pushes it away until it's at the full extent of his arms, blurry and red-hued against the rising fire.

When he comes to the end of the second page, his mouth is chalk; pain throbbing in tingling pulses in the muscles at his shoulder blades and neck.

THIRTY-TWO

They keep saying I should write to you, which is stupid, because you're dead. I don't know what I believe outside of that. Maybe you're somewhere else, sitting on a cloud, playing a harp. Maybe you're already a caterpillar crawling along a leaf. Wherever you are, I hope you're happy. I don't know if dead people still suffer with depression. I hope not. You've suffered enough, Dad. And I want you to know that – actually no, Dad, fuck that I can't say it yet. I am angry. I'm so angry I can feel it in my teeth. Every single moment of every single day I'm just this ball of unexploded hate. It fizzes in me. Makes me giddy. If I wasn't an actor, they'd all see it at once – how I'm just this monster wearing a skin-suit; how all I can think about is what's been taken from me, what's been done to me.

That day, Dad, when you told me why you'd always loved me so hard, so much, and you said what you said . . . that one of you had to love me and it may as well be you. It was like a punch, Dad, and I knew you knew as soon as you'd thrown it. I should never have walked out. Shouldn't have got myself so drunk and so hurt and so angry that I didn't know where I'd been or who I'd seen. I shouldn't have gone with the police to the station. Shouldn't have told them why you are so upset. It just spilled out, Dad. I told them about Le Gros and the arrangement and how he'd said he wasn't going to pay any more, and I couldn't stop asking questions, and . . .

I had to stop for a moment. I'm at Redburn. I've got my back to the wall you used to let me climb on. I tried earlier. Got right up to the tree that grows from the old wall. I looked, but I couldn't see where your noose cut into the bark. I feel strangely empty, now I sit here. I don't know what I'm supposed to feel. I don't know why I'm doing this!

Wulf's the man you said he was, Dad. He's kind. Listens to me. Puts up with me. I know he has his secrets and there's things we can't say to each other – not until it's all . . . I don't know, Dad. Will it ever be over?

I'm going to keep trying, I swear. I'll make you proud. Alec has got me a try-out for a role as a tour guide. I'm bringing him to life, Dad. Remember how you used to do the voices. The limp. How you'd tell me the story by torchlight under the covers until Mam came in and started roaring at you.

We're trying our best, Dad. It's . . . hard, I suppose. I think it was easier for her when she wasn't seeing my face every day.

I have to stop, Dad. It's making it worse. I can hear it again – the voice you used to do. Sometimes it seems more real than my own thoughts . . .

I can feel you here, I think. Just a trace of you. On the windy days, sometimes I pretend that you're swirling around me, wrapping me up in one of your hugs.

Don't hate Alec. Please. He was there when you left. For me too.

I wish things were different.

I'm going to try something, I think. Something that might make it all . . . bearable, I suppose.

Do you think it's still there? The place we found? You holding me by the ankle, swinging me out against those narrow walls, down to the rock and the mud and the skulls and the rats and . . .

I love you, Dad.

I'm so sorry.

'It's made up, isn't it? Just made up.'

Hagman looks at Nola, reading over his shoulder. Stares into her big, open eyes. Watches the flames reflect and dance. He slides the pieces around in his mind. Sees only one picture.

Feels the question flow out of her and into him. One word: Sal.

'Come on,' he says, his voice catching. 'Let's see if we can get the old Landy started, eh? Maybe take a drive?'

'I thought we were doing the spell?' asks Lottie, aghast. 'And that Landy's got squirrels living in it. It's just rust! And the spell, Uncle Wulf, please . . .'

'Later,' says Hagman, a moment before Nola does. 'We'll get marshmallows while we're out, eh? Just a quick run out while the fire builds.'

Nola takes her sister's hands. Pulls her towards the trees.

Hagman waits until they've both got their backs turned.

Bends down.

Picks up the axe.

THIRTY-THREE

Sal uses the light from her mobile phone to illuminate the path which cuts across the lawn to the low stone circle at the centre of the little courtyard. Spies an old wheelbarrow; trees in ceramic pots; a great black lacquered cartwheel hammered into the brickwork beneath the apex of the roof.

'That was the well,' says Theo, at her side, nodding towards the circular structure. 'Dad filled that in when he was a kid.'

Sal glances at the pale, handsome face that appears at her side. Stumbles slightly as she catches her foot. Feels him catch her, nimbly, by the elbow and forearm, taking her weight as if she were a fragile grandparent. She feels the strength in him; the wiry muscles beneath the cloak.

'Do I make tea?'

Sal snaps a glance at the figure in the doorway. Sees nothing of the woman she knows from the newspaper articles and TV bulletins. She seems depleted. Drained. Seems like a straw has been punched into her marrow and her essence slurped away in great hungry gulps.

'Tea would be lovely, Tara. Thank you.'

Sal lets Alec hold the door for her. Ducks under his arm and into a high-ceilinged room: deep red walls and timber floors; sagging L-shaped sofa crowded with cushions and blankets. She checks her exits, instinctively. Hears the door click closed and is surprised to feel a little trill of fear in her chest, her gut.

'We've been expecting it, of course,' says Alec, crossing to the fireplace, where a small flame dances in the dark hearth. Its lights pick out the ornaments on the thick, uneven walls – cutlasses and pikes; shields and swords – crammed into the space between faded tapestries and dark, hard-to-discern portraits of men with curly hair and frilly collars. Sal doesn't like the energy in the room. There's a hollowness to this place; an air that feels strangely soporific, lifeless.

'Expecting it?' asks Sal, as she hears the clink of crockery coming from the room beyond the dark wooden door.

'You're not breaking any news to us – that's rather the thing of it.'

Theo throws himself down on the mound of cushions and rugs.

Puts his feet on the little cartwheel-shaped coffee table and earns a reproachful look from his stepfather. He puts his feet down on the floor. Runs his hands through his hair, pulling down his hood. Sal watches him pull something from one of the folds of the robe. Watches as he twists the crinkled leather mask in his hands.

'You knew I was coming?' asks Sal, unsure whether to sit.

'Juris Project, God love them. Tweeted to say how appalled they were that Theo is once again a suspect in a high-profile case.'

Alec stares into the fire as he speaks. He doesn't raise his voice. Keeps his composure.

'Did Cumbria Police put out a statement?' asks Sal. She feels her guts churn.

'Not a word,' says Alec. He selects an implement from the brass bucket by the fire. It's a short, blunt poker, set into the handle of an old cutlass. Alec squats down, painfully. Pokes at the flames.

'These things do tend to get out,' says Sal, wincing at how hapless she makes the police sound. 'High-profile cases, I mean. There'll always be an interest.'

'We were just getting somewhere,' mutters Theo, from the sofa. He's unfolded the mask and is staring into its sightless eyeholes as if reading a prayer book.

'Getting somewhere,' says Alec.

'Mum,' shrugs Theo. 'You saw the state of her. Jesus, she was starting to get . . . if not better, then maybe something . . . something that she could have sustained. And now this, dredging it all back up again . . .'

Sal crosses to the wall opposite the fireplace. She suddenly doesn't want to be here. Doesn't feel safe. She knows how the pressure builds before violence, can read the nearness of danger like clouds. She knows she's caught up in something much bigger than herself. Wishes to God she were somebody else – that she could let go of her own pathetic self and give herself over to Jarod. He'd know how to behave. Would know what to say.

'It would be best if you arranged to voluntarily hand yourself in at a specific police station,' says Sal, sweat prickling her skin. She feels wrong. Feels like there's a high buzzing nearby; a wrongness to the warm, joyless air. 'Or you could come with me now. We can make sure you're looked after.'

'We?' asks Theo, tearing his eyes away from the mask. 'You're on your own. There's just you.'

Sal glances up as Tara enters the living room, holding a single mug of tea, filled so high that it slops over the lip with each little step. She walks as if her bones have come apart inside her skin, each step slow and painful. Sal hurries towards her, reaching out for the mug. Tara raises her head. Sal manages to catch her gaze as she looks up. Stares into blue eyes that shimmer with a reservoir of tears. Sal tries to see some sign of the impassioned, vivacious woman who had waved banners and placards in the faces of prosecutors, judges, home secretaries and monarchs; who kept fighting until the fight was won. Sees only her ghost, dusty and fragile in her supermarket pyjamas and fluffy robe.

'Always knew they'd come back for him,' mutters Tara, and silent tears spill on to the maze of capillaries and wrinkles at her cheeks. She makes no attempt to wipe them away. Since the night her son was arrested, her face has bathed in salt water more often than not.

'We're not coming back for him,' says Sal, as gently as she can, sipping from the mug and scalding her top lip. 'There are some questions to be answered and I thought perhaps Theo might feel more comfortable answering them with somebody he knows.'

'He doesn't know you,' says Alec, standing up with an audible crack of his knees. 'He's Wulf's friend.'

'Which is why I'm here,' says Sal, looking from one face to another in turn. She suddenly doesn't quite know what she believes. What she came here for. What she expects to happen next. 'I've seen what happened to Wulf. I've seen the lengths some people go to to make a conviction stick. I know what happens when you try and make the old guard look silly. I want to avoid all that, and if you come with me now, we can make sure that everything is done properly and above board.'

Alec raises the poker and stares at its glowing tip. It reflects back in the thick glass of his lenses. 'That's a useful thing to know, Ms Delaney,' says Alec, with a faint smile. 'You distrust your colleagues so much that you're willing to put your neck on the line just to ensure things are kept whiter than white? That's quite telling, really. It might be the sort of leverage that Theo can use to his advantage.'

Sal raises the mug again. Realizes that she's shaking a little. She gives Theo another imploring look.

'Mahee Gamage,' she says, not letting herself look away. 'He's in a very bad way. He'd been kept somewhere – almost certainly against his will. Hurt himself very badly trying to get free. If he recovers, he can tell us what happened. If he doesn't, there are going to be lots of questions, Theo. For all of you. Whatever happens, you're going to have to explain your movements.'

'He could always just say "no comment",' says Tara, breathily. She's sat herself down next to her son and is gazing at him as if trying to soak up every last detail. 'That was what that pervert . . . that stupid, nasty, hopeless pervert . . .!'

'Steady, Tara,' says Alec, gently. 'It's all going to be OK.'

'Pervert?' asks Sal.

Tara's face twists in disgust. 'You know what he got struck off for, don't you? Watching pornography at work. Pornography! As if it was a surprise to anybody. Theo saw what he had in his suitcase the first night he was saddled with him as duty solicitor. Didn't even have the grace to look embarrassed! Wouldn't surprise me if some dirty so-and-so had got carried away. You never know what some people get up to, do you? I mean, live and let live, but he'd half the reason. He ended up in the hole he was in. He could have explained it all away that very first night. He had an alibi and his phone showed him somewhere else at the time that poor man was killed, but Mahee didn't want to hear any of that – told him not to answer a single question, so that's what the poor lad did. Could have all gone away, that's what I think, and these two don't disagree, do you? So many years, all because that useless bastard gave my boy bad advice. That was what nigh-on did it for Paul.'

First husband, thinks Sal. *Theo's biological father. He'd taken his own life while Theo was inside . . .*

Something rises up inside Sal – an ugly, cancerous thought; a slimed tuber climbing up from her worst imaginings.

'As far as we're concerned, all those sods who let Theo down – they may as well have put the rope around his neck themselves.'

Theo looks up, eyes flashing with hurt. He cocks his head, hearing the sound from outside. 'Sirens,' he says, under his breath. He clutches his mother's hands in his own. Presses his forehead to hers, noses almost touching. 'It'll be OK, Mam. I did nothing. I did nothing.'

'You didn't do anything last time,' says Tara, voice catching. 'You've always been a good boy.' She wraps herself in her dressing gown. Pats her pocket and seems to find reassurance in whatever she feels within. 'Been hard, hasn't it? All of us cooped up together, living in each other's pockets. Taken some re-adjusting, hasn't it?'

'We're getting there,' says Theo, looking at her with eyes that seem starved of something they crave. Sees him all but yearning to be patted on the head and told he's a good boy. 'Sometimes I think it would be easiest if we all just pressed reset. Forgot the past. Started again.'

'We can only do that if you tell us the whole truth, Theo,' says Sal, kindly. She pushes her luck. 'Is there anybody else down there?' she asks, reaching out to put a hand on his arm. 'I understand. What they took from you. What you lost. But Theo, this isn't the way . . .'

'I can't let this happen,' states Alec, audibly making up his mind. He hasn't moved from the fireplace. He's pushing the metal-headed mace into the fire.

'Do something, Alec,' says Tara, desperately. 'He can't do more time. The things they did. The things he endured . . .'

Sal hears the sirens drawing closer. She pulls her phone from her pocket, hoping for a signal – a message from the world beyond this red room, its walls inching closer with each passing moment. She doesn't know what to do.

'Theodore Myers,' she hears herself begin, 'I am arresting you on suspicion of the abduction of Mahee Gamage . . .'

Theo looks up at her from the sofa. There's something like heartbreak in his eyes.

'We can still make this right,' says Alec, slowly turning to look at Sal. 'He knows the woods. He can keep his head down. You never found him. He was gone when you got here.'

'I can't,' says Sal, wishing she could. 'I'm trying. I know what it feels like, I swear. But I'll try and protect you.'

'You?' sneers Tara, fixing her with a look of pure disgust. 'You're a traffic cop, for God's sake. How many bodies are in your ledger, eh? Your boyfriend's real wife – you think we should ask her about whether to trust you, eh? Or your brother? The one who might be dead or might not? Your big fat mam with her throat slit open and your blood still on her knuckles. You turn up here like you're our fucking white knight and think we can trust you because you've got daft old Wulf eating out of your hand. All the same. All liars. Bastards. Perverts!'

Sal shrinks from the lash of each name, each accusation, each skewering, invasive truth. Feels her throat closing up. Feels her eyes sting as the dam behind her eyes threatens to break.

'Theo,' says Sal, pleading. 'I can help . . .'

Tara looks up as blue lights flood the garden, the sirens wailing, discordant screeches deadened by the trees and the dark.

'Go, son,' says Alec, staring at his stepson. 'Go, and I'll make everything right . . .'

Sal steps forward, reaching out. If she can get him under control, if she can have him safe and sound when they come through the door . . .

'You're under arrest . . .'

Alec throws the poker. Tara snatches up the mug of tea from the table and throws the still-hot liquid in Sal's face. The poker misses her head by inches, clatters against the far wall. Sal recoils, sodden, scalded, rubbing furiously at her eyes.

'I didn't do anything!'

Theo kicks out, smashing his heels into her shins. Pain shoots up both legs and Sal tipples backwards, tumbling over the edge of the cartwheel table and thudding against the hard wood floor.

'Run, lad! You know where to go.'

Sal pulls herself up as Theo darts past her. Tara throws herself at her from the sofa, fingers seeking her throat, her eyes, her hair. She feels Alec grabbing for her legs, holding her down, jagged nails puncturing her skin, scraping at her flesh.

'Theo. Theo, this is Cumbria Police. Open up!'

Magda's voice, muffled by the door, punctuated by sharp raps and hammered fists.

'He didn't do it,' hisses Tara, lips and teeth gnashing against Sal's cheek. There's something animalistic in her eyes: the primal form of mother's love; the sort Sal never knew and doesn't feel.

'Open the fucking door!'

Sal thinks of her mother. Of Trina Delaney, with her big ham-hock arms and fists like trotters. Thinks of the beatings she took, and those she escaped. Thinks of the one lesson she learned from her monster mother.

She jerks her elbow down and feels the point crunch against the side of an unprotected head. She swings her head like a bowling ball, dizzying herself with the thudding impact against her captor's jaw. She feels the pressure ease upon her legs and frantically wriggles to her knees. There's a sudden searing pain behind her calf.

Tara is biting, clawing, still trying to pull her down, to stop her going after her precious boy. Sal raises her boot. Sees the bloodied face; the ugly, yawning chasm of regret turned to hate. God how she would love to stamp down . . .

Somewhere, above the din and the chaos, she hears a door bang.

'He can't get away!' she shouts. 'There's nowhere for him to go. Let me help him.'

Tara tries to haul herself upright, blood staining her dress. She looks past her at her husband. 'Don't let her ruin everything, Alec.'

Sal turns. Sees Alec staring at his wife as she sobs in pain, blubbering redly into her cupped hands, blood beneath her nails.

'*Right, we're coming in!*'

Sal looks down at Alec's right hand. Sees that he's grabbed the mace from the floor. He's holding it like a club, the top still spitting, hissing.

'You don't get to hurt us any more. We don't want any of this. Why can't you just leave us alone. Let us forget. Let them all be forgotten . . .'

Sal raises her hand to protect herself. Braces for the blow, eyes screwed up tight.

The door bursts open. Sal feels the world fragment. Her world becomes splintering wood, creaking metal, running feet, bright lights.

Sal opens her eyes.

Sees Alec jerk as the taser-points take him in the back of the neck. He twists. Drops the weapon upon himself as he dances, briefly: a fish on dry land.

There's a whoomph, as his clothing goes up as if covered in brandy.

'Put him out! Put him out!'

And then Sal is throwing herself at the burning man, rolling him over across the hard wood floor.

She feels herself catch fire.

Thinks: *So this is how it ends.*

THIRTY-FOUR

Theo runs. He feels the brambles snag at the long tails of his cloak; wet branches clutching and clawing at his hair, his face, his hood. He can hear himself making little whimpering noises as he pushes deeper into the copse. Can hear himself praying, pleading.

'I've done nothing. It's not me. It's not me.'

He can hear people shouting his name. There are lights flashing, split by the tree trunks into slices of lurid blue. He thinks about Mam. About Alec. It's been a mistake, he knows that. Alec will make it right. He has to. He won't go back to prison. Can't. Thinks, fleetingly, about his cell. About the showers. About the things they did to him inside.

'Theo! Theo, stop! We just need to talk to you!'

It's a woman's voice. Refined. Cool. Urgent. He pushes on, arm in front of his face. He realizes he's sobbing. Snot drips from his nostrils, salt-water flooding his cheeks. He wants to put the mask on. Wants to feel like Blindworm.

He lets out a shriek as he tumbles over a risen root. Cuts his hand on something sharp. Drags himself to his feet and throws himself through a tangle of bramble and teasel. He glimpses the ruin beyond. *Redburn.* His secret place. The place Dad told him about in case he ever needed a place to hide.

'Theo, you're only making things worse.'

He realizes his face is bleeding. Snatches his hand across his cheek and feels briars puncture his wrists, his scalp, the fleshy meat at the back of his calves. For a moment he thinks about stopping. He's done nothing wrong. He can make them see. Can explain himself.

He thinks again of Mahee Gamage. Poor bastard. Wasn't his fault. None of it was his fault. *It just happened . . . something bad happened and now it's over and I want to move on . . . Mam, please, you've got to drop it – he's going to leave. Or kick us out. He's going to take this all away if you don't get a hold of yourself and start being the wife he signed up for . . .*

'Theo!'

The voice comes from further away. They've taken a wrong turn, following the path towards the stream. He lets himself believe he might make it. He ducks under a fallen fence pole, feeling the barbed wire snag at his exposed skin. Whimpers, bloodily, as he slithers through the twists of metal and thorns.

He thinks of his father. Thinks of Blindworm. Of Alec.

He limps through the long, wet grass. Stumbles. Rises. Glances to his left and sees the dark smudge: the spur of uneven wall that skewers the name of Redburn Castle to the land it once bathed in blood. Feels another burst of desperate anguish squeeze at his insides. He could have made a life for himself. He'd been so close! A little place in the wilds; a job that allowed him to imagine, to inhabit, to escape. There might have been a girl, some day. Kids. He'd promised Mam that he would make the best of himself. He'd show them all that he didn't need compensation – didn't need to be compensated for what was done to him. He'd make it on his own. He'd make her proud, on his own. Would become the man his father would have stuck around for, on his own. He'd show Alec he was right to take a chance on him.

In the centre of his skull, he senses a slow, slithering presence. Hears something approximating a voice; a fork-tongued hissing that makes his insides tickle.

You knew, Theo. You knew all along what he was doing. And you let him do it because he did it for you. For Mam. Even for your dad . . .

He drags himself onward, bursting across the open ground to where the crumbling remains of the old tower lie. Glimpses toppled, green-slimed stones, crumbling masonry; saplings emerging from the gaps in the sagging walls. For a moment he thinks of his father. Thinks of the things he did, here, when he was still a boy. Thinks of the weight of it, sitting in his father's chest like hot stones. Wonders whether he forgave himself, at the end.

Theo stops, feet slithering on the wet grass. He remembers Dad, taking him behind the mound of masonry, mud, grass, into the furthest reaches of the sunken space. He starts to claw at the earth, seeking the planks of wood that same long-forgotten workman had used to cover the opening. The earth feels wrong in his hands. The smell of turned crops; of mud and blood and filth and shit rises to shove its rude stench down his nostrils, throat. He punches down at the mulch. Gags afresh on the reek of corrupted flesh, dead earth.

'No,' he whispers, as the realization stabs into his skull. 'No . . . not like this. Not down there . . .'

He turns at the sound of footsteps behind him. Looks up, face wreathed in blood and tears, his fists sunk into the wet earth up to the elbows.

Quinn leans against the toppled tower wall. She's breathing heavily, hair plastered across her face like the tails of a whip. But she's smiling. Grinning, even, as she holds the phone in front of her and films his every move.

'It wasn't me . . .' gasps Theo, letting the tears come. 'It's a place to hide. A place to put myself if I want to be forgotten about. A place where it never has to happen again.'

'A place to put people who wronged you,' says Quinn, stepping forward, a look of triumph and anger on her face. 'They're down there, aren't they? Constance? Didier?'

Theo recoils at the names. 'I didn't do this! I swear!'

'We can make sense of it all together, Theo. Come on now, let's not make it worse.'

The wind drops. For a moment, the ancient place is silent. They both hear the sound at the same time: the desperate, plaintive song that rises from the hole at Theo's feet.

He sags, folds in on himself. He hears Blindworm. Twitches, as the snake tongue flickers again inside him.

Kill her, Theo. Nobody else knows. Take the phone, hide away. Come out when everything is better . . .

He glances down. He's exposed a small square in the earth. He can glimpse the darkness below. Remembers the distant plink and splish when he dropped a rock into the nothingness, his dad's hand in his. Their little secret, he'd said. Nobody else would ever know.

But Alec had known, hadn't he? Alec had read every letter. Listened to him for countless hours as he filled himself with fond memories, happy recollections. Alec, who'd promised he'd make everything right. He wouldn't turn his back. He'd get him free; he'd make sure he had a life. He'd marry Mam, if Theo would permit it. And Theo, so pitifully grateful that somebody believed in him, had given his blessing.

'Theo,' says Quinn. She reaches out a hand. Raises the phone to her mouth. 'Got him. He's at the ruin, urgent back-up required . . .'

Theo reacts instinctively as soon as the light is snatched away. Picks up a handful of grit and dirt and throws it at Quinn's face. She shrieks, raising a hand, and Theo punches down again through the earth. His fingers find the rusted metal, closing around the rusted grid. He anchors his feet and tries to haul up the wet, rusting hatch. The stench climbs inside him. Above, the moon slithers from behind a cloud and – in the sudden wash of yellowish light – he glimpses something far below; some crude assemblage of meat and blood and bones. He stumbles backwards, retching.

'I didn't . . . it wasn't me . . .'

He turns just as Quinn reaches him. Doesn't even get the chance to raise his hands before she brings her phone down like the handle of a knife, smashing it into his cheekbone. He stumbles backwards, pain exploding inside his head. Falls back against the metal grille.

Hands at his throat, now. Fists raining down upon his face. Quinn, teeth bared, blood on her cheek. He feels the ground beneath him falter and tilt. For a moment he sees Blindworm. Mask, cowl, coffin nails clutched in one dirty, deformed fist. Sees Alec, opening up the space in the floor and rolling in his victims. Thinks he can hear the screams, growing weaker, far beneath the old, bloody earth.

Blindworm, at his ear: *She's going to kill you, Theo. Going to squeeze your throat until it closes. Let her do it. Give in to the dark . . .*

She holds his gaze as she throttles him. There is purpose to her actions. This is what she wants. This is what she has always wanted.

'Stop it! Stop it, you're killing him!'

It's a child's voice. A little girl, pleading for his life. For a moment the pressure at his neck relents. Through one bloodied eye he sees Wulfric Hagman. Sal's kids; sodden, dirty. The oldest one is holding out her phone, filming every movement.

'You,' sneers Quinn, glaring holes in Hagman's skull. 'You know he'll get you next, don't you? Whitehead. He won't stop. Whatever you did to him, he won't relent . . . we've already fucked you, you moron. It's already happening. Everything you care about, it's all going to come down . . .'

Hagman steps forward. Picks up Quinn's phone from the muddy rocks. For a moment, he does nothing but stare into the screen. Eventually, he shakes his head. Blinks. Throws the phone into the long grass beyond the wall.

From nearby comes the sound of barking dogs. Running feet. Shouts for help.

'Inspector Quinn! Inspector Quinn!'

Quinn's face twists. She snatches up a rock. Hagman clears the gap between them in three strides. Clatters into the two figures; a tangle of limbs and blood and earth. The ground tilts beneath him. The rocks slide. Timbers slip and crack. The ground opens up as the metal grille slumps off its moorings. For an instant, the three of them are scrabbling for something to cling to; something to anchor themselves to as the earth begins to cave in.

Theo feels himself fall. Grabs for the tip of the oubliette. His fingers find the mark embossed on the highest stone: a perfect Catherine wheel, chiselled into the stone.

He sees the pale-skinned, blood-streaked figure beneath: a church candle against the dark. She's huddled in on herself, eyes wide.

And then he's dangling in the dark, skin scraping against wet stone. He's looking down at the pit of bones, of shimmering brown fur and blood-red water. He's thinking of Mahee Gamage pulling himself out of this place of filth and wretchedness, dragging his skin from his bones as he wriggled through the grille.

And then there is pain. Pain at his wrist, at his ankle. He looks up. Hagman is holding his gaze. Holding his wrist. Clinging to the edge of the hole in the earth with one hand and Theo's arm with another. Theo looks down.

Sees Quinn, clawing her way up his leg; face white with terror as she angles within the void, kicking desperately at the slimed, bloodied walls.

'Don't . . .' she hisses, looking up at Theo. 'Don't you dare . . .'

He wants to kick out. Wants to do what his dad would do. What Blindworm would do. What Alec has done, in his own feeble way.

He looks up. Sees the children at the lip of the hole. Sees Hagman. Hears him.

'Hang on, lad. It'll be OK. It'll be OK . . .!'

He feels Quinn begin to climb up his body. Feels nails puncturing his skin. Feels Hagman's grip loosening at his wrist.

He feels himself slip.

Feels the big hand losing purchase on his wet skin.

From below, Quinn screaming, screeching, kicking against the walls of the ancient prison.

He closes his eyes.

Lets go.

Tumbles into the darkness.

A scream, as he bounces off the walls and clatters, bloodily, into the rocks and the bones and the wreaking water. Feels his limbs jar and shatter. Feels his skull strike stone.

THIRTY-FIVE

For a time there is just the silence, and the pain. In tiny increments, he becomes aware of the quivering shape to his left.

Hears a whispered voice; hair upon his face, tears falling upon his cheek.

'Mahee,' she whispers. She presses herself against him. He feels sandpaper skin; flesh that hangs upon bone like raw bacon. 'Did he . . .'

She stops. Recognizes him. Sees something in the ruins of the once-pretty face.

'Theo,' she breathes. Dissolves in on herself, withdrawing into the horrors behind her eyes. He tries to rise. Pain grips him. Spies bones. The swollen, bloated corpses of dead rats, bellies torn open, flesh exposed, chewed. Flicks his glance to the girl.

The moon slides into the ragged hole at the top of the shaft. Dazedly, drunkenly, he tries to make sense of it. Of Mahee and Constance. Uncle Callum . . .

He looks again at the mass in the corner. At the pile of fallen bricks; the broken shaft leading off into the latrine shuts. Hears his dad, patient, calm, explaining how it all worked; the tunnels underground; the endless chambers and tombs hidden beneath the carpet of the valley.

One eyed, bloody, he looks up. Sees the moon fill the space at the top of the oubliette.

Sees Quinn, clutching the stone wall of the prison, feet wedged into a crumbling gap.

Sees Hagman, reaching down . . .

Hears his father.

Home, son. Home at last . . .

THIRTY-SIX

Sal's sitting on the grass at the front of the Devlin house, staring at the sky like a festival-goer watching a stage. She's soaked to the skin; the water seeping up from the sodden turf while simultaneously pummelling down from the heavy-bellied sky.

She tries not to listen to the weeping from inside. She's allowed to sit here. She's earned the right to sit here, wrapped in a borrowed fluoro-coat, letting the rain soak the bandages upon her hands, making a sticky mess of the newly applied salve beneath. The paramedic said her hands will be OK. He hadn't vouchsafed any opinion on the rest of her.

'She's going bloody mental, Sal.'

She forces herself to turn back towards the house. A tall, bearded constable is looking at her with a thinly veiled desperation. 'Seriously, we can't bloody cuff her . . . not with what's gone on . . .'

Sal winces as she hauls herself up. Feels the rain run down the back of her collar. Casts off the jacket as she moves from the grass to the rain-blackened paving stones, wiping her feet before stepping into the chaos of the living room.

'I told you,' says the PC at her ear.

Tara Myers-Devlin is on the floor, pinned beneath the weight of another, frantic constable, whose blonde hair is smeared across her face as she tries to keep hold of the writhing, bloodied mother.

'I don't want to arrest her but she went for me with a bloody sword, Sal. Off the wall!'

Sal takes a moment to process what she's seeing. She finds herself staring intently into the anguished, hate-filled face: the strings of saliva suspended between her teeth like the venom of a snake. She sees something she recognizes – something she glimpsed in her expression as she sought to sink her teeth into her leg. Feels her gut lurch.

'Off her,' says Sal, forcing herself to move into the room. 'Let her go, Jenny.'

'She went for John, Sal. Went for him with a fucking sword!'

'I'll do it again, you bastards! Do every last one of you! Not content with the years you stole . . . have to kill him too! Have put a good man in hospital!'

Sal keeps her eyes locked on Tara's, watching as she struggles, her bony arms straining as she tries to push herself up. Squats in front of her.

'If she lets go and you go for any one of us, you're going to be arrested,' says Sal, as gently as she can. 'And you don't want that. You've been through enough, Tara.'

'I'll kill every last one of you,' hisses Tara, lunging forward towards Sal, teeth snapping. Jenny tries to pull her back. Loses her grip and stumbles back. Tara lunges forward, trying to sink her teeth into Sal's face, hands scrabbling at her clothes.

Sal can't bring herself to hit her. Doesn't ever want to hurt anybody again. She grabs at her wrists but the slime from the salve makes her grip slide off and she loses her footing. John, inert at the door, rushes forward, tripping over Jenny's flailing legs and clattering against the armchair.

'You killed him! My husband!'

She rains down double-handed blows, striking down with her spindly forearms, bunched fists. Sal takes the blows on her forearms, shoulders, chest. Covers her head.

'Harder,' she hisses, when Tara slows, gasping for breath. 'Let it out. Go on. Go on!'

For a moment she is a child again, bloody-lipped, gap-toothed, goading her mother to do it one more time. For a moment, all she wants is to be hit.

She locks eyes with her. Jerks her chin at her. 'Come on then,' she says. 'Come on!'

John and Jenny tackle her from behind, dragging her away, still kicking, still spitting.

Sal drags herself up. Wipes the goo from her hands on her fluoro-coat.

'He's not dead, Tara,' says Sal, catching her breath.

Tara stops struggling, going suddenly limp in the tangle of entwined arms and legs. The two PCs look at each other, then slowly lower her to the floor. Tara pulls her legs up. Sits on the floor, wet-faced, mad-haired, half undressed. Rocks herself.

'He will be,' she says, into her knees. 'He'll die.'

'He's a survivor,' says Sal, rubbing her arms. She sits down again, cross-legged, their knees almost touching. 'All those years in prison didn't kill him.'

Tara raises her head, snot smearing her top lip. 'Prison?' She sneers. 'Bloody holiday camp, that's what that was. What sort of prison has a drama society? By Christ, he had the time of his life.' She lowers her eyes.

Sal stares at her until she raises her gaze. 'Easier though, wasn't it? Having a son in prison. Having a cause. Having a purpose.'

Tara swallows. Glares at Sal. 'You'll pay for that, girl. My Alec . . . he'll have your job for that. Doesn't matter to me about your sob story . . . poor Sal, with her mad bitch mother . . .'

Sal lets the blows land. Takes them full in the face.

'I think we both know that Alec isn't going to be around much longer, Tara. I think he's had enough. He's leaving you, isn't he? Leaving you unless you let go of the past. Is that why Theo did what he did, Tara? Why he took those poor sods and dropped them in the earth to be forgotten about?' She angles her head. 'You knew, didn't you?'

Tara hugs her knees. Whispers dark threats into the hem of her dressing gown. When she raises her face, her cheeks are flushed red; sodden with fresh tears.

'Leave me? *Leave* me?' She shakes her head. 'That man would do anything for me. For Theo. He loves us like . . . like love should be. And he's got time. We've got time.'

Sal watches as something starts to break inside her. Watches her shiver as all the bottled-up bile and poison floods her. She grimaces. Gasps.

'I shouldn't have . . .' she sobs. 'Shouldn't have let it, let it get me. It was just so . . . so necessary. They had to see you can't do that. Can't tell lies and destroy a family and not . . . not have consequences . . .'

Sal moves closer. 'You were tormenting Mahee Gamage.'

'Useless bastard,' she sniffles. 'Gave Theo the advice that got him locked up! And then he just had to comment on that bastard article, didn't he? All that shite about "no comment" defences – some glossy nonsense written by some London lawyer who doesn't understand how the world really works. Had to have an opinion, didn't he! Cruel sod wasn't even sorry! Said he would do it again! People were "liking" it online, you know that? Couldn't just say sorry and leave us alone.'

'And Constance; Didier . . .?'

'Dangling us from a thread, the pair of them. How were they going to make it sound on the documentary, could we maybe help them make up their mind . . .'

'So you started threatening them.'

'It was . . . a distraction. A release. Alec said I was better for a while.'

'And you needed that release, did you Tara? After your son came home. After Paul died and you got the big house and you became the woman who used to be on the telly . . .'

'Don't you fucking dare! My Alec . . . my Alec . . .'

'Your Alec would do anything for you, wouldn't he, Tara?'

Sal stands up. Looks to the two ashen police constables.

'Call Quinn. Don't tell her I was involved.'

'Sal . . . this isn't right . . .'

Sal looks back at Tara, snivelling into her hem. 'Theo didn't know, did he? None of it.'

'He's got no bloody clue,' she says, eyes flashing with the same angry hate. Sal sees it. Knows it.

'Didn't really want him home, did you Tara? It was all about the campaign, wasn't it? Not him. Not the actual boy.'

'Boy? That's not what I got with that one. I can raise a boy, love. What do you do with that waste of space, eh? Teach him to bloody dance? Too bloody soft. Paul gave me hell for it but one of us had to show him how life was. I mean . . . what's the point of him! What do you want a lad like that to be?'

Sal lets her talk. Hears the change in accent: repeating shameful words she's stored up in the core of her being ever since she bawled them at her husband.

'You hate him,' says Sal, flatly. 'Hate your own son. Hated him even when you were telling the world about how you wouldn't stop until you brought him home.'

'It was the principle! You think I wanted to be known as the mam of the soft bastard who kicked a tramp to death?'

'Fucking hell,' breathes Jenny, still motionless at the sofa. John is beside her, phone in his hand.

'And Alec . . .?'

She gives a girlish shrug. 'He forgives me very easily. Of course, he was very upset with me. But he said he would help me stop. Take away the temptation. Help me forget about them.

Promised me a new beginning. We could do what he wanted. Get away . . .'

Sal tries to make a picture from the pieces. Watches as Tara clutches at her stomach. Below. Cradles her womb. 'Had to blab,' she whispers. 'Had to tell him why.'

Sal thinks of Tara's dead husband, Paul, the doting dad who took his own life before he saw his son freed. Thinks of the timeline: Theo and his father, drowning their sorrows in a Middlesbrough bar . . .

'What did he tell him, Tara? That night. What changed everything?'

'Why I'd always fucking hated him,' she says, the words coming out in a rush of blood-speckled, fetid air. 'What he was.'

Sal wonders if anybody ever thought to check. Ever ran Theo's DNA against those of his family members.

'Whose is he?'

Tara shrugs. 'Could have been any one of them, love. You'd have to ask the genial host.'

'I don't understand, Tara.'

Tara stares at the carpet. Her words seem distant, hollow. 'All the fun and games up at the castle, back when his father was lord of the manor. Trip down memory lane for the valley, eh? Back to the "good old days", eh? Threw a fancy-dress shindig for friends and family, some of the lads who worked for him – just like his dad used to. Told Paul it were all just some silly fun – that he could bring the missus and have a grand night out. I was excited, if you can believe it. Felt all glamorous in my medieval gown, sewn from old curtains, and a pair of court shoes I'd found. All the regulars were there. His pals. Me and Paul, feeling like we'd suddenly become big shots. I don't know if it was planned or if they just saw my dress and reckoned I'd be up for it. Sycamore's never said.'

'Sycamore Le Gros?'

'Went from a banquet to a Roman orgy before we'd finished the mead. We tried to leave.' She lowers her eyes. Chews on her tongue. 'We had to play along,' she says. 'Had to pretend we wanted to be there – that we liked it. All those men. What they did. What they made Paul watch . . .'

'Sycamore must have felt bad. He said he would make a contribution to putting things right.'

'You got pregnant.'

Tara holds her stomach. 'I would have told,' she says, quietly.

'In time. But he kept paying, each month, right as rain. And it was all we got for him, you see that? I had to look at the face of a bright little lad who only wanted to be loved, and I had to know deep in my bones that every time he looked at me, I wanted to poke his eyes out because he reminded me of what we did. What was done! To us. To me. All those years, chewing it down, pushing it down, and when I finally found the courage to call Wulf, our friendly neighbourhood police officer, he's off in a prison cell having stabbed his fucking lover.' She rocks on her heels. Clutches at herself. 'I wrote to him to tell him what I thought. Wrote back telling me he could never suffer enough for letting me down. Told me that whatever I wanted from him, he would always be there to offer whatever he could. That he didn't deserve my forgiveness, even if it was forthcoming. Told me to make friends with that mad social worker down the youth club – that she'd be good for me. The fucking nerve!'

'And Paul raised him?'

'Took whatever cruelties life threw, did Paul. I couldn't love the little bugger, so he had to love him twice as hard. He just took it. Stood by. Did the lot. Loved him because I couldn't. That's what did him in, more than anything else. Not that night in the pub, not the mistakes with the phone and the alibi . . . it was seeing me in the papers saying how much I wanted him home.'

'And he was going to tell the truth,' says Sal, slowly. She lowers her voice. 'And Alec?'

Slowly, Tara slides her hands into the pocket of her dressing gown. She pulls out a crumple of patched leather. Lets the mask slide to the floor.

'He made it better. Took care of things. Them in the ground. No little reminders. He's a good man. Easily led, you might say. Bit of a romantic. Thinks love conquers all. So did Paul. That's why I know it's all fucking bollocks in the end.'

Sal swallows the words. Feels her stomach clench.

'Will you make a statement to that effect, Tara?'

Tara gives a snuffled little laugh. Giggles, as tears fall. 'No comment.'

Sal turns away. Walks to the open door.

John trying to talk to her: 'Sal . . . you've got to call her . . . Sal, she's telling the chief constable that it was Theo! Sal!'

She walks out the door and into the rain. Looks up through the trees to the dark hump of the hill. Thinks her way beyond and into the little forest, bleeding darkly onward to the gloomy grey walls and blackened timbers of Redburn Castle. Le Gros's land.

She looks inside herself as she walks. Thinks of Jarod. Of Dagmara. Of Mam. Wonders what it would be like to hate your own child. Thanks Christ she doesn't know.

Hagman's waiting at the end of the lane, hands in his pockets, jiggling from foot to foot. As she approaches, two shapes detach themselves from behind him.

Sal glances at where her watch would be. 'They're meant to be in bed!'

Nola and Lottie run forward. Wrap her in damp, sweaty hugs. They smell of chips. Smell of the peat fire. Of Hagman.

'It wasn't Theo,' she says, over the bobbing heads, making sure Hagman hears. 'Alec took care of things.'

Hagman gives a tight nod. 'Will Theo live?'

'He'd better. They'll blame everything on him if he doesn't.'

Hagman breathes out, slowly. 'He told me some stories. It was a . . . difficult relationship.' He shakes his head. 'She wrote to me a long time ago, Sal. I don't know if I wrote back. Everything's such a blur from that time. But . . . I know she wanted help and I wasn't there to give it. Not like you, love. You're always there.' He sucks his lower lip. 'Alec, eh? Her too.' He shakes his head. 'That poor boy.'

Sal strokes Nola's cheek and she pushes her hand away, grimacing.

'What are you covered in? I doubt it's glory, love,' says Sal, and squishes herself against her. Steals a little warmth. Through the dark line of trees she sees the gathering vehicles; the forensics tent being hoisted through tangles of bracken and bramble, teasel and thorns. Bodies have already been found at the base of the oubliette. Two corpses, huddled together, skin and bone. Didier. Constance. It would be a career-making case for any cop who wasn't about to announce the name of a different killer on live TV.

Sal finds herself grinning, madly. Feels the tears begin to flow. Stops as a shape appears behind Hagman, walking slowly forward from the darkness.

Sal narrows her eyes. Feels a hand at her throat, a fist in her stomach.

'Wulf told him what had happened,' says Lottie, making a face. She knows things might get awkward. Tries to find a suitable way to break the tension. 'Shout it out . . .'

'For your ocean animals,' finishes the quiet voice from the darkness.

Sal walks forward on legs that barely support her. Inside her head: *don't you dare . . . don't you dare break this fucking easy . . .*

And then her arms are around Lewis, and he's pressing his face into her hair, and kissing her sore cheeks, her ears, the frames of her glasses. And he's sobbing. Sobbing against her as if he were made of nothing but salt water.

She holds him close. Squeezes until her arms ache. Swaddling him with her coat, wrapping him up, stroking his head in a way that feels more like an act of love than a thousand kisses.

'I'm sorry,' he whispers. 'I'm . . . I'm not right . . . I'm not who I was.'

She strokes his razored skull. Runs her fingers over the indentation; the steel plate; the ridge of stitches. Kisses his forehead.

'Then I'll love who you are.'

Behind her, she hears Lottie pretending to be sick.

Thinks: *this is good. I could live with this. This feels awesome.*

Closes her mind to the other voice. The one that recognized the eyes of a mother who despised her offspring.

Thinks: *you can't do this. Can't be this.*

She puts out an arm. Doesn't mind who gets to hold her hand.

EPILOGUE

She sits in the high-backed chair like a discarded teddy. She's short. Squat. Lumpy, in her grey jogging trousers and shapeless, too-big hoody.

'Nowt going on, is there? You could stare through one ear and out the other.'

The woman in the chair pulls herself up, smiling in the general direction of the gruff voice.

'Her teeth are orange. What's happened?'

'Very independent,' comes the female voice: brisk, efficient. 'Doesn't accept help without a fight. Likes to take care of her . . . ablutions.'

'Ablutions?'

A sigh. 'Some confusion over her Steradent and her Berocca. Rather unsightly, isn't it?'

There's a snort. 'By Christ. Always was unsightly. Even when she was young.'

The woman in the chair lets her gaze linger on the two figures in the doorway. The light from the big windows is patterned by the overhanging leaves from the maple tree. It makes the old man and the young, white-coated woman look as if they are caught in a great dark mesh. It makes it hard to define what they look like. Everything shimmers.

'Under the hat?'

'Staples are holding. Graft has taken.'

'But still gaga.'

The woman moves away from him, stepping fully into the cheerful room.

'Take a look,' says the woman, picking up a leather folder from the coffee table and passing it to the white-haired figure. 'It's all in there. She can see snatches of her life but can't make any sense of it. Responds to her name. Likes the garden. Likes children. Enjoys a second pudding.'

In the doorway, the man starts leafing through the pen-and-ink sketches. He holds one up for closer inspection. A man hangs in a cramped kitchen; blue cord at his neck, bearded face turning purple.

He holds up another. Sees a shaven-headed figure in the front of a little car, one sightless eye glaring up through a mosaic of smashed glass.

'It won't . . . bleed through?'

The young woman gives a little shrug. Crosses to the woman in the chair and squats down in front of her, staring intently into her eyes.

'How are we feeling today? How are the headaches?'

'Hurts, love. Hurts like owt.'

'Doesn't sound like herself,' says the old man, stepping forward. His belly noses through the front of a blue blazer. He forces himself to meet her gaze.

'You know me. Know my face?'

The lady smiles, eyes barely focusing. 'I think . . . I think you do the floristry with me. On Thursdays. I like Thursdays.'

The man laughs, hands at his waist. He gives a shake of his head, as if the sight saddens him somehow. 'Fucking waste.'

The woman wrinkles her nose. Looks at the tall man. 'Bad language. I don't care for it.'

'Aye,' he replies, with a wry smile. 'Aye, there she is.'

The woman in the white coat rises from the floor. A whiff of expensive perfume, of some creamy bergamot skin lotion.

'Take care of yourself, Dag,' says Callum Whitehead, turning away. 'I wish you could have seen it . . . could be there at the end. Don't you want to see how it ends? Who wins out? Can't you come back just long enough to see whether you were right or wrong . . .'

He walks away without an answer. Grumbles as a care worker blocks the doorway. Pushes past him: Old Spice, port, Germolene.

The doctor follows him out, jumping a little as the leather folder slides off the desk and on to the floor.

The care worker waits patiently in the doorway. Doesn't enter the room until the visitors are at the far end of the corridor.

Closes it, softly, behind him.

Steps into the little space and cocks his head, staring at the woman in the chair.

For a moment, time stands still. The air seems to fizz: the whiff of burnt filament, singed hair.

Slowly, she rights herself. Straightens her back. Jerks her head: a Northumberland hello.

'Hello Jarod,' says Dagmara. Then she smiles, the intelligence flooding her eyes. 'I've been waiting.'